Pra

"Amy Dupcak's prose is precise and taut, yes, but it teeters at the edge of some precipice, some crucial border between control and disaster. The characters in *Dust* are complicated: passionate, scornful, smart, fickle, loving, manipulative, impulsive, and wry. Sometimes they enact the worst kinds of betrayals; at other times they approach redemption. Reading these stories is like looking in the mirror." —Nelly Reifler, author of *See Through* and *Elect H. Mouse State Judge*

"*Dust* reads like a perfect scar of time-softened pain. You'll find old friends between these pages, cool ones who watch obscure movies and listen to vinyl and remind you of days when you felt too much. From an abducted fourth grader to a maniacal, unignorable voice inside your head, Dupcak's characters leave you in thrall with the possibility of darkness." —Jordana Frankel, author of *The Ward* and *The Isle*

"Amy Dupcak has a relentless commitment to illuminating life's quirky, raw underside. In her searing debut story collection, Dupcak unflinchingly gets under the skin of a tribe of fascinating young characters that offer insights beyond their years. Anchored with lush tangles of prose, Dupcak's stories not only touch but often scorch the heart." —Scott Alexander Hess, author of *The Butcher's Sons*

"The characters in Amy Dupcak's beautiful, smart collection *Dust* often find themselves both connected to and estranged from one another and themselves. A dynamic personal tension fuels each of these finely-taut stories, which are, like many of the characters in them, sometimes sweet on the surface, yet fraught with an underlying emotional weight. A jaded man begins to feel comfort from reading the diary of a woman he's never met. A girl who feels paralyzed by her own beauty struggles to name the unnamable and become invisible through her stories. A young boy works on writing his own dictionary to better express himself, yet can't find the words to identify his own grief and sadness. These are characters striving to understand themselves and their world through language, but who are often unable to find the perfect words. Lucky for us, Dupcak does." —David Olimpio, author of *This Is Not a Confession*

dust
short stories

Amy Dupcak

Copyright © 2016 Amy Dupcak

All rights reserved.
Lucid River Press
www.lucidriverpress.com
ISBN: 9780988854321

CONTENTS

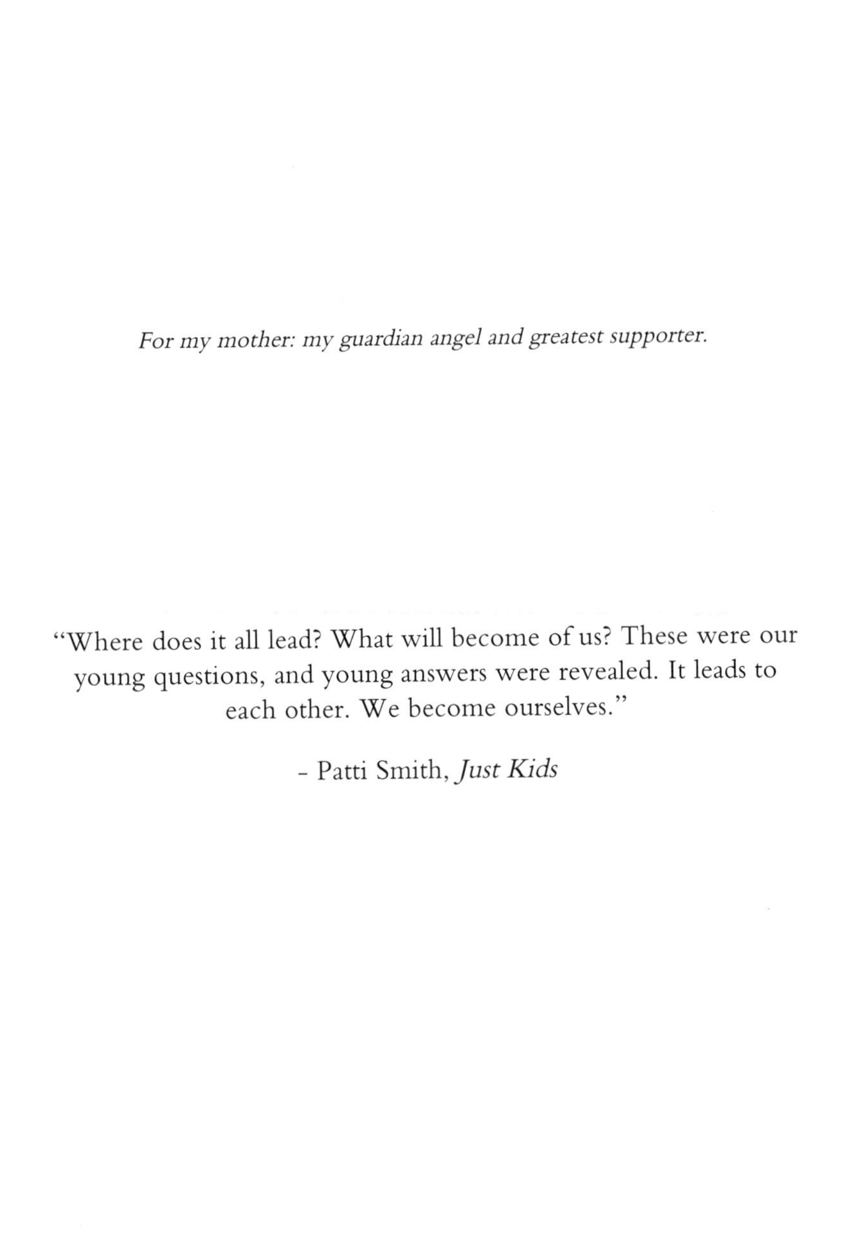

For my mother: my guardian angel and greatest supporter.

"Where does it all lead? What will become of us? These were our young questions, and young answers were revealed. It leads to each other. We become ourselves."

- Patti Smith, *Just Kids*

THE GARDEN

BECAUSE EVE IN THE GARDEN took the first bite, we planted apples. We wanted to be close to sin, to invite it to live with us. It only seemed appropriate. Nothing in our lives had gone according to plan, yet there we were: two near strangers in an overgrown garden, clutching apple seeds.

Theo had stolen the seeds that morning, wandering into the nearest neighbor's barn half a mile away. We were unwilling to spend money if we didn't have to; he'd been searching for supplies when the seeds called out.

We knew we were lucky to have found this place at all; we'd heard it was abandoned after its occupants died. Together we decided not to feel guilty about pretending to be their orphaned children, come home to mourn. We were old enough to know better, yet young enough to exist in such a lie.

"Do you want to say some kind of prayer?" Theo asked, looking down at the Eden we had claimed.

"I don't pray," I reminded him.

He crouched and plunged his hand into the earth, creating a chasm the size of his fist. He started dropping the seeds one by one, a perfect hailstorm. Theo lingered, caressing the dirt, petting it, and touching the crown of his head as if he had buried someone he knew.

I imagined the evil fanning out instantly. It would spread throughout the garden, infecting the tomatoes and spinach and whatever else our dead "parents" grew, until reaching the farmhouse where we would sleep. The evil would creep under the floorboards, snake into the plumbing, greet us in the morning as we washed; there it would enter the tips of our fingers, invade our blood, and engulf our cells until we too had transformed. This is what we deserved.

When Theo stood, his knees and palms were covered in soil. He turned toward me and smiled. It was this smile I had trailed for days like a famished fawn following its mother doe. I had confided in Theo that my life back home had nothing more to offer. I was his family now, no one else's. I was his Eve, or he was mine, and our apples would come. We would wait here watching rain impregnate the earth, and by the time our apples bloomed we would no longer be strangers. This is what I hoped.

"I prayed anyway," he whispered.

"What did you pray?" I asked.

Theo didn't answer. He simply walked through the garden and into the farmhouse.

Before going inside, I decided to spread my prayer atop his like a second layer of skin, but I didn't know how people prayed. I tried to feel the seeds beneath my feet, grasping hold of the dirt—this patch of earth that held us in place. The evil was taking its first tiny breaths, the apples small as pinpricks. I could hear it.

Because Eve was born of Adam's soil, we made love at dawn. The early light crept between our ribs, slick with sweat as they slid back and forth beneath the surface of skin. No one saw us, but I wanted to believe the garden was watching, or at least the ivy climbing the walls.

It was our first time together, yet something about it felt final, as if there would be no need to resume this rhythm once it had stopped. I found myself surprised by the strength of Theo's hands, the quickness of his breath, and the soil caked beneath his nails.

I thought, Now I *know* him. Then I felt the urge to scream, but who besides Theo would receive the sound? The unborn apples might perk up, their new roots shaking with fear like the veins in Theo's hands. Those snakelike veins twitched as the blood inside them tunneled into mine. I could feel his heart sing out: old blood mixing with new.

When we lay there spent, I wanted Theo's voice to fill the hollow space where his breaths had taken shape. He seemed more capable of words than me, the way he was more capable of decisions. He was the one who had freed me from the dirt and dust of my past, pushing me heart-first into a future that did not allow a lifeboat. For this I wanted to be grateful.

But I also wanted to believe that I was not surrendering like so many women before my time. I was not simply relying on promises of light uttered halfheartedly by a man I hardly knew. In some ways, we were too young to be "man" and "woman" anyway; we were merely playing a game without rules.

Together we stared at the ceiling, becoming acquainted with its particular water stains. They seemed ever changing, like clouds. First, a tooth. Then, a staircase. Soon, a ship with symmetrical wings. Always a surprise.

"Maybe it will rain today," he whispered.

My stomach moaned as life and death fought inside my body. Which of them would win?

"I'd like that," I replied. I imagined the tiniest storm raging over our precious hole in our garden, which he had closed up tight.

I had to admit that the two of us might not make it to the time of apples. Perhaps we would cave and retreat, heads hung, to the wicked places we once called home, the places that held our ghosts. Perhaps the ghosts of *this* place, the ones that had made love on this very mattress, were poisoning our bones, or whatever parts of us hadn't already been poisoned.

I wanted to ask Theo all sorts of questions, but only one escaped my lips: "Was Eve really evil?"

For several minutes he looked at me sideways, then left to check the garden. I went to the sink and offered myself to the water.

Ten Days

Day 1

I SING IN HER SHOWER and lounge naked in her bed.

From what I can tell so far, Alana's left the place spotless, save for a build-up of grime in every corner of the shower. I've been given specific instructions from Justin: collect the mail, receive (mysterious) package next Monday and, most importantly, take care of the plant. The plant is key. When people go away, they need someone to feed their cat or walk their dog. She needs someone to babysit an aloe vera plant. His name is Vadim.

Of course there's the whole don't burn the place down, don't leave garbage, don't eat her food, don't invite people over, don't bring in my bike, don't smoke in the bedroom...basically, don't make it look like I've been squatting here for ten days. Justin handed me the key with a look of terror in his eyes. "Kyle," he said, "if she comes back and finds that you've destroyed her apartment, I will kill you. Kill you dead and then resurrect you and kill you some more." I swore on the soul of Allen Ginsberg and reasoned it's only because he's fucking her.

From what I can recall, which isn't much these days, I've encountered this Alana chick once. It was at a bar, so I was drunk, and she didn't make much of an impression. What I do remember though is that she only drank water. At some point I offered a shot, but she shook her head firmly and said, "No thanks." I thought that rather odd. I asked Justin and he told me she doesn't drink...ever! I remember thinking, this girl thinks she's better than me. I mean, who does she think she is? Then Justin said that they'd gone to another bar the week before and she'd ordered tea. Tea! Who knew a bar even served tea?

I forget how Justin met her...not that it's any of my business, but I like to know the general goings-on. In any event, he's doing me a big favor by letting me take advantage of the situation. As far as I'm concerned, I am Couch-Surfer Champion, Squatter Extraordinaire. They just started renovating the abandoned apartment where I've laid my head for two weeks. I've become adept at climbing down fire escape ladders in the nick of time.

Alana's ladder is broken. There's a step turned sideways and the railing is inching out from the brick, as if about to fall off completely. I sit cross-legged in the middle of the landing to smoke a rolled cigarette and study the distance between this building and its cousin.

The night is eerily quiet in between streets. This is largely undiscovered territory—hidden from sidewalks or passersby. A slice of sky, hazy and unsure, is star-deficient, as usual. Of the fourteen windows I count, only two are lit. In one, a man irons pants. Thick blue curtains barricade the other. There's a tree down below, two if you count the dead one, and dirt patches with objects loosely scattered.

The plant sits dumbly in its clay pot, staring. Leaves like octopus tentacles reaching out. I take long concentrated drags and hold the cigarette in the corner of my mouth.

Day 2

Her kitchen cabinets make promises they probably can't keep: gluten-free, soy-free, non-dairy, 75% organic (ha!), all of it sans preservatives or any real flavor. Plus vitamins upon vitamins, none of which are FDA approved. A juicer and rice cooker sit on the counter, cords limply coiled.

It's dinnertime and I'm broke again. The weekend drained my wallet clean and I have to make it to Friday on five bucks. This health-aisle concoction of cereals will have to do. I add cinnamon, vanilla extract, low-glycemic agave, and carob chips in an attempt to make the meal as interesting as humanly possible. She has only rice milk to offer. The paper towels are pre-recycled. The toothpaste in the bathroom deemed "sensitive care."

I wander the confines of the apartment, chewing loudly, the bowl like a baseball in my palm. Her front door lands you smack-dab in the kitchen. A short diagonal hall leads into the bedroom and living room, on opposite sides. The bathroom is crammed into the kitchen's far corner. Everything must be Alana-sized: living room's short red couch, bedroom's twin mattress, bathroom's precious porcelain sink. For some reason, she only has baby forks and spoons, with little cartoons on their plastic handles.

I count a total of sixty-seven books on the vertical bookcase, which occupies a wall of the diagonal hall. This doesn't include a pile of *Time Out* magazines, or the poetry books on the top shelf. More shelves in the living room contain an overwhelming amount of DVDs (documentaries and foreign) and CDs (post-punk, riot grrrl, indie rock) perfectly alphabetized. This is disgusting. Who has the time or patience or motivation to *do* this? I'm tempted to rearrange them for the sake of mediocrity.

There's no TV, only an expensive projector hooked up to a DVD player. No video games, no pack of cards, no alcohol. Nothing to provide mindless entertainment. Anatomical posters and a series of abstract drawings hang on the wall. No pictures of her, though. Maybe the full-length mirror remembers her reflection.

I set the empty cereal bowl on the bedroom floor and take to opening and closing her dresser drawers. In the very top drawer I find cotton underwear in various colors. I spin a lacy pair on my fingertip and dig some more. Women always think the underwear drawer is the perfect hiding place. Why is this? Just where I expect, I find condoms ("For Her"), a zebra-print vibrator, and a wad of twenties. I drop the panties and avoid the vibrator. Hungrily, I count the folded bills. Eighty bucks! For now, she won't miss twenty.

The bottom drawer isn't brimming with clothes, but more books, art supplies, and typewritten pages laden with ink scrawls. At the top of the pile sits a slim black book with a rubber band to keep it closed. I rip off the band and turn to page one. It's a journal. Bingo! Instant entertainment.

Grabbing my tobacco from the kitchen, I roll myself a cigarette and plop down on her bed, leaning on my elbow. Are the stars on her sheets meant to compensate for this starless city? Hmm. I flip to a random page and press my eyes to her tiny handwriting. You need a fucking magnifying glass to read this.

June 13

Everything and everyone exists in a story with infinite plotlines and overlapping dialogue. The omniscient, overindulgent narrator sits with his decaf coffee and ripened banana, planning the next climax. Ballpoint pen in hand, he creates every superfluous character and idiosyncratic episode. All of the incidental actors in this story interweave as he, our narrator, intervenes. One day, you might just get a chance to read the hefty novel, but only when it's much too late to matter. It contains some noteworthy tragedy. Some mastermind innovation. Some beautiful mistakes.

Words fall off cliffs inside my skull and bump their puny heads on the edges of my tongue. I can't get them out fast enough, can't sell my soul quick enough to compensate. I'm a word-girl; it's not my fault. Excessive use of commas, overindulgent-metaphor, surrealist-imagery, stream-of-conscious babble, iridescent-syntax: my tools of the trade. I wish I could draw well enough to illustrate every phrase and waking dream. My imagination is bloodshot. My mouth upside-down. Yesterday, I saw a green-lit firefly floating above a neon ATM sign.

—A

I scratch my head in the proverbial sense. I've known girls like this. They want to disguise their privileged lives and college degrees and twenty-dollar bills lying uselessly in their goddamned underwear drawers. She thinks she's an *artiste* when she's just another spoiled Amerikan who lacks real-life experience or valid grievances and thinks she can find it in books. She deems herself a quirky downtown poet, but look...cherry-wood floors, expensive agave, exposed brick wall, dimmer lights, marble tiles, and a dishwasher, not to mention prime location next to all the best subway lines. She's on sacred ground where *true* poets once gathered with something revolutionary to say. Now the area is swamped with rich kids and costs two grand a month, which I highly doubt she can afford on her own. I mean, what does she do besides try to write?

What makes this entire situation worse is the fact that Justin's fucking her. Probably right here in this bed. He should know better.

I toss her pretentious journal to the floor and walk to the bathroom to flush the tail end of my cigarette. Then I fill a cup with tap water and approach the windowsill where the plant resides. Its thick green stems stick upright like zombified arms. "Here," I announce, dumping the water. The greedy dirt gulps it down.

Day 3

For some reason, the old hag in apartment 15 never stops screaming. When I stopped back here earlier the screaming went on for nearly an hour. "I know why you don't like it," she started, in her nasally New York screech. "It's because you're drunk. You're always drunk and *that's* why you don't like my cooking anymore. This is the last time, Harry. You're just a big, fat drunk." Then I see good ol' Harry (or at least a man who fits the bill) slumped on the staircase gasping for air and clutching his chest. The man can't make it up one flight of stairs without a rest stop. Poor guy. Wonder if Alana helps him.

Their domestic turmoil, however irritating and probably abusive, reassures me that relationships are bad news. Right now, I'm in the best sort of situation. No long-term girlfriend to drag me down, no loyalties, obligations, or conformity to the status quo. On the flipside, I'm not the kind of single guy who needs to sleaze his way into picking up girls who drink too much on a Saturday night. I've got a healthy list of phone numbers to choose from when necessary. Maybe I'll spare a quarter for one of them tomorrow night.

In all honesty, I don't like to overthink the past or the future. What's done is done and what may become is out of my hands. A few nights ago, I was sleeping on a bare mattress in an empty room, with only a string of half-broken Christmas lights the previous occupants disowned. For now, I'm tossing a paper airplane around Alana's bedroom, smoking a joint, feet propped on a pillow, lights gently dimmed, freshly jerked off, flipping again through her journal.

Somebody once said people with tiny handwriting are intelligent creatures. I don't buy that for a second. Alana just grips the pen too tight.

June 24

Woke up depressed again and less than thrilled about life (generally or specifically speaking), but was able to cheer myself up…the beautiful summer weather helped, as did the fact that it was Saturday. I cleaned the apartment vigorously because it was begging for it, especially the kitchen corner by the A/C, picked up my laundry and put it all away, made a pharmacy trip, and finished Sam's mix-cd. I looked up art classes online because I'd like to take one somewhere this fall. I always feel the need to prove myself, and I never expect people to take me seriously. Then I met Jayne and we walked to Sam's juice bar so I could give him the mix and score myself a beet/apple/ginger juice (he makes it best) and bag of raw granola. Jayne and I wandered awhile, browsing through records even though neither of us owns a player. One of these days, I should ask Dad for his old one. That is, if I ever make it out to visit him. At night, we sat in Washington Square Park's empty fountain until a creep asked us to have a threesome, and then we watched The Little Unicorn on my projector, eating oatmeal cookies until I felt ridiculously full. Now I'm debating whether or not to call you-know-who (Alana, resist) and wondering if anyone wants to accompany me to MoMA tomorrow.

Random thought: I feel like I've been delicately eased into adulthood, and I think I'm mildly self-conscious about it. I really hope I get into grad school…

—A

I close the book and readjust my eyes after holding them inches from the page. Is there something cathartic about recapping the lackluster details of the day? I bounce around the room in search of a pen and fresh paper. In large, sprawling lowercase letters:

september 27

woke up depressed as anybody ought to be on this shitty falling-to-pieces planet. boo-hoo. showered, used alana's fish-shaped soap, opted against the "organic" shampoo that smells like shit. rode my bike, delivered messages from 11 to 6 just like any other pointless day. stopped by union to make a special delivery to skater-rob, watched some skater kids jump orange cones and scrape their knees. rob almost got his ass kicked by this big lady who called him a motherfucking faggot for flipping off her kid. rode to tribeca to make a couple more deliveries. my stash is gone, need to replenish. came back to the pad and listened to the old bag and her lush argue while eating my italian hero (thanks for the dough alana). hung around wash-square for a few hours, watched the rats scurry. gave bam the squatter 2 bucks for pizza. corey-sensitive was out playing guitar and we shot the shit, he was all hyped up on speed or something. gave lawrence the street-poet pills he was asking for. ran into shaggy from tompkins who told me johnny and him were in jail for trespassing past midnight when they lock the park gates. he looked like hell.

what else? i held a letter someone wrote to alana up to the light the way i used to with report cards but it didn't work. also tried on a pair of her glasses but they hurt my head.

and no alana, i never feel the need to prove myself. what's there to prove? who cares? everyone in this city is out for themselves.

I reread my sloppy words before folding up the ridiculous entry. This new paper-airplane loop-de-loops and lands behind the dresser.

Fishing the last nug out of my Ziploc bag, I speed-roll a spliff and give it a good smoke on the fire escape. The sky is still opaque. I count two planes and zero stars. The man isn't ironing his pants. I bet he passed out with the light on. No other insomniacs out here smoking. I fetch the plant from the sill and place him by my bare feet. "Hi," I whisper. He has sixteen big leaves and twenty-five baby ones. Well, two of those are adolescents. I watered him (or them) twice today.

A humming sound lingers. A far-away siren, the Doppler effect. Echoes cling. Energy emissions—various lives ducking in and out of air-vents. Cable wires run the lengths of these buildings like ivy.

Day 4

She's got a hoop septum ring and dreadlocks tied with ribbon. Her jeans scrape the floor and a flimsy top reveals this sliver of belly I can't stop staring at. When she smiles, she scrunches up the freckles on her nose, which is cute. Aside from the fact that she talks too much, I'm glad I called her.

"Can we watch a movie on the ceiling?" Leigh asks, marveling at the projector and ashing her cigarette on the floor.

We met at Astor Place in June. Justin had climbed the cube and hung onto its side while a bunch of touristy teenagers plus Leigh's friends banded together to spin it. Leigh ignored them and sauntered over to me.

I always seem to attract a certain type of city girl...the kind who dig Bukowski-esque boys with dirt-caked fingernails, someone they can either clean up or get dirty with. It's my rolled-up jeans (the only pair I own), grungy t-shirt, hair to my chin, and perpetual scruff. Plus, I've maintained a lean muscular build from biking. She offered me her number then and there, but we've only gotten together twice. She's free-love like me and it's well worth a third go.

"How about *Baraka?*" she asks, displaying her find. "It's great to watch stoned."

It takes several minutes to figure out the projector and then angle it up. We strip the bed of its blanket and pillows to arrange spontaneous padding on the floor, and I retrieve my newly purchased dro, which I've yet to divvy up for tomorrow's sales. I roll some as she tells a story about a friend of hers, which I'm only half-listening to.

On the floor side-by-side, I inch closer until our arms touch. We're lying on our backs like corpses, passing the joint back and forth while she oohs and ahhs at the wide-screen images overhead. A spineless cloud of smoke lifts towards the ceiling's time-lapse sky, where daylight speeds into night.

"This is killer," she says, pointing through her visible exhale to the indoor moon. "And whose apartment is this?"

"Oh, it's my sister's."

"Pretty cool."

For a while we lay silent, staring through dilated pupils. I always feel awkward before a first kiss, even if we've kissed before. It's like getting a shot when you're a kid. You dread it and dread it, but the big day comes and your old disgruntled doctor says, "This won't hurt a bit" through his ugly smile. You flinch and flex and look away as he shoves in the needle. But then it doesn't hurt nearly as much as you expected, and it's over in five seconds. You unclench your jaw and realize, "Hey, it's not that bad. Guess I got all worked up for nothing." The problem is that it's another six months until you need your next shot, so you completely forget that it wasn't so bad and the same thing happens again. Not that a shot is the same as a kiss, but it gets me worked up all the same.

Honestly, the best part is the momentary after-glow—the post-coital cigarette, when she's half-naked and fastening her hair, resting her head on my leg and smelling like my sweat. It's like getting that lollipop in the waiting room.

This time, though, the glow feels stickier. Muted. We're sitting in our underwear with our backs against the couch and she's ashing into the hollowed-out shell of a candle. She smokes her filtered stog and I my rollie and the never-ending montage of images still dances overhead, but neither of us cares to look at it anymore. I feel hung over even though I didn't drink. Her little sex noises echo in my ear canals.

"By the way, Kyle," she says, turning her head toward me and adjusting her bra strap, "how old are you?"

"Why?"

"Because I don't remember."

"Twenty-nine."

Her eyes pop out and she retracts her neck like a turtle. "Holy shit, are you serious?"

"Yeah, so?"

"So I thought you were like twenty-five at most."

"Not like that's much of a difference."

"But you're almost *thirty*."

I cringe. "How old are you?"

"I just turned twenty."

"Oh."

I can't help but feel mildly offended. Most people would take it as a compliment that she thought I was younger, but the matter-of-fact nature of my age stings like a bee. A constant truth I can't escape. The countdown to eventual decay. Something inside me begs to play musical chairs with time and space.

Her bracelets rattle like coins as she scratches her skull. "Wait, so you're a bike messenger, right?"

"Uh, yeah."

"I remembered when I saw the bike in the kitchen."

"Right."

"So, is that all you do? Ride around and deliver messages to people?"

"Yeah, I work for a service. And then I deliver weed for this guy."

She laughs and does that flat-handed thing girls do when they try to hold cigarettes like movie stars. Now I'm more than offended. Who needs a girl getting judgmental on me, especially one who can't even legally drink?

"Cool, cool," Leigh responds, placing her free hand on my thigh and squeezing. "I like guys who ride bikes. Very sexy."

I want to snap, "I don't find you sexy anymore," but I don't. Instead we smoke another joint, gaze absently until the film's end, touch each other half an hour more, feel around the room for our clothes, and high-five goodbye.

I lock the door. The microwave tells me it's four a.m. Tomorrow is pay-day and then I can give Tobias what I owe.

Splashing cold water on my face, I press myself as close to the mirror as possible. Pellets of water trickle into every crevice. I pinch the skin around my mouth and search for signs of aging. The only new evidence is unflinching shadows beneath both eyes and sunken indents that make my cheekbones stick out more.

I brush my teeth with the "sensitive care" paste while filling up a glass in the kitchen. The plant is on the landing, so I walk to the window and pour water onto his chlorophyll fins. "Drink up," I mutter, with a mouth full of suds.

I spit and rinse and realize I've dripped onto the tiles. Rather than sop up the puddle, I switch off the lights, stretch out like a sunbather on Alana's bare mattress, and imagine myself retrieving the pillow and blanket Leigh and I brought to the other room.

Day 5

One by one I'm dipping Alana's low-sodium animal crackers into organic apple-butter. I feel more comfortable sitting cross-legged on the floor than upright in the kitchen chair. I'm getting crumbs everywhere, but I figure she doesn't have mice.

It's finally the weekend. Since I'm conveniently lodged in Manhattan, I'll just ride east in a few. Avenue A on a Friday night is my jam, unless there's a show happening elsewhere. Last Friday I was in Williamsburg heckling my buddy's band and drinking cheap beer.

For now, I've got the journal again. Just smoked my evening

joint on the fire escape and the plant and me shared a cup of water. With one hand, I plunge a zebra headfirst into the jar, and with the other I trail Alana's tiny words.

July 16

I feel too loosely tied to half-sincere apologies, art for art's sake versus this maddeningly oversaturated commercialized industry of artistic mass marketing (the opinions of unskilled others) poisoning my brain, eating so-called holistic foods (raw? vegan? macrobiotic? opti lipotropics?). Imbalanced, predisposition to dot dot dot . . . alchemical excuses.

I want to be less:

distracted, internalized, incessantly heartbroken (or at least put the pain to good poetic use), wishy-washy, self-judgmental, "meta-thinking" in my own head.

I want to be more:

inspired, validly artistic, confident, outwardly eccentric, focused, financially independent, healthy, and wise.

I want to stop making these lists and get more sleep, visit Dad, stop harboring residual anger, stop biting my nails, go to the dentist, watch more Godard, submit my film, stop missing the past and start embracing the future...yada yada yada. I'm not fully dressed and ow(!) something hurts. Big surprise there!

Alana versus internal gravity.

—A

I smack my palm against my forehead. Alana Alana Alana. These over-achieving obsessions are doing you no good. Every girl wants to be skinnier, smarter, more popular, don't they?

I wish I could take her to the squats and bridges and park benches and makeshift punk houses so she could see what it's like for the rejects, addicts, the truly uninspired who live moment to moment and not to impress. Though with her no-drinking policy and analytical mindset, this might make her feel even worse.

I wish I could explain that I've been on my own since I was sixteen. Even though I haven't much to show—no cell phone, computer, insurance, or place to call my own—I'm damn proud. Home is my travel pack and bicycle and I wouldn't have it any other way. Who needs the bills and responsibilities? Who needs to be tied to society? Who wants to be cooped up in a hip apartment oblivious to the raw asphalt down below? You know, it makes me sick to my stomach when people like Alana piss and whine about how difficult their lives are.

I raise a tiger cookie to all the kids who have struggled for everything they have. We can rest our heads easy knowing we owe nothing to no one (except maybe our dealers), knowing we've made it on our own and that nothing's been handed on some silver platter. Here's to true freedom. People like Alana will feel lost for the rest of their lives, even though they're square on the map.

I tear a blank piece of paper from the journal's end, intending to write all this down, but the words have already dissipated from my brain. Leaning on her book, I write again about my lackluster day.

september 29

"woke up fell out of bed, dragged a comb across my head"... sped off to midtown dirty and half-asleep. nearly got side-swiped by a car and shouted "fuck you" but his window was up. work work. saw poet-lawrence in a new location with his typewriter on the sidewalk. he's still selling his soul. told him i'd buy one next time and mean it. after work met skater-rob for a split second. he introduced me to this chick marissa. she was pretty hot, gave me her number on the back of a receipt and told me to call. probably will. hung around wash-square waiting for tobias to show at our usual time. saw an old man in a spiderman costume, all the usual bums, some guy jerking off under a towel, a living statue painted silver, oblivious tourists with dollars to spare, fucking tic and tac spinning on each other's heads, decent cellists and a crummy band wearing matching bandannas, hippie-man weaving bracelets, entitled NYU brats, and johnny good as new after his stint in the big house. he's avoiding cops around tompkins for now. at union rob and i ran into dawn, seems like she's on heroin again. sleeping in the squat on c, her track marks clear as day. i should have given her a few bucks but she'd probably spend it on dope. tobias showed. gave him his money and he handed me the beeper and green for the weekend. not enough. showered, shaved, blasted one of alana's cds. old couple still

at it, something about "you're going to kill me one of these days!" tried out alana's shampoo and it didn't smell as shitty as i thought. sat on the fire escape with the plant, smoked, dropped my new butane lighter. must remember to go down and get it.

kyle vs. kyle.

I leave my entry on the table and search the living room for my sneakers. Lingering at the bookcase, I glance sideways at the titles. *Healing with Whole Foods. Lovers of Cinema. Steal This Book*...whoa, Abbie Hoffman just gave her points.

I leaf through my good ol' friend. She's underlined some phrases with blue pen. Page 117: "Remember, the *New York Times* in its low format represents the Death Kulture." Page 144: "Guerilla TV is the vanguard of the communications revolution, rather than the avant-garde cellophane light shows and the weekend conferences." Justin and I stole this book ourselves when we were sixteen. It showed us how to score free food and make weapons for street fighting. It taught us better ways to hitchhike and shoplift and sneak into shows, basically to rip off and condemn "the system." This, of course, was back when I really cared about that shit. Back when I had what some might call punk rock ethos. Now I know that nonconformity is still, in the end, a form of conforming.

In the back of the book there's a whole "fuck new york" section with helpful lists for squatters and radicals, though it's mostly outdated. Once, Justin and I went to 125 Sullivan to meet "a poet named Delworth" who housed kids if he had room, but of course he wasn't there. Probably died like Hoffman.

My question is: why does Alana own this book at all? Curiosity? Maybe for school? I mean, she underlined it. Justin and I studied the book but we didn't fucking underline.

Something falls out of the last few pages and lands by my feet. It's a photograph. A Polaroid. A girl is sitting on the red couch with her knees bent, wearing only a bra and what could be shorts. The person taking the picture is on the floor; her eyes look down, into the lens, as she leans forward. I know it's Alana, but I don't remember her like this. Not an ounce of detectable makeup. Dyed black hair just above her shoulders and a purple barrette like little girls wear. Band-Aid on her knee. Square glasses. Pale skin. I can't tell the color of her eyes. She has skinny arms and small breasts you can practically see through the black transparent bra.

I'm not as turned on as I am intrigued. She is sad...not disappointed, but like she's not sure what to make of the person taking the picture, or her own self trapped inside. She doesn't want to be captured, remembered, stared at. The sides of her mouth turn down and her forehead is crinkled. There's sincerity to her seriousness. She isn't posing, isn't playing to the camera. Everything around her is static and unchanging, but a thought zips through her skull. I can almost see it. She's about to say something profound sitting there in her bra.

I tuck the picture back into the pages and shove Hoffman between *Timeless Reality* and *Dada & Surrealism*, pushing Alana's pretty face out of sight. Raising an arm above my head, I shout, "Onward to Friday night!"

The sneakers are by the front door after all.

Day 6

My body weighs twice as much as it should. Sleep is the only cure, but it's six p.m. and I can't sleep anymore. So far, the day has been filled with a series of uncomfortable dreams. Every now and then, a pounding headache poked through, and I'd press my fists to it. Veins polluted, tight.

Though the headache has ceased to pound, a dull ache remains, like somebody's stepped on my temples. I feel black and bruised. My body is mad at me, and who can blame it? I can't say exactly what happened last night, though I'm sure it wasn't anything new. Another bar, another one too many drinks, another acting like a fool, another riding my bike drunk, another night with people who don't mean that much to me. Justin and Emily were there. A couple of Emily's friends—girls who were nice, but horribly boring.

I rise off the bed and take a much-needed piss. It's dinnertime, but I'm not hungry. In the mirror my eyes look red and puffy. My hair's matted down. I brush my teeth hard and fast until I draw blood, but they still feel filthy. Can't get clean enough.

I pull back the glass to reveal three shelves of a medicine cabinet. Why didn't I think of this before? Hair ties, Q-Tips, nail polish, nail polish remover, hydrogen peroxide, Band-Aids, acne cream, mouthwash, eyeliner pencils, plastic thermometer...and all along the top shelf are bottles and bottles of pills, lined up like soldiers. Carefully, I lift each prescription for inspection, and discover a row of empty bottles behind the first. Percocet, Vicodin, Valium, Ativan, Ambien, Belladona, Klonopin, Xanax, acetaminophen with Codeine. How the hell did she get all of these? All I want is aspirin.

I rattle the Percocet. I could make a lot of money off this shit if I just took a couple pills from every bottle. She'd never even notice. I imagine showing up in Tompkins tomorrow and making fifty or more bucks between Shaggy and friends. Or offering Lawrence a special cocktail for free. It'd sure make him happier than buying any poems.

I put the pills back and click the mirror closed. I don't want to make this decision right now. Instead I glide into the kitchen and accidentally kick Alana's journal. I pick it up and pillage her kitchen for caffeine. The only source is peach black tea, so I boil water. Taped to the kitchen cabinet is a slip of paper that says, "When you know that all is light, you are enlightened." Hmm. Yesterday I noticed fortune cookie prophecies taped to various surfaces: one on the light switch, another on the microwave, two on the closet door. I hadn't bothered to read them until now.

I carry a Snoopy mug and her journal to the living room. The sky out the window is deep gray, thick with clouds. I settle down on the couch and get to reading.

August 23

My life is eternally frustrating. It feels like I'm going through a second adolescence; my skin is bad, my teeth hurt. The boy I'm sleeping with has a girlfriend. I'm lonely and cynical, achy and lethargic, stressed and nostalgic, harboring resentments, wondering why I always self-sabotage. I wish I could live inside old photographs. I wish I were a child, but I've lost the ability to exist in a fantasy world.

I really do feel adolescent, except for the fact that no one's around to stop me from making terrible decisions. I want to dissipate. Disintegrate. Create, collect, inspire. I don't want to work tomorrow. I'd rather take a five-hour train-ride to nowhere's land, or travel through time.

I wish he'd call (I miss him). I wish there was a way to more eloquently and elaborately express the sentiment (all of this) trapped inside. I need to write more. I need to go to the dentist. I need to lose five fucking pounds...dumb dumb dumb...and then quit my whining.

Alana, calm down. My thoughts play chutes and ladders. My nails are bitten to their cores. I cannot find my footage from June, even though I've lost interest in my own ideas and don't have the guts to make another short film. I am choking, hitting myself over and over until invisibly bruised. I'm afraid of being a cliché of myself. Oh well whatever nevermind.

Sometimes déjà vu is deafening.

—A

Nothing like Alana's inner monologue to make me even more depressed. She's so fucking lucky and she doesn't even know it. I want to shake her little shoulders and tell her, "Stop tormenting yourself. Lighten up."

I shuffle back into the kitchen to find my scribbled-upon paper from the night before, then sit down with Alana's clicky pen.

september 30

feel like shit today. everything else feels shitty too. it's saturday, i should be out making runs but the sky is gray and cold. don't want to do anything at all.

dreamt i was sitting on a rooftop with devangi. haven't had a dream about her in a year, maybe more. at first it was like replaying a memory...this one night when we climbed onto the scaffolding of a random building so we could fool around. i remember her friends shouting up at us from down below. in the dream the sky was eerie yellow and devangi was mad. she had this wild look in her eyes. she was controlling the weather, controlling me too. i tried to talk, tried to hold her but couldn't move. couldn't speak.

that kind of dream leaves you with all this feeling. aching. loss.

like somebody just plucked some organ and you need it back. like punching yourself in the gut. like listening to a song you used to play over and over and remembering how it sounded the first time you heard it. i can't handle the history.

unfortunately alana, everyone's a cliché. life is just that predictable sometimes.

——k

The neighbors are fighting. A dog begs for attention. I wander back into the living room and tap the doorway seven times. I stand motionless, horrified. I haven't had to do that in awhile.

The plant looks mopey. His leaves are hanging limp and his skin's a tinge brown. I can't remember whether or not I watered him yesterday. "Vadim, you're not looking so good buddy," I whisper, petting one of his flippers. Maybe he's having a bad day too.

Dashing to the bookcase, I search for a book on plants. She's got to have one somewhere. Ah ha! *Aloe Vera: Nature's Soothing Healer.* I sit cross-legged on the floor and read the appropriate chapter aloud. "Aloe vera is a succulent plant similar to a cactus, and shouldn't be over-watered." Oh.

For some reason, I feel really shitty about this. I wish Justin had told me not to over-water the damn thing, but I guess he didn't know either. "Vadim, I promise you sunlight tomorrow. No more drowning."

I shove the book back where it belongs and glance at the poetry shelf, where an inconspicuous Ginsberg section sits alongside Cummings and Plath. For some reason, *Ariel* calls out to me. I've never read a chick poet before, let alone the goddess of misery.

For the next hour, my eyes absorb poem after poem in Alana's bed before I fall asleep with the light on. I wake up to piss at eleven p.m. and find that I'm hugging her stuffed hippo. It smells like childhood.

Day 7

The birds squawk like babies and rouse me out of sleep. The sky is blue-blue like I promised, and I place Vadim in the sunniest spot on the fire escape so he can soak up all the rays. He looks so happy, glowing bright green. I can't help but smile.

I shower and shave, listening to another Alana CD and dabbing her "stress-free" lotion on my elbows. As I'm buckling my belt, a piercing sound sprints through the apartment. I rush to the video-intercom by the front door and Justin's black-and-white face pops up on the monitor.

A minute later, Technicolor Justin barges in like he owns the place. "What's up, man?" he asks, flinging his jacket on the table.

"Nothing, just about to go out. I didn't get to make any runs yesterday so I'm gonna head to Alphabet City."

"Alright, just came by to check on things. See how much damage you've done in a week. Already I see your dirty bike in the kitchen." He laughs loudly and smacks me on the back. I pour tap water into an *Alice in Wonderland* glass and trail behind him.

"Not bad, not bad," he says, looking around the living room. "You left some ashes on the floor over here."

"Yeah yeah, I'll clean that up."

"You haven't been fucking any girls in her bed, right?"

Well, Leigh wasn't technically in her bed, so that couldn't count. "No," I answer.

He drops onto the couch, folds his arms behind his head, and stretches his grasshopper legs. Justin's long and lanky body makes the entire room shrink. "Want to smoke a blunt before you go? I bought a cigar from that tobacco shop down the street."

"Sure."

"Pass me a book or something."

I hand him a photography book and he lays it flat on his knees, taking a Swiss Army knife from his pocket and slicing the cigar like a surgeon. Cross-legged on the floor, I look up at him. His hair is mangy and his brown eyes are too big for his head. What the hell does Alana see in him? And was it Justin snapping the photo of her on this couch?

"Hey, where did Alana go anyway?" I ask, trying to sound nonchalant.

"Why?"

"I'm curious."

"California."

"Oh...why'd she go there?"

"I forget."

I consider my next question before opening my mouth. "What does she do for a living?"

"Um," he bites his bottom lip while disemboweling the cigar, "works for a publishing company."

"Oh, that explains all the books."

"She's a brainy one. An indoor kinda girl."

"Is she in grad school?"

"Not sure."

"How'd you meet her?"

"Um, how *did* I meet her? Oh, it was when I was also working at Yaffa Café. Remember that?"

"No."

"That job lasted about three weeks. Anyway, she was nice and fucking cute so we met up after my shift and I took her to a show on the Bowery or something."

"She takes a lot of pills, you know."

"She's into that. Also, she's always in pain."

"Why?"

"I don't know. Headaches. Backaches."

"How old is she?"

"What is this, twenty questions? I don't know, twenty-three?"

"So...okay." I pick at the hole in my jeans while Justin pulls a dime bag out of his shirt pocket.

"Good stuff here. OG Kush." He holds it out for me to sniff.

"Nice," I respond, though I honestly don't care. I don't even feel like smoking. For some reason I feel like punching Justin in the face, even though I haven't punched anybody in years, not since that junkie picked a fight with me on Coney Island. "How's Emily?"

"She's good."

"Yeah, what's she doing today?"

"She went uptown."

"So she doesn't know you're here right?" I can't keep my voice completely level; it's rising up out of my throat.

"Of course she doesn't know I'm here. Are you crazy?" His eyes stare into mine as his tongue licks the paper.

"I mean...I just don't understand the situation."

"What's there to understand?"

"You living with Emily, but fucking Alana."

"What the fuck do you *care*, man?" Justin gets this crazy look sometimes, but it's hardly ever directed at me.

"I don't...I don't care."

"Give me your lighter."

I reach into my pockets and then remember how it fell to its death. "There's matches by that candle."

"Fuck that, I think I have one." He stands up to rummage through his pants and the room gets even smaller. He's about six inches taller than me. I don't usually notice things like that.

We smoke and joke about getting wasted Friday night, but my mind is elsewhere. Something's knotted in my ribcage, like a gnarled tree branch. It's Alana in California...I've always made it my mission to go there, but never got far enough west.

Justin leaves soon after our smoke and by the time I make it back from my runs on the Lower East Side it's 10:30 at night. I leave my bike chained on the street and open the mailbox even though it's Sunday.

The first thing I do is fetch the journal. It's waiting for me face-up on the table. The second thing I do is make myself a bowl of Alana's corn-flour macaroni. I stand at the stove, stirring.

September 2

I am all backwards today. I ate cereal at 6 am and then took Percocet and went back to bed.

I am making a vow, here and now, never to speak to an ex-boyfriend ever again. Make that, never to speak to boys again (uh huh, right).

I wonder if I have generalized anxiety disorder, or just a propensity for hypochondria-induced self-diagnoses. And ineffectual obsessions. And (psychosomatic?) chronic pain.

I feel old.

—A

Before I can stop myself, I'm clutching the pen and scribbling sideways in the margin.

alana...you're going to be okay.

Day 8

Dripping water and blood, I run into the living room and wrench open the window. "Shit, shit, shit. Fuck!" Vadim is soaking wet. I pull him inside, bang the window shut, and sop up his leaves with the bottom of my shirt. "I'm sorry, I'm sorry," I moan, working to dry him as fast as I can.

I waited for Alana's package this morning and rushed to work late. The sky was decent until around three, when it just fucking cracked. Torrential rain. Pounds and pounds of it slamming down on me, like god spiting my sorry ass. Then I remembered Vadim. I didn't care that the workday wasn't done. Racing downtown from West 73rd, I hit a huge puddle and dove to the pavement, cutting up my hands and forearm and banging the shit out of both knees and nearly breaking my fucking face, but I got up and kept going.

I've let the goddamn plant down.

Suddenly, I'm crying. I'm actually *crying* over this. I haven't cried in years…not since Devangi. I sit here with my bloody arm and bruised knees and dirty palms and drenched clothes and beet-red cheeks and watch the raindrops pummel the landing. "Vadim, I'm such an asshole. I can't do anything right." He looks at me unblinking, probably unthinking, and doesn't say a thing. My mind is wrapped around her face…

Sometimes I forget that I haven't been on my own all these years. Sometimes I forget those two, almost three years in Baltimore, before this city caught me by the throat and refused to let go. Unlike a more conventional breed of squatter, I always refused to dart south for the winter. After squats and park benches with Justin and before bouncing between couches, consistently overstaying my welcome with buddies who actually make rent, there was Devangi.

Everything about her was romantic. Surreal. She wasn't one of the dyed-hair, neo-hippie girls I attract now. Her name meant "like a goddess." She was tall and thin and wore a bright red stone and had this dancer's sashay to her walk. She used to tell me Indian fables when I couldn't fall asleep. She'd gone to college, but never made me feel bad about not finishing high school. Whenever we'd go out, I felt immensely proud of her…and better about myself, too. I couldn't believe someone like her could love someone like me.

I didn't know she'd get pregnant. I didn't know she'd want to keep it.

We were living in a one-bedroom down in Baltimore's Chinatown, near Lombard where she grew up. I was working all kinds of odd jobs, but Devangi was basically holding us up. She worked at the Baltimore Museum of Art and loved it. I wanted to marry her. The night we found out, when she told me what she was going to do, I proposed with a twist-tie from a loaf of bread. She laughed. We never spoke of that again.

It was 3:46 in the afternoon on April 21. Devangi's mom was there in the hospital. She gave me this icy stare that meant, "I can't believe *you're* the one who did this to my daughter."

We named her Kavita, which means poem. I'd never held something so tiny before. So vulnerable. Something that needed my help. At first I worked during the day—janitor, waiter, grocery bagger, selling knives door-to-door—but Devangi's parents had to help us out. I felt really shitty taking money from them. I was the father, the man. I thought I should have been able to do this, even though I was just twenty-four.

After a few months we switched roles, and Devangi went back to work while I stayed home with Kavita. She cried all the time. She just couldn't stop. She cried and cried. I felt so bad; I didn't know what to do. I gave her milk, rocked her, sang songs, made silly faces, but nothing worked. I started crying with her every time. I thought maybe she was mad at me; maybe she only needed Devangi.

The night I left, I wrote a letter of apology. I meant every word, but I can't remember what I even said…how I was able to justify…part of me thinks Devangi knew all along. She knew I wasn't the one. Part of me thinks she was glad I took it upon myself to leave when I did, before Kavita's first birthday.

"I shouldn't have given up," I tell Vadim, "but it's too late anyway."

I strip myself of the wet clothes and wash my hands with scalding hot water. I pour Alana's hydrogen peroxide onto my arm and watch the scrapes fizz and foam, then cover it all with two Band-Aids. Alana has Batman Band-Aids, and they almost make me smile.

I take her journal to the bedroom and lie naked under the warmth of the blanket.

September 17

I bought a rubber-ball for 50 cents from the supermarket vending machine, and it's a microcosm of the universe. A red and white swirly universe. Or perhaps hurricane season.

The air is gray and heavy with imminent rain. I am completely and utterly devoid of energy, yet I want to do something grand and crazy. This is what happens after my 4-day menstrual migraine. I'm lonely and sad…and how terribly redundant, but god I just feel broken. My spirit, my body, my soul. Everything. I am trapped in this body, and nothing I attempt for relief helps…analgesics, opiates, anti-inflammatories, anti-depressants, caffeine, acupuncture, massage, nerve blocks, triptans, vitamins, marijuana, mindfulness, muscle relaxants, yoga, sleep, feverfew, lavender, sex, psychotherapy, discontinued vioxx, shall I continue?

I know that I'm a lucky girl. I have a great apartment. I have a fairly important position at an independent company. I have friends and a supportive family…but I'm fucking miserable sometimes. I feel too much and keep it all inside. Time is deceptive and we're dying second by second, and I hate whining and complaining, but what am I supposed to do? People don't understand. They say, take an aspirin! Have a drink! Be grateful you have legs! Ok thanks, but when you wake up and you feel like someone is stabbing you in the innermost crevice of your head, stabbing you so hard and so incessantly that you can't think let alone see, and you can't lie down and you can't sit up and not only that but you have pain shooting through your neck and back and all down your body into your hands and hips and feet and you can barely stomach plain toast so you can gulp down two useless pills you wish you didn't have to take, and then you have to rely on your mother to come bearing more pills and saltine crackers, and she drives you to her house in traffic and the obscured-by-clouds-sunlight hurts the backs of your eyelids and you think this is the longest car-ride of your life and you are so completely carsick and dizzy by the time you make it home that all of your extremities tingle and you hit the bed clutching your neck because this is what you do when you cannot breathe…..then all you want, all you really want, is someone to curl up behind you and pet your hair and tell you that it's going to be okay. But you're afraid of that too, because you're a fucked up mess of a girl, and who wants to deal with that?

It's time for some dinner. Maybe I'll steam vegetables. I should go rent a movie or something. I just need get out of this place. Soon...soon.

—A

Day 9

"So then I said to him, 'You're totally missing the point. You don't understand pure rebellion, the whole philosophy of living life the way you want and not giving a fuck what anyone thinks, or what society says you're supposed to do.' Like, we're only here for so long, you know?"

"Yeah."

"Like, I don't want to grow up and get married and have babies and become this quaint domestic housewife in the suburbs somewhere and cook my husband dinner until I die. I just don't get how people are sucked into actually *doing* this...like, it's totally revolting."

"Yeah," I sigh.

Marissa is a brunette valley girl, wannabe revolutionary beatnik. She's got patches on her jeans and a homemade t-shirt that says "Anti-War." I was hoping she'd take my mind off things, but so far it's not working.

"The whole planet is going to die soon and we're all totally helpless and totally fucked so like, why bother conforming to societal norms? Why not just go crazy and lead the life you deep-down want to live?"

"Hm. Is that what you're doing?"

"I think so...like, I'm actively trying to." She talks with her hands and touches my arm every so often. She smells like Nag Champa and nicotine. "So Kyle, tell me something fascinating about yourself."

"Um..." It was a mistake to call her. "I don't know."

"Something, anything. I'm sure you're just full of stories."

Well...I could tell her about getting gassed at a protest, thrown in jail without food or water for fifteen hours. I could tell her about recklessly checking the payphones for quarters and riding the trains all night to stay warm. I could tell her about stealing food and clothes and a TV, about throwing Molotov cocktails, about shrooming in the park, about trying heroin with Justin and feeling galaxies away. I could tell her about bringing Dawn to the ER when she'd OD'd. I could tell her about setting up hospitals for wounded fireflies in my backyard. I could tell her about my father's fists. I could tell her about the campground where Devangi and I met, and how we'd talked in the glow of a fire. I could tell her about the nervous compulsions and counting rituals that started after I left her that note. I could tell her...there's a little girl out there who's half me and half Devangi. Instead, "I gave myself a tattoo when I was sixteen."

"Where is it?"

"On my hip."

"Ooh, let me see," she purrs, lifting my shirt and trailing her fingers along my ribs, all the way down to my belt. She pulls at the top of my jeans, exposing my hipbone and tracing the shape.

"It's a faded anarchy symbol," I say. "Pretty stupid, I know."

"No no, it's cool. Makes total sense." Her hair falls into her face and she pushes it back seductively, the way girls do. She giggles and leans into me. Suddenly she's kissing me, but I can't kiss her back.

"Yeah, um, so," I stammer, pulling away.

"What's the matter?"

"I'm sorry...I've got a lot of shit going on in my head. I can't really do this right now."

She gives me a puzzled look. "Okay, we can go chill in the park or something."

"No...I think I just want to be alone."

Marissa stands abruptly and glares at me on the couch like I'm her punished kid. "Maybe you shouldn't have called me then," she says sternly. For some reason, I give her a long hug, too long, while we're standing in the middle of the room. Then I lead her to the door, over-and-over apologizing for my lack of doing something wrong.

Later, the walls whisper. Vadim sleeps peacefully in the dark. I'm curled on the couch, counting the green blinks of the DVD player's pulse. The dishwasher's oceanic humming makes me feel safer and not all alone.

I haven't smoked weed in two days. Haven't written a journal entry either. What's the point of writing something only *you* are meant to read? Why did I start doing it at all?

My mind drifts back to the bar. The music was loud. The room smelled like any other bar I've ever been to. Drunken frat kids played pool. I remember now Alana's dyed black hair and pale skin. I think she was wearing a dress with black stockings. She stood idly, sipping ice water, watching Justin and me take shots. I remember now that I felt intimated by her stares, as if she was trying to figure me out.

I wish I'd said more.

I don't remember where I stayed that night, or who I went home with. I know I'd been mostly at Emily's, crashing on her couch while Justin occupied her bed, but I hadn't put two and two together. Hadn't thought about Alana and Justin, or Justin and Emily, or Alana as someone worth knowing.

I fumble around the bedroom for the journal. It's wedged between mattress and wall. Back in the living room, I yank open the window and climb onto the fire escape. An eerie light rises from the ground like mist. None of the windows bear life.

September 22

I am sitting on the fire escape with Vadim (he's telling me secrets no one else can hear).

I am licking a strawberry ice pop.

I am a boy inside girl-skin.

I am a mousey cat.

I am a balloon, translucent green.

I lose buttons, rings; use safety pins, staples.

I feel like dancing, and

screw you (and you and you and you) for my fantasies, my needs, my fear of rejection and mutual love.

I am more than someone's secret.

I don't belong on your pedestal or bathroom floor. Squeeze me inside your closet, let me curl there.

I'm still that girl, after all.

And...I miss my self. All of my selves.

And I carry lead in my chest, tension in my jaw, my mind is in the gutter again.

All I ever wanted to do was make peace with this body.

I am changing color and shape before your eyes, and you can't hold me down, can't claim me for your own.

I am not for show.

Hello....sunshine.

—A

There's a buzzing in my ears, the clamor of complete silence. Yes, I want to write you. I want to write her. I want to write Kavita.

October 3, 2006

Dear Kavita:

I wish I knew what to say, how to explain everything to you. Truth is, I made the wrong decision. I shouldn't have left, shouldn't have run off with my tail between my legs. You're five years old now and I'm sure as beautiful as your mom. I would like to see you. I would like to be part of your life again. No matter what it takes.

One morning we shared a Rocket Pop on the balcony. You had this really big smile on your face and I got this really big smile on mine. That was the best day of my entire life.

I love you.

—Kyle (daddy)

Day 10

Sweep every inch. Take out the trash. Put away dishes. Dust windowsills. Windex mirrors. Scrub down the shower. Make the bed. I don't even care if Justin gets the credit. Set the hippo on her pillow. Place the journal back in its bottom dresser drawer, rubber band intact.

I call in sick to work. When I woke up this morning, I almost expected to be somebody else. A whole new person. Like all of this, living here, could have somehow transformed me. But no, I'm not a new person. And the saddest part about this is Vadim. Oh man, Vadim. "Goodbye buddy," I tell him, shaking his slender green arm. "It's been real. Stay strong."

I tip an imaginary hat to the room, to the floor, to the ceiling, to the cabinets and the last remaining animal crackers crammed inside their opaque box. I double-check my pocket for the letter and my entries, then lock the door.

The day is warm and bright. Pedestrians are all smiles, walking two-by-two and holding hands. I've got my travel pack and bicycle, but I don't feel much like riding. I need to meet Justin at the uptown hotel to hand off the keys. When he first got that job years ago, we used to room-hop to watch TV and steal amenities. These days, things like that just aren't worth it anymore.

I walk my bike to the A train and stand inside by the doors. An old man in a blazer sits across from a young Latino girl holding a baby on her knees: pigtails, pink overalls. The old man smiles at the baby, and she smiles too. Across the way, only my reflection stares back.

In Limbo

SHE AWOKE WITH A FEVER. A small one, with distant burning.

Naoko's palm touched her daughter's forehead. Her earrings made tinny click-clacks as she shook her head. "No, no, no," she declared, pulling the scrunchie out of Tara's tangled hair. "There are too many things to do at the office and you've made me miss work two days now. Go to the bathroom and get ready."

"But Mom, I still feel sick."

"You're fine, you're barely even warm anymore." She turned Tara around and nudged her toward the staircase.

Tara stomped off in mismatched socks, pulling herself up the banister. Her legs felt like clumps of wet sand and her tongue tasted salty. Whenever she had a fever, Tara imagined large claylike shapes rubbing against small rough-edged shapes. She could feel their friction all throughout her body, like bare feet dragged along a carpet. She shivered.

In the sunlit bathroom cluttered with her sister's makeup, Tara brushed her teeth slowly to avoid a loose molar. She shoved a brush through her hair and blew her nose into toilet paper. Then she stumbled back to her bedroom and found her mother sitting on her unmade bed. Naoko was holding Tara's starchy blouse and navy jumper. "They're a wrinkled mess, but they'll do," she said, tossing the uniform at her daughter.

Tara turned toward the closet to pull her nightshirt over her head. She didn't want her mother to see her naked anymore. Whenever she took a bath, Tara made sure to lock the door.

The jumper felt scratchy, like the lining of her throat, and smelled of gerbils doused in Lysol. Tara eyed her Social Studies textbook swathed in a purple book-cover. She suddenly remembered the quiz Mrs. Hayes had planned for Thursday.

"Mom," she said, spinning around.

Naoko held out a pair of knee socks as if they were her stepson Ethan's underwear—gingerly between the tips of two fingers and far away from her face. "Is it too warm for these today?"

"Mom, I didn't do any homework," Tara said, grabbing the heel of one sock.

"Of course you didn't, you were sick."

"But there's a test on Native Americans today...I didn't study."

"Okay, I'll write you a note."

"But Mom...I don't know...what if she makes me take it?"

"She won't. Where did your loafers go?" Naoko pulled down the hem of her skirt and kneeled on the carpet. She twisted her neck sideways, lifting the bedspread with one arm.

"Mom..."

"*What* Tara?" Naoko threw a size-two penny loafer and kept her head down to rummage for its match.

"I still feel sick." Tara sniffled and forced a dry cough.

"You'll feel better today," Naoko responded, tossing the left shoe and approaching the mirror above Tara's armoire. She fastened her pin-straight hair with a clip, the kind with plastic teeth that pinched the skin. Tara pulled her fingers through her own dark hair, but they caught stubborn knots.

She watched Naoko wipe lipstick from the itty-bitty corners of her mouth. She knew that her mother had a *career* now, a career that required makeup and fancy jewelry to impress "the boss." She didn't know what her mother did, just that it involved endless stacks of paper. Naoko loved to mention that she was the only Asian woman ever to hold her position in the company. In marriage number one, she'd been forced to stay home with her daughters Hana and Mika; in her current marriage, she finished school and pursued this career. Then along came Tara, creeping up inside of her.

"I'm not sure who's picking you up," Naoko said to the mirror. "Maybe me, maybe Mika, maybe Ethan, maybe even your father, but I wouldn't count on *that*."

Tara shrugged and coughed forcefully for good measure. This one sounded a bit like the electric can opener and tasted like Robitussin.

Naoko swung around with hands on her narrow hips. "Alright, off we go."

Tara packed her purple knapsack and followed the ticks of high-heels down the stairs. Already the morning seemed blindingly blue, with a lonely seahorse-cloud swimming along the sky's curve. For the entire ten-minute ride, Tara leaned her head against the window's cool glass. The seahorse faded while she tried to remember whether the Iroquois or Cheyenne made longhouses.

The cafeteria smelled like a swimming pool.

At exactly 12:25, a hundred and thirty girls lined up single-file to walk through the cafeteria's backdoor, along the path by the parking lot, and into the fenced-in playground and field. The playground was a mixed ensemble of new plastic equipment and rusted metal apparatuses. The chains of the swings were particularly antiquated.

Kristen and Jenny, with matching ponytails, held Tara's hands and pulled her to their spot behind the swings, which squawked like hungry birds. They sat cross-legged on the blacktop while Tara hugged her bare knees to her chest.

"Make another keychain, we need a lot more to sell at Jenny's tag sale on Saturday." Kristen pushed her lunch-box, filled with plastic lanyard, toward Tara's feet.

"I'm tired," she protested, squishing the bottom of her face against her knees.

"Oh, come on," Kristen persisted.

"She doesn't have to," Jenny said.

"Whatever." Kristen took her half-finished lanyard out of the lunchbox. "What was wrong with you? You missed the math quiz when you were absent. It was easy though."

"No it wasn't," Jenny mumbled.

"I don't know, I guess I had the flu." Tara rested her chin sideways and sniffled as evidence.

"Did you get to watch a lot of TV?" Kristen asked. "Soap operas and stuff?"

"Or those shows where guys throw chairs at each other?" Jenny added.

"No," Tara sighed, tugging the ends of her hair. "My mom said she didn't want me to infect the whole house, so I just stayed in my room."

She remembered how she'd lingered in a state between wake and sleep for most of the week. At night, she'd watch iridescent particles flutter around the room like moths. In the interim hours between Monday and Tuesday, she'd woken with the weight of gravity pulling every muscle. A landscape of shapes buzzed and hummed and bubbled on the ceiling. She'd tried to rise, but crumbled to the carpet. Half crawling, she inched down the hallway until she'd reached her parents' door, only to find it locked. She'd knocked softly, careful not to "wake the entire house," but then her heart picked up pace and something caught in her chest: trapped, frantically beating its wings. She knocked three more times. Still no answer. She'd imagined her mother and father lying dead like supermarket fish.

Mika had entered the hallway wearing a t-shirt and socks. She'd picked up Tara and carried her to bed, wringing a wet washcloth and placing it on her forehead. "Go back to sleep, you'll be okay," she had whispered. In the morning, Mika left a note for Naoko, who took Tara's temperature and reluctantly called in sick for the both of them.

"That sucks," Kristen said, "I always get to watch TV when I'm sick."

Jenny nodded in agreement.

"Hey Tara, I can see your underwear!" The voice could have only belonged to Natalie, who had been teasing Tara exclusively since second grade. It used to be about her glasses, which Tara refused to wear anymore, though she had to squint to see the chalkboard and faraway people were immersed in fog. Other times it was about how quiet she was, which made the teasing all the more possible. Mostly it centered on Tara being the only East Asian girl in the entire grades 1-8 Catholic school. Half-Asian, actually, with a non-practicing Jewish father.

Natalie walked closer with her friends giggling nearby. Her corkscrew curls caught the sunlight, shining storybook gold.

"I don't care," Tara said, stretching her legs and covering her knees with the navy jumper. The blacktop felt warm under the noon sun. She wished she could lay every inch of her skin on it.

"Of course you don't care. That's because you're a slut!" Natalie and friends erupted in laughter. Tara knew she should feel offended, but she wasn't sure what this new word meant.

Kristen stood, gripping her keychain and narrowing her eyes. "Leave her alone, Natalie, she didn't do anything to you."

Natalie's friends cried, "Oooh," with hands over their mouths. Tara's fourth grade class and Natalie's fellow fifth grade girls were craning their necks from various spots on the playground to witness the showdown.

"You better watch your mouth, little girl," Natalie threatened, moving closer to Kristen. "Who wears red underwear anyways? Tara is *such* a slut, she probably makes money doing it."

A possible meaning clicked in Tara's mind as Natalie pinched the pleats of her skirt and performed a small curtsey. The big girls strutted, still laughing, back to their clique camped out by the parallel bars.

Kristen sat down again, obviously shaken. "That girl is so immature!" she gasped, gripping the lanyard. "*She's* the one who's a slut, right?"

Tara could only sigh in response. She didn't think Kristen really knew what she was saying, and she tried not to care what Natalie thought. It was old news, and she felt so very tired.

When the bell rang again, the girls formed a crooked line and Sr. Lucille led them back into the building. Before ducking inside, Tara caught a glimpse of two clouds swimming in sync, stilled in slow motion. She reached out to grasp them, but they were much too far away.

Tiny creases appeared at Mrs. Hayes' eyes whenever she smiled. While the rest of the class took her Social Studies test, she let Tara sit with her head down on the desk. Between folded-over forearms, Tara watched her classmates chew their pencils and swing their legs, until she lingered in a lucid dream.

She and Mika were in the midst of a carnival. Under phosphorescent lights from revolving rides, Mika's hair shone like a polished jewel. A long skirt danced around her legs. She took Tara's hand and led her to a ride, where they sat side-by-side in a two-seater cart on a metal track. The silhouette of a man pulled a long lever and off they went, tiny lights above their heads. *Hold on tight*, Mika said, so Tara gripped the railing. Their cart gained speed and lifted from the track, gliding into the fluttering lights, up into the midnight blue. The wind ruffled their hair as the carnival became a distant city, like an aerial view from an airplane window. The world below revolved without them.

A loud *achoo* startled Tara. She wiped her eyes, took the bathroom pass from its hook on the wall, and made her way down the hall. The bathroom smelled like stale Play-Doh. She splashed water on her cheeks and blotted them dry with a brown paper towel. Sitting on the windowsill, she watched a crow peck at something in the grass. A moment later, it parted its dark wings and flew off.

When the tests were passed to the front of the room and the girls restlessly kicked each other's desks, Mrs. Hayes allowed them to play 7-Up. For one round Tara walked up and down the rows of desks, choosing whose thumbs to push down. Then the final bell sounded and the class scrambled to collect books, bags, and lunchboxes. "Don't forget to do Chapter Four in your Vocabulary books," Mrs. Hayes shouted over the racket. Girls sped through the halls, ignoring Sr. Lucille when she reminded them to walk like ladies.

Immediately, Tara spotted Kristen's mom waiting by the school sign. She always arrived early wearing sweatpants and carrying snacks for Kristen and her sister.

After Kristen waved goodbye and Jenny scooted to her bus, Tara ambled to the sidewalk in front of the school, where other students waited for their parents. Car after car crept past, stopping to scoop up children. Tara caught sight of Natalie buckled in the passenger seat of her mother's Cadillac. Natalie stuck out her tongue.

Tara walked down the road, balancing on the curb. A large oak tree marked the edge of the school property, and she stood near its exposed roots. Her mother's car was silver, her father's black, her brother's red, and her sister's metallic blue. Many cars were these colors, but none stopped for her. She gnawed the insides of her cheeks and shifted her weight from foot to foot. The tops of the trees, now autumn-orange, glittered in the afternoon light. Above them, clouds interlaced like crochet.

Tara decided to wander farther to the corner. Behind her sat the church topped with an ornate cross. She thought of the dim halos that hovered above the Virgin Mary in all the church's paintings. Whenever the school had mass, Tara stared at those intricate oil portraits: round moonlike faces set against swirling backdrops of no real place. Above the archway of the altar, Jesus hung naked, beaming an embarrassed grin. Sometimes Tara imagined him crashing down on everyone in the pews.

One by one the teachers drove away; the buses, too, had long since gone. Her stomach whined, her legs felt heavy, her uniform itched, and her chest rattled with every inhale. Tara slouched forward, desperate to lie down. She counted the road's cracks, or those her faulty eyesight could discern, crisscrossing like a spider web.

A black car pulled up. It didn't look quite like her dad's. The window rolled down and Tara peered inside.

"Are you waiting for someone?"

A voice like the priest Tara always tuned out. A Rubik's Cube jaw. Shiny brown hair, parted in the middle, tied back in a ponytail. Feminine cheekbones. Black collared shirt, top button undone. No wedding ring, no jewelry of any kind, and no facial hair. Skin as white as chalk. Round eyes behind rounder glasses with black frames. Thin eyebrows, slightly arched. Older than twenty-five-year-old Ethan, but much younger than her father.

"Yeah, I am," Tara answered.

"Who are you waiting for?" He reminded her of Molly C, who whispered even when Mrs. Hayes told her to speak up.

"I'm not sure," she heard herself reply.

"I think I'm supposed to come get you...what's your name?"

She knew better than to tell him, yet an aura of fever remained. She imagined the softness of her bed, only ten minutes away.

"Tara Dresner."

"Tara Dresner, yes, I've found the right girl!" He made an elegant circular motion with his hand and patted the leather seat twice. "Hop in, okay?"

Tara stood rigid, feet planted on the curb.

"My name is Will, we've met before. Don't you remember me?"

She couldn't settle him into any crook or corner of memory. *He must belong there somewhere.* She found herself lifting the door handle, tossing her knapsack to the floor-mat, and sitting down beside him.

Upon closer inspection, Will's skin was marred by tiny indents. *Chicken pox scars.* Tara had one of those on her thigh. His hand gripped the steering wheel so tightly she feared its bones would break through the surface.

They crossed two intersections, through dual green lights. She pushed the button for the window, but it didn't budge.

"How was school today?" Her mother hardly ever asked.

"Um, it was okay."

"Why just okay?"

"Well...this girl made fun of me again at recess."

"Why did she do that?"

"I don't know. She doesn't like me."

"Maybe she's jealous."

"Of me? Why?" The thought had never crossed Tara's mind.

"Why not?" Will said. "Do you have a lot of friends?" He glanced at her sideways. His irises were colorless, a blue so faint you could hardly call them blue at all. Like water.

"I have two best friends."

"Two best friends? See, that's great."

"I guess."

She tried to read a street sign to figure out where they were; she hadn't noticed they were going the wrong way. At least, it wasn't the usual way home. They drove onto an entrance ramp and quickly accelerated to sixty on a highway; they should have been nearing Tara's house by now, the last one on Lakeland with a stone chimney, Japanese wind chimes, and her purple bike on its kickstand in the driveway.

He switched on the radio. "You can pick anything you'd like." Naoko never let Tara choose the station.

She watched luminous digits speed up on the dashboard and settled on a song she thought she ought to know. A high pitched voice sang about love.

She wanted to ask Will how he knew her. Maybe he was a client of her dad's, or someone at Naoko's job. She couldn't imagine that he'd know Mika or Hana, who was living on campus in another state. Maybe he knew Ethan? She wanted to ask him about the last time they'd met—perhaps she'd been too little to remember—but her voice folded like origami in her throat.

He drove a straight trajectory, without switching lanes. "Do you know what you'd like to be when you grow up?" He had a funny way of asking questions. An accent of some sort. He offered a smile as boxy as his chin.

"I don't know."

"You don't know?"

"Maybe a teacher," she answered.

"That's very nice. I'm an artist."

"Do you draw pictures?"

"Yes, but mostly I paint, and I take photographs too. Lately I've been experimenting with different kinds of art. Do you like art?"

"Yeah, I can draw koi. And I like to make bracelets and stuff."

"That's wonderful. I hope you like what I do then." He kept checking the rearview mirror. Glancing all-too-often at the cars behind them.

She felt her words rise through her: "Where are we going?"

He gripped the wheel even tighter. Bluish veins mapped out his hand. "We're going to my art studio."

"Why?" A moth was trapped between her ribs, stuck in the concave pit of her chest.

"See...your mom asked me to watch you until she gets home. She has some errands to run."

Whenever Naoko worked late, Mika fetched Tara after high school let out. Ethan was home most afternoons, too. He slept until three because he worked the night shift at the hospital. Their father arrived home around seven, just in time for dinner. Naoko would usually order Japanese and Tara had her own polka-dot chopsticks. Some nights, she'd help Mika make noodles or sushi. There was a TV in the kitchen, nestled in the corner of the counter, which her father always tuned to the news. People fought in the desert. A newscaster lost. If company came over, they ate in the dining room, with fancy plates and cloth napkins instead of paper towels.

"You okay, Tara?" he asked, turning onto Exit 9. They caught their first red light.

"Yeah," she answered.

"Don't worry," he said, his voice as smooth as glass, "this'll only be for a little while."

The lobby smelled like dog pee. Floor tiles gleamed. They

approached an elevator, which sat open and waiting.

Ethan had told Tara an elevator story. Someone at the hospital sent the body of a man down to the morgue. It lay on a bed with steel railings, covered by a sheet, bare feet sticking out. A tag on its toe like a t-shirt. Ethan had entered the elevator and stood next to the body. He didn't touch it, he said, but could feel its coldness creep into his bones. Suddenly the entire hospital had a blackout for twenty minutes. Ethan was stuck. Just him and the body. Just him and death.

Will pushed a button and the elevator door closed. Tara bit her lip and watched the numbers light up, fearing they'd get stuck somewhere in between. Stopped dead. When the doors opened on the fifth floor, she breathed a sigh of relief.

"Here we are," he said. She followed him down a dimly lit hall. After turning a key, he held open his door and flipped a light switch.

The first thing she noticed was the cage.

The second thing she noticed was the bird inside. Two birds, actually. Naked white, behind thin bars. "That's Ophelia and Persephone." She couldn't tell one from the other.

He wandered off through an archway, shouting "I'll be right back" over his shoulder. Tara stood motionless. Her knees felt like rubber bands.

She surveyed the room. It had deep red walls on which several paintings hung, a leather two-seater, a plain table holding an antique candelabra and glass-blown cylinder, and a large bookshelf full of cans, bottles, and tubes in every color of the rainbow. Between the bookshelf and the birds were several blank canvases, some big and some small. In the corner sat stacks of books and crates of art supplies. A smell of burning plastic clung to the room.

All of the paintings bore abstract shapes; some were suspended amid watercolor swirls while others were crowded in a sea of formless blobs. In one painting they looked like fluffy clouds. In another, stringy creatures swam amongst coral. She trailed her finger along raised, oily strokes.

"Do you drink milk?" He called out from the next room. Tara tiptoed across the wooden floorboards splattered with dried paint.

Will stood in the kitchen with a full glass of milk. He'd let down his hair and it lay in waves at the tips of his shoulders.

"Thanks," she whispered as he handed her the glass. Milk was for babies, or so Natalie had said, but Tara drank it anyway.

"You must be hungry too...I could make you some eggs really quick. Or, let's see, I might have a bagel somewhere." He rummaged through a cabinet with a black and white photograph taped to its surface. In the photo, a long shadow slithered up a staircase like a black snake.

"Oh!" he exclaimed, producing a box of Girl Scout cookies. She hardly ever got an after-school snack. "I have Trefoils left. Want some?"

"Sure." She sat on a stool by the sink and dunked a cookie. Will leaned against the refrigerator with his milk. His skin was nearly as pale.

"I live alone here, so boxes like this one last awhile. I used to have..." His voice trailed off as his eyes searched the air.

Tara coughed and his gaze flew back to her face. "How old are you now?"

"Nine and a half."

"Wow. You're almost double digits." He took a long sip and wiped his mouth with the back of one hand. "Would you be willing to help me with an art project before I take you home?" His voice was still smooth, but the hand by his hip trembled.

"What is it?"

"It's a new idea I'm playing with...see, I want to combine photography and painting, using live subject matter. A central focus obscured, blending in like a ghost. Let me explain. Art can transform reality...like alchemy. The artist is essentially an alchemist. Do you know what I mean?" He wove his fingers together to form a little web.

"No," she mumbled.

"An alchemist, in the Middle Ages, the time of Robin Hood and all, concocted elixirs, or potions, to turn anything into gold. Now an artist can take all sorts of objects and shapes and ideas, even people, and concoct something equally as valuable. For example, I could take energy from someone like you and capture your vitality, your spirit, on film or on canvas, and in that way you can escape mortality and live forever."

Tara nibbled her third cookie and stared at a metal bird hanging from the ceiling. "Like magic?"

"Exactly! So, do you want to help?"

"I guess so."

"Okay, what's your favorite color?"

"Purple. It's my number one favorite."

"Oh, purple is beautiful! We *could* do purple, but I think it's a little too mature for you yet. I was thinking green. Green is a spiritual color and a youthful one, too. It represents birth and rebirth in nature. I mean, what's green? Grass and leaves and plants of all kind, right? Everything grows green. It's balancing, soothing. Essentially, it's life." He paused and took another sip. "So is green fine with you?"

Tara nodded, closing her eyes.

While Will prepared the materials, Tara dozed off on the loveseat. She could hear the birds banging their bodies against the bars.

In limbo again, she envisioned a tank of blue water. A single iridescent fish swam upside down, its sinewy tail rippling like satin. Mika and Hana were there too. Together they dove into the tank headfirst—dark hair fanning out like black halos. Mika tried to catch the fish, but it glided away untouched. They breathed tiny air bubbles as they spoke to one another, but Tara, with her palms pressed to the glass, couldn't hear her sisters' words. She waved to them, but they pretended not to see her. They didn't wave back.

Someone tapped her shoulder. "Tara? Sorry to bother you. Are you ready for the project?"

Everything looked a bit misty. She swung her legs sideways and sat upright on the cushion, stretching and rubbing her eyes. The room was darker and it took a few seconds to remember where she was. Will had changed clothes; he wore a faded gray t-shirt and paint-splattered jeans. His hair was tied back again and the glasses were perched on his head. He'd draped a towel over his forearm like a fancy waiter.

"I'll take you to the bathroom to get ready," he said, gently pulling her up and leading her to a new door. "Here's what you need to do. Take everything off and wrap this towel around you." He said this like a secret and she felt her face redden. "Don't worry," he murmured, "nothing bad will happen. I promise, you have nothing to worry about."

She took the towel and shut the bathroom door. It didn't have a lock. Through a small window she watched the silhouettes of clouds drift in an indigo sky. On any other day, Mika would be out of school, her parents would be home from work, and Ethan would be heading to the hospital. She wondered if they knew, or cared, where she was.

Shoes, jumper, blouse, undershirt, underwear, knee socks, and headband in a pile. She blew her nose, wrapped the towel around her torso, and crept into the kitchen. "I'm here," she heard him say and followed his voice. On the way, she looked around for a telephone; she knew she should probably call her mother, even if she was busy running errands. But there was no phone to be found, so Tara tiptoed through a long beaded curtain, which opened into a back room.

Sponges and brushes lay scattered on a plastic sheet covering the floor. A tapestry, with intricate lines spiraling into knots, masked the wall where the windows should have been. A large canvas, painted green, was propped against it. Tara stepped closer. Various shades of green formed frenzied billows, glistening wet.

Will lit a candelabra on a stool, its flames licking air. Then he grabbed a bucket and spongy paintbrush.

"Will you take the towel off please?"

"Huh? Why?"

She felt the winged thing beat again, battering her rib bones.

"I'm going to paint," he said calmly.

"Paint what, paint me?"

"Yes, paint you."

"Why?"

"Trust me, you'll see."

Her throat felt like sandpaper. She felt a faint glow like a fever in her ears. A chill ran up the backs of her legs. She forced her fingers to loosen their grip and the towel fell with a soft thud. She wanted to cry, but no tears came. She rarely ever cried.

"Are you embarrassed?" he asked, dimming the overhead lights. "Don't be, please. Are you cold? Wait, let me get the space heater." He put down the bucket and plugged in the heater, facing it toward her. Tara watched its metal coils redden like a toaster.

Kneeling on the sheet, Will held out his brush. The paint was cold like a doctor's stethoscope. Damp too, with a sterile scent. He trailed a map of her arm, smooth and slick, around the crook and to her wrist, where greenish veins intersected.

The space heater's warmth was like an embrace, protecting her from the coldness of paint as it seeped into her pores. She thought of Mika in their bathroom at home. Sometimes Tara sat on the edge of the tub to watch Mika smudge silver dust atop her eyelids, tracing the bottom lid with a black pencil. Naoko wore lipstick to work, but she did her makeup privately in her bedroom. Tara would watch Mika powder her cheeks and laugh about the boy who was taking her out. *He's so cute and such a good kisser,* she'd gush, changing her top and blotting her lips. *Do you think he'll like this?* she'd ask, modeling a shirt that stretched around her newly bloomed breasts. Tara wondered when her own body would start to look like that.

Will hummed a vague tune while he worked. For a moment Tara forgot she was naked. Then the idea of it, the undeniable reality, washed over her anew. She wanted to scream. Moss-colored paint continued to seep. She felt unveiled, exposed, but then giggled as he ran the cushioned brush along her ribs.

"Sorry, does this tickle?" His voice sounded serious, like Sr. Lucille's.

"A little bit," she whispered.

"Tell me if anything feels bad and I'll stop." He made his way to her hip and she tried not to move. "Oh and will you put your hair up, please? I don't want to get it sticky with paint." He handed her an elastic band and she made a ponytail like Kristen and Jenny.

In the dim light, Will looked different, no longer like the stranger from the car. Tara wondered what he thought of her. Did he find her pretty? Naoko always said that Tara had boyish legs, with hard little calf muscles exactly like her father's.

"This is water-based paint I'm using," he told her, picking up a second can. "It comes off quite easily." He started the strokes on her arm again, traveling now to the tips of her fingers. This green was a warmer tone, like leaves infused with sunlight. The color mingled with the mossier hue. More and more of her swathed in paint. She marveled at her brand new skin.

As the paint dried, he told her to stand still against the giant green canvas. Then he thoroughly wiped his hands and grabbed an old-fashioned camera from a shelf.

"I want you to close your eyes," he instructed. Even her eyelids had been painted. "I'm going to take a few photos of you and then we'll be done. Ready?"

She nodded and flattened her back against the painting. Bursts of light burned bright behind her eyes. Something electric coursed through her veins.

"Stretch out your arms a little."

His voice and the clicks of his camera were the only sounds in the entire room. Maybe the entire world. She parted her arms like wings, pinned back to the paint. She wondered what Kristen or Jenny would think. Mika or Hana. Natalie. Naoko. Her *father.* When Will had journeyed the length of her torso, along the invisible seam that separated east from west, down to her very center, she'd almost asked him to stop. Had they been "doing it?"

"This looks great, Tara," he exclaimed like an excited teacher. "From some angles, I can hardly see you at all. It's as if you're invisible. Lost in the green."

Tara's mind raced back to her most recent dream. It suddenly made sense now, the logic rushing quickly. To her older sisters, Tara had been the one underwater.

They kept the windows down the whole way home. She heard the *whish* of passing cars and crickets snap their legs.

"It ain't easy being green, is it?" he teased.

"Nope," she answered, letting her damp hair blow in the chilly gush of nighttime air. She felt as giddy as a teenager and woozily awake. She'd never stayed up this late.

"Do you have school tomorrow?"

"Yeah. I didn't do my Vocabulary homework."

"There's still time."

The digital dashboard read 12:21. It was already tomorrow.

She wore her uniform again, without her headband or socks, and he wore the black collared shirt and spotless pants. After he'd finished snapping photographs, Will had left Tara alone for a shower. The paint had run like liquid streamers around her legs and down the drain. She had turned the water green. Like magic.

They stopped abruptly at the same curb where Will had picked her up. The church sat like a bored onlooker, towering above them.

Will turned to face her. "I have something to ask you now," he said, his voice serious again.

"Okay."

"Please don't tell anybody about this, especially your family. They might find it very strange. They wouldn't understand what happened. I think it's best that we keep this, our *art*, to ourselves. Is that agreed? Can you do that?"

"I can do that." Tara knew she could keep a secret. *Besides,* she figured, *no one would believe me.*

Will leaned over to unbuckle her seatbelt. For a second, his forehead nearly touched hers. "Are you going to kiss me?" she heard herself ask. His lips were so close.

Will jumped back, widening his eyes and putting up his palms. "What?" he stammered. "No, no, I was just helping you out."

"Oh, okay...sorry."

He took a deep breath and pushed a button to unlock the door. "Tara," he said, more composed, "I had a nice time with you. Thank you for all of your help, you did beautifully. Maybe I'll see you again. Somewhere."

She stepped out of the car, and he drove away.

Tara sank to the sidewalk. Everything was still. She rubbed her eyes. Across the street, an orange halo wavered around a streetlamp. She thought she saw moths dancing in its silent glow. She rubbed her eyes again, and the moths were gone.

India

THE OBVIOUS IRONY was that she wasn't from India.

She didn't know where she was from, ethnically speaking, but she could pretty much count on not being Indian. Why her adoptive parents named her India was not a story she liked to tell.

She bore the burden of being beautiful. A burden few others could stand to hear about. Her friends said she didn't have the right to complain. She didn't have the right to downplay it either, but that didn't stop India from trying. She donned low-brimmed hats and lopped off her hair. She wore chapstick, oversized sweaters, and ugly shoes. Somehow this only added to her charm. There's nothing more beautiful than a girl who doesn't know she's beautiful.

Everyone she encountered said she needed to model, as if the world would suffer a terrible fate if her face failed to grace its glossy covers. She had been granted the mysterious genes of physical perfection, so she had to pay her dues. It was the right thing to do, and she only had so much time to make it happen.

But India didn't want to model, or act, or stand in any spotlight. She would use and reuse the same analogy: "Does a tall athlete *have* to play basketball?" People would laugh politely, appreciating her modesty. Didn't they know that calling someone pretty could be just as damaging as calling them ugly? How could she live up to such a label, such an enviable identity? And what *was* beauty, anyway? Was it something in her facial symmetry, something subliminal like the golden ratio? Was there an underlying pattern to the usual culprits: the feline eyes and plump lips?

She knew everyone possessed their own concept of *beautiful*, yet somehow the world had joined hands in her name. So she kept on fighting her so-called beauty—or the stigma of beauty: the envy, jealousy, and decisions other girls had made about the kind of girl she must be. People asked about her parents—"Is your mother a model? Your father then? That must explain it!"—as if her face had belonged to someone else first. As if she couldn't claim it as her own. *Well*, she'd think, *I never met my biological parents, so how would I know?*

Deep down, India wanted to write—an art, people said, for the old and ugly. Or at least it didn't matter if you were old and ugly, especially if you eschewed the quintessential back-cover photo. In fact, the older and uglier, the better the writer. Or at least that's how it seemed. Relatives laughed when her mother told them about her writing goals, and India knew why. She wasn't born to be an observer; she was born to be observed. What did she know about rejection and suffering and character flaws, which were all prerequisites for budding writers? How could she capture the messy and degrading human experience? And what kind of idiot would throw away such beauty to pursue the solitary act of writing?

The biggest problem, though, was that India's stories never had a point. They got off the ground, sure, but they never went anywhere. What was the angle? Where was the *story*?

Her vignettes were plot-less character sketches of protagonists who were universal yet bizarrely specific. Not one of them was beautiful. Each bore the names of countries they weren't from and had never visited, and none explained why their parents had chosen those names.

Morocco licked the bathroom tiles after taking a shower. Laos built miniature birdhouses. Brazil was allergic to rust. Syria abhorred nudity and kissing. China was terribly pee-shy, suffered recurrent UTIs, and sprinkled apple cider vinegar in her nightly bath. Nepal was schizophrenic and held frequent conversations with the mirror, imagining his reflection as an identical twin. Angola sang lullabies to her pet goat. Israel collected Styrofoam packing peanuts and glued them to his walls.

Did any of these characters resemble the *real* people walking along Sixth Ave, darting in out of subways, ordering coffee with extra milk, hovering over public toilets, smacking themselves on the forehead, chewing nicotine gum, burning toast, chopping garlic, jumping jacks, popping Tylenol, tying shoes, setting alarms, falling up stairs, using the wrong card, breaking their vows, cracking their necks, testing the water with their big toe...or did India's characters exist only on the page?

After falling into a sickening depression and dropping out of college, she began taking semester-long "advanced" writing courses at the Y. Her mother tried to be supportive, but cringed whenever India asked her to read a new piece.

So there she was, taking seminars with people much older and uglier and therefore more entitled to the business of words. Week after week, the students tried to perfect their chosen art. *I didn't choose the art,* India wrote, *the art chose me.* Then she crossed out that line and wrote, *How pretentious, yuck!* with a sideways frowny face...still, she thought it had to be true. She didn't simply decide one day that she wanted to be a writer, like a stay-at-home mom might decide freelance medical transcription is the perfect job to suit her current situation. No, India had always wanted to write, long before she made her first attempt in tenth grade, at the start of the "you have to model!" mantra.

Back then she had penned a four-page story about Yemen and Somalia: they were very much in love, but their bodies rejected one another like a failed kidney transplant. Eventually the two learned to make love without physically touching, which solved the problem of their apparent anti-magnetism. After handing in the story, her Global History teacher called her mother, not only to discuss the possibility that India might have been inappropriately touched (*who hasn't?* India thought), but also to profess her sincere confusion since the assignment was to spotlight a country in need of American aid.

In the quiet of her bedroom, India came to her own secret wonderings: was she really just looking for her Benin, or Peru, or Cyprus, the way a girl named Juliet searches endlessly for her very own Romeo? Or was it that she'd rather write *about* love, naively and abstractly, than experience it directly? She'd never had a problem attracting boys. But as for their stares, letters, wilted flowers, and uncreative compliments...she didn't want to deal with it. She fended off all prospects of love, although love—or a false idea of love, a Halloween mask of love, a Top-40 lyric of love—wouldn't quit knocking at her proverbial door.

At the Y, India scrawled all over her classmates' pages, requesting they do more to describe the characters, even the minor ones whose names appeared once. "What is Conrad's biggest fear?" "How often does Faye call her mother?" "Why did John become a mailman?" "Does Emerald like her name?" "When you say here that Vanessa is 'pretty,' what do you mean? How pretty are we talking? Does everyone, everywhere, find her beautiful, or just a select few? How often does this word pop up in her daily life? What does she think about being called pretty? Does she actually think she's pretty, or that there's such a thing as physical beauty—one person being nicer to look at than another? To whom does she compare herself? Does she ever feel suffocated, with no way out?"

When people turned in revisions, it became obvious to India that her questions and suggestions had not been helpful. Few felt the need for extraneous detail, backstory, or internal dialogue, especially when it didn't advance the plot. Plot was the important thing. "Plots are for dead people," experimental writers said, yet nearly all published novels contained them. Plot might be for dead people but they were also for successful writing careers—for the hope that someone, somewhere, would someday take you seriously.

Whenever it was India's turn to workshop, a sigh rose up from the round table. Her stories were winding, with misplaced metaphors, missing indents, excessive lists, and unanswered questions. Was it worth the time it took to critique them? Were these really *stories*? "Could something happen here?" someone wrote. "What is the arc?" "What does the narrator want?" "Where are we going?" "What is the conflict?" "Why should we care?"

She developed a sort of trickery, though. She could trick people into reading her stories by way of a light tone, or by making promises she didn't keep. This was a serious no-no, teachers told her. If she showed a gun in the opening paragraph, the gun had to go off later. But in India's tales, the metaphorical gun remained in the opening paragraph and nowhere else. In other words, the gun never left the table. The gun collected dust. Often, she tried to employ her idea of a funny writerly voice, though she knew she wasn't naturally funny—ironic yes, cynical yes, ill-fated yes, but not *funny*. Her stories weren't good enough to be taken at face value, so they were assumed to represent some kind of self-reflexive mockery. Some carefully wrought meta.

Still, she kept at it. Wasn't it important that Morocco felt a compulsion to drag his tongue along the wet tiles? What did it matter that he never left the bathroom? Sure her characters were suspended by shaky strings, tied to no real setting and no imminent conflict, but they were *real*, weren't they? They had landscapes of thought and patterns of behavior. They had habits, hang-ups, dreams, phobias, pimples, pets, regrets, birthmarks, body odors, and oral fixations.

Life wasn't a tidy chain of cause-and-effect leading to some tied-with-a-bow ending. Life was amorphous and monotonous. Life consisted of microwaved leftovers and misplaced keys. Life was doodling on your fingers, throwing salt over your shoulder, nodding "yes" when you couldn't hear the question, trying to choose the right jacket for the weather, accidentally buying an overripe avocado, and signing your name as illegibly as possible...even if your name was some foreign country you'd never been to. Life was a myriad of characters milling about, unsure of who they were, where they came from, where they were going, or why they were there in the first place. No one knew this better than India, despite being blessed with the gift of beauty, that bewildering affliction.

So maybe she wouldn't be known for her writing. Maybe China's good-luck underwear and Brazil's phantom cavity and Syria's habit of pretending she was blind and Nepal's secret language and Angola's high-pitched sneeze and Israel's affinity for the sound of hissing soda didn't matter to anyone, didn't amount to anything, didn't alter India's fate or help conceal her barefaced beauty. But still the characters came, still their names graced her page. As for India, she wanted to be nameless, to be wholly undefined. And so she was, or at least on the page, in the truth that was fiction.

Anything To Save Her

ON THE FIRST DAY OF SCHOOL I wore a Batman t-shirt.

I'd passed by the junior high building for years, wondering what went on in there. My small elementary school had colorful murals of kids jumping rope and playing hopscotch, but this new building was large, gray, and squat like a prison. Cammy gave me a few details about it when she started two years ago, but she was terrible at telling me what I wanted to hear. She thought she was supposed to protect me from the truth. Maybe that's why superheroes never had sisters.

So I'd spent hours—days, to be honest—deciding what to wear and finally settled on my favorite Batman shirt (I owned five). It had a picture of blue-caped Batman above the yellow words: "Batman says 'Be Cool, Stay In School.'" I thought that was pretty funny. Also, I was hoping the slogan would distract people from noticing my hearing aids, which sometimes poked out of my hair. It was bad enough when new teachers called me up for a "chat" to make sure I didn't need to sit closer.

I was trying to unlock my locker after homeroom, which was a lot harder than it looked, when a tall kid with spiky hair and a shadowy mustache approached me. He looked at least fifteen! The guy smiled and said, "Sick shirt, bro."

I tried not to look stunned. "Thanks! You like Batman too?"

That's when his face totally changed. "No, I don't."

He paused for a second, then burst out laughing. I watched helplessly as he high-fived the kid next to him, who wore an earring.

"Superheroes are for six years old," he said.

"He looks about six, though!" his friend added.

I'd never felt so *bollific* in my life.

I later learned that spiky-hair was Sean and earring was Keith and the two of them more or less ruled the school, especially now that they'd started eighth grade. I didn't expect either of them to like me, but I held out hope that my Batman shirt would score a nod from *someone* that day. It never did. No one talked to me more than they had to and I barely saw the kids from my elementary school, who weren't friendly anyway. I spent most of the day trying not to get lost, and of course I sat alone at lunch. Good thing I had a comic book with me.

As soon as I hopped off the school bus, I avoided my stepmom's "So how was it, Jacob?" and ran straight to my room. I ripped off my bad-luck shirt and slam-dunked it in the trash. I stood there breathing hard and fast, then eventually dug it out and brushed off the cereal flakes clinging to its fabric. None of this was Batman's fault; he didn't deserve it.

After placing him in the hamper, I sat down at my laptop and added my new word to the ever-growing Jacob Farrow Dictionary (JFD).

bollific (adjective) – feeling simultaneously moronic, awkward, and nauseous

lone-loon (noun) – one Canadian penny in a handful of American pennies

pland (verb) – to fall off your bed

aero pulse (noun) – a plane mistaken for a star

I had recently pledged to create one new word a day. I got the idea last week after my stepmom, Yasmin, said the Arabic word *gufra*, which means "the amount of water you can hold in your hand." I'd never thought of something like that, so I decided to pay extra attention to my surroundings. Eventually, the Oxford English Dictionary (OED) would come to the JFD when they needed help creating words for complex emotions and common phenomenon that had gone undefined for centuries. As their top contributor of new words, I'd gain respect from people far and wide. So at least I had that to look forward to.

By the end of the first week of school, I'd added four more words to the JFD.

declask (verb) – to make a declarative sentence sound like a question, or to sound unsure of what you're saying even when you know it for a fact

soof (verb) – to get stuck in a door

soofer (noun) – a person who frequently gets stuck in doors

duhmiss (noun) – something that is new to you but obvious and apparent to everyone else

margle (verb) – to make a loud stomach or throat noise in the middle of class

Suffice it to say I hadn't made a real friend, though a few of my teachers were nice and the janitor smiled in my general direction. I got a lot of reading done at lunchtime. I'd switched from my comic book to *Lord of the Flies* so I'd look smarter and ahead of the curve. So far no one had asked about it. Sean and Keith, on the other hand, had an awful lot to say to me.

It didn't matter what shirt I wore (superheroes were out) or what book I carried, the two of them always found *something* to joke about. It usually happened in the hall near my locker, which they'd obviously memorized, and once it happened on the lunch line in the cafeteria, since they could easily spot me from across the room. It seemed like they wanted to shake me up in front of as many other kids as possible.

"Are you feeling sick, Batman?" Sean asked at my locker on Tuesday. He hadn't bothered to learn my name.

"No, I'm fine."

"Because you look a little pale and sickly."

"A little weak and wimpy, too," Keith chimed in. "What is he, sixty pounds?"

"I think he might faint! Quick, let's get him to the nurse."

Sean scooped me up and flung me over his shoulder like a sack of laundry. He paraded me down the hall for a good twenty feet. I couldn't see much beside the backs of his legs and the floor's gleaming tiles, but my hearing aids picked up echoed laughter from the students we passed. Blood rushed to my face and I worried that I might actually faint.

I heard a man say, "Put him down right now," and I was swung onto my feet, wobbling like a seesaw.

"Mr. Randall," Sean said politely, "we were just helping him get to the nurse's office. He doesn't feel well."

"Yeah, doesn't he look sick to you?" Keith said.

"Is that true, young man?" Mr. Randall asked. Standing between

Sean and Keith felt like lying in a pit with two dangerous giants I didn't dare piss off.

"Yes," I said meekly, "but I'm feeling better now."

A small part of me hoped that Sean and Keith would respect me after I'd saved them from detention, but the next day they made fun of my eyelashes, which were apparently girly, and then my voice, which was apparently squeaky, and on Friday they noticed my hearing aids, which I'd been fearing all along.

"What are those things in your ears?" Keith started.

"They're hearing aids," I *declasked.*

"Oh no!" Sean said, putting his palms to his cheeks. "We haven't been talking to him in his special language. He can't understand us!"

He and Keith proceeded to "talk" using ridiculous hand gestures and speaking in garbled voices like brain-dead idiots underwater. I wanted to come up with a witty comeback or at least walk away, but I'd gone mute and limp like a rag doll. So they kept doing it for another minute before high-fiving each other and ambling down the hall.

I knew they were targeting a few other kids and that I was simply a cat toy for them: easy practice for the real kill. I knew I was smarter and more observant than they'd ever be, and I knew Sean and Keith would eventually tire of their games; some day, they might even regret what they'd done and feel ashamed. But that didn't stop me from wanting things to change. As soon as possible.

When I got home that Friday, I bypassed Yasmin for the fifth time and locked myself in my room. I had a lot of homework for the weekend, and while I usually got down to it, no part of me wanted to open a book.

I lay on my bed and stared at the ceiling, where my poster of Spiderman stared back. He was hanging upside down, effortlessly clinging to a brick wall. Spiderman used to be a normal kid, too—a kid without parents, like Batman and other superheroes. Peter Parker's parents died in a plane crash set up by The Finisher. Later in life, Spiderman killed The Finisher in self-defense.

I remembered dressing up as Spiderman for Halloween; I must have been six years old then because Spiderman was my favorite superhero in first grade. Mom had taken Cammy and me trick-or-treating in our neighborhood while Dad stayed at the house to hand out candy. She was never one of those moms who stood on the sidewalk and waited impatiently; she came with us to every doorstep and shouted "trick or treat!" with glee. She'd painted her face green and wore a crooked witch nose, so she didn't even look like Mom anymore, but her voice was the same, and her touch and her laugh, and who could be scared of a witch like that?

I realized that I was one parent away from becoming an orphan like Peter Parker. I took out my hearing aids and let the distant voices of Cammy, Yasmin, and the TV fade to a dull hum. Other sounds took their place: whispering waves of white noise like holding a conch shell to your ear. Sometimes the white noise became shrill and piercing like ghosts screaming in echoes. But mostly it sounded like wearing earmuffs made of Styrofoam.

White noise was such a perfect term for the collection of sounds that sounded like nothing yet still like something. I loved the simplicity of words—that was my goal for the Jacob Farrow Dictionary. Why say three or four or more words to describe something when you could just use *one*? Sometimes you only had one shot at explaining yourself.

I flinched when Cammy knocked on my door, which shook the whole wall. I knew it was her because she always knocked three times, hard and fast, no matter what. One, two, three: "Jacob, open up!"

Scrambling off my bed, I put in my hearing aids and unlocked the door. She was clutching her phone in its sparkly blue case. I could hear that phone pinging all over the house; it vibrated my teeth. If there was a fire, I was pretty sure she'd save her phone before me.

"Hi Cammy."

"Ew, stop calling me that."

"But I've always called you that."

"I'm Cameron now, okay? I've told you that like sixteen times."

"But you always said Cameron was a boy's name."

"Well I think it's cool now. Cammy's, like, lame. Anyway, Dad just called from work and said he's taking us for pizza to celebrate my first week of high school and your first week of junior high."

"Oh, great."

"I know, it's thrilling. We're going early because I'm staying at Annabel's and I promised her I'd be there before eight."

"Okay. Can I come with you?"

"To Annabel's?"

"Yeah."

Cammy had been friends with Annabel Wong since first grade and they used to invite me to play with them too. We loved pretending we were mermaids in her pool and superheroes on her trampoline.

"For real?" She threw her head back and laughed. "No Jacob, of course you can't come. God, we're not like eight years old anymore."

"Oh. Right."

I looked at my sister for a good long second. Everything about her appearance had changed. I couldn't pinpoint when or how this change had happened, but her hair was blonder and her boobs were bigger (I tried not to notice, but they were right in front of me) and she wore an undersized shirt and gunk around her eyes. She looked almost nothing like the girl I'd grown up with, while I looked like the same ol' Jacob Alexander Farrow.

"Sorry for my *duhmiss*," I said.

"Your what? Speak English, weirdo."

I didn't know what had happened to my best friend, the one person I could trust in the entire world. Was she still the girl who woke me up on Christmas morning, squealed when I said "juice," let me win at Uno, offered me the burned corners of her Pop Tarts, and performed "the worm" when I felt sick? Where was that girl? Had *Cameron* taken her place?

"Nevermind," I said.

My stranger-sister walked away and I returned to my bed, sitting up and staring into space. Spiderman was still looking down on me.

According to the dictionary, a hero was "a man of distinguished courage or ability, admired for his brave deeds and noble qualities" (and also the "bread or roll used to make a sandwich" but that was beside the point). The dictionary never mentioned how to go about becoming a hero, let alone a *super*hero, but that's where movies and comic books came in. In all the movies I'd seen and books I'd read, the hero saved civilians (usually girls) and killed villains (usually guys) and then everyone endlessly praised him whether or not they knew who he was. The hero was strong and smart and suave and speedy, and he wore a cool costume that made his muscles look more muscly. Hair gel was also required.

A tingling sensation invaded my skin...that was *it!* All I needed to do was save people—no, *one* person—and I'd gain respect, praise, and adoration with or without a cool costume. It was better than waiting for the OED to publish my words and much more likely than standing up to two bullies. Once I saved someone, the local news stations would interview me and my face would appear in the paper—or ideally in a viral video like the one of that golden retriever saving a drowning child—and then Sean and Keith would stop harassing me, and Cammy would lovingly bring me to Annabel's, and everyone everywhere would want to be seen with me forever.

By the time Dad took us for pizza, I already had a plan.

When I asked Yasmin if I could tag along to yoga, she looked at me with remorse.

"You know my class is for women *only*," she said delicately, like she might crush my soul.

"I just want a ride to the mall," I explained.

"Oh, sure!" she said. "Are you meeting friends?"

Yasmin knew perfectly well that I didn't have friends, not since Finn moved to Colorado in fifth grade and all the other kids started leaving me out.

"I just want to look at comics and stuff."

I put on the bookbag I'd packed the night before. It contained an empty binder that could double as a shield, a mini baseball bat I got once at a game, and very sharp scissors that could inflict some major damage. I also had Sour Patch Kids for diabetics and bandages for bloody victims. I even packed my toothbrush in case I got kidnapped while saving someone else. Hygiene was important no matter what.

Luckily Yasmin didn't ask about the bag; she just grabbed her yoga mat and found the keys to her Honda. She also didn't notice the gel I'd worked into my hair, or if she did, she didn't mention it.

I'd always liked Yasmin, though I used to pretend to hate her because Cammy didn't think Dad should replace Mom. Yasmin's cinnamon eyes and seesawing laugh were a lot like Mom's, but that's where their similarities ended. For most of Yasmin's childhood, the Iran-Iraq War was in full swing. Bombs wrecked her neighborhood.

Her best friend was paralyzed after debris crushed her spine. Her father carried a gun everyday. Two uncles and three cousins—the youngest fourteen like Cammy—signed up to be soldiers and died. Yasmin often stayed home from school, reading books under her bed. At twelve, my age, she left Iran for good and came to the United States for the first time. Looking at her now, wearing fuchsia yoga pants and singing along to Adele, you'd never think she had seen so much death and destruction in her life.

Were her uncles and cousins "heroes" for deciding to fight in the war? Was her father a hero for protecting her? Was her mother a hero for getting her out of that country and starting over in America? Could I ever do something like that?

Yasmin parked and we headed inside the open-air mall. "Meet me at Starbucks at exactly one o'clock," she said as she handed me two crisp twenties.

"What's this for?"

"Whatever you want, kiddo. Comics, a game, or maybe a new Batman shirt?"

She pinched my cheek and waltzed off to the yoga studio. Once her fuchsia legs had turned a corner, I walked to the center of the mall's first floor, where the bare sun poured onto potted plants. Pennies glimmered at the bottom of a fountain and I tried to telepathically receive the wishes they contained. I wondered if any of them held a wish like mine.

I switched my gaze from the drowned pennies to the dozens of people strolling about. On all three floors, people lugged bags, sipped straws, checked phones, and held hands. It was a sunny September Saturday and no one appeared to be in any distress.

According to my digital Iron Man watch, I had fifty-five minutes until Starbucks. Would anyone need saving in the next fifty-five minutes? There had been plenty of terror attacks in malls and I was certainly prepared to handle one, but if I just kept standing alone at the fountain, someone might suspect *me* of planning something crazy. Of course, I could have created a scenario that would necessitate heroic deeds. For instance, I could have struck a match—or rather, I could have tried to buy matches, then tried to light one—and secretly thrown it into one of these stores, like the Pottery Barn with all its fluffy pillows and billowy drapes and wooden tables. Then I could have rushed in and pulled out a toddler who got trapped in the blaze. But in that case I'd also be the villain, and that just didn't sit right.

I consulted Iron Man again: ten minutes had passed! I commanded my legs forward. Sniffing out danger like a bomb dog, I searched for puddles and banana peels, dangling wires and broken pipes, creepy men and suspicious packages. I made note of the exits. I looked for bulges in pockets. I searched faces for fear. I turned my hearing aids to the highest volume, in case someone let out a high-pitched scream.

Then I saw him: a shaggy-haired, nervous-looking man in his twenties or thirties sitting at a table near Auntie Anne's, trying to screw (or unscrew) some kind of cylindrical bomb! I flattened myself against the wall and sucked in my breath. *What would Batman do?*

Just as I began reaching for the baseball bat in my bookbag, I saw that he wasn't holding a homemade bomb but a bottle of iced tea. His hands didn't work right; they were too straight and awkward, so he kept twisting and twisting the cap between his palms like a frustrated two-year-old. I switched modes: I didn't have to hurt this guy, I had to help him! I puffed out my chest, deepened my voice, and prepared to save the day.

"My name's Jacob Farrow and I'll help you with that."

The guy looked up at me, sweat shining on his forehead. "Sorry?"

"I said I can help you," I repeated, reaching out to grab the bottle.

"No thanks. I got it."

"I can do it, really."

"I said no thanks." He turned back to his bottle and struggled some more, like wrestling a slippery fish. I stood there, stock-still. Eventually the cap came off and he smiled to himself, then returned his gaze to me. "Are you still *here*?"

I darted off, cheeks aflame. I had thirty minutes left. Even if no one needed rescue, some animal or human *must* have needed help! And helping someone was just as good as saving them, so long as a bystander snapped a photo, got my full name, and then circulated the story. The cruel world craved such a story these days.

Downstairs by the bathrooms, I noticed a frazzled mom. Her infant son was squirming in the carrier strapped to her chest while her daughter threw a tantrum. These kids were about the same age difference as Cammy and me—was this what Mom had gone through with us? I bet she would have appreciated assistance from a selfless stranger.

"Daisy, get off the floor *now*."

"Noooo!" The girl kicked and screeched and slammed her tiny fists. Meanwhile, the baby squirmed so hard that the mom had to unstrap him and put him down. Now the whole family was on the ground, getting in people's way.

"You said you had to go three times. We don't want another accident."

"Don't wanna! Want dots!"

"You are not getting the Dippin' Dots until you use the potty. Stop making a scene."

While the mom tried to calm her daughter, the baby started crawling away. I blocked him the same way I'd stop my grandma's dog from going outside. "I can help you," I called out, but the mom didn't hear me over her daughter's screams, so I bent down and lifted the baby. He was bulkier than a miniature poodle, and way heavier than I thought babies ought to be, like a bowling bowl with legs. I didn't know how to hold a baby either, so he was just kind of flapping around, limbs akimbo, while I held onto his pudgy midsection.

The mom's head spun, searching for the infant. When her eyes locked on me, she gasped and jumped up.

"I can hold him," I said, my voice strained, "while you take Daisy…to the bathroom."

"Who are you? What are you doing with Liam?" she shouted as she rushed over.

"I'm Jacob…Farrow, and I got…him," I repeated, though both Liam and me starting sinking to the carpet. "Take…Daisy."

The mother tried to pluck Liam from my arms but I was gripping him too tight.

"Let go of him," she said through gritted teeth. I released the boy and he fell from my arms into hers. All around us, people *blarked*. "What were you thinking?" the mom said brusquely. "You don't just pick up other people's children."

I started to back away, though I knew it made me look shady. The mother returned to Daisy, who was standing up and no longer crying. At least I'd solved one problem. Maybe the mother would remember my name and thank me later.

My body felt like an overstretched rubber band, both flimsy and taut, as I accidentally bumped into three people, including an old lady, on my way to Starbucks. *Sorry, sorry, sorry.* Ten minutes to go and the line practically wrapped around the store. I practiced my order: one Iced Skinny Mocha (for Yasmin; yes, I paid attention) and one Sweet Tea Lemonade (for me). As I waited patiently, I noticed how poorly people treated the baristas. Nobody smiled or said, "How are you today?" Nobody thanked them in a meaningful way. And from what I could tell, nobody tipped, even though there was a tip jar sitting smack on the counter.

I pulled a twenty from my pocket and a pen from my backpack. I started writing on the twenty, but then I realized that wasn't smart...would they still accept the cash with words all over it? New plan: I darted off the line, took a napkin, weaseled my way back in, *sorry sorry*, and started writing on that instead.

Dear Starbucks baristas,

Thank you from the bottom of my heart. You deserve tips like this all the time. You are wonderful human beings and you look nice in green.

Sincerely, Jacob Farrow

I folded the napkin around the twenty to make sure they stayed together, that way they'd know I tipped twenty bucks and not just extra pennies I didn't feel like throwing in a fountain. Finally, it was my turn.

The barista had long hair on one side and a shaved scalp on the other. I wondered if she'd had brain surgery recently.

"How's your day, Jimena?" I asked, reading her nametag.

"It's *hee-MEH-na*," she said, with a huff. I thought about how Yasmin always said, "it's *yaz-MEEN*" when asked to spell her name at the drug store or over the phone.

"Oh, sorry," I said, blushing. "My name is Jacob. It's cool that our names both start with J, right? Even though yours sounds like an H."

"Uh huh. Can I take your order?"

"Oh, um," I racked my brain for the order, trapped in there somewhere. I managed to eke it out, bit-by-bit, tripping on Jimena's questions about grandes and ventis.

"That's $7.23."

I grabbed the other twenty. "How are you feeling?" I asked in my most sympathetic tone.

"What do you mean?"

I pointed to the shaved side of her head. "Your…surgery," I whispered. I figured she didn't want everyone to know.

"Are you serious?" She shook her head and turned to the cash register. There was a tattoo of a swallow on her neck. Maybe she was secretly a pirate.

"Jacob, there you are." Yasmin squeezed past the lumpy bags of coffee beans.

"I got your favorite drink," I said cheerfully as I took the change from Jimena.

"Oh…I'm trying to cut back on caffeine on the weekends." My smile faltered. "It's okay, I'll drink it anyway."

"Pick them up over there," Jimena said.

Yasmin and I went to stand near the other customers when I remembered that I'd forgotten the tip. The tip was the whole point! I took it out of my pocket, making sure the napkin was still folded with the bill, and did a little electric-slide back over to the register.

"You again?" Neither Jimena nor the man now ordering looked pleased.

"I just wanted to say *thank you.*" Slowly, I placed the money in the jar—*Thanks a latte*, it read—so she could glimpse how much it was. Before she could say anything I slid back to Yasmin, who looked puzzled.

"What was that about?" she asked.

"What was what about?"

"Did you just put a napkin in there?"

"Yes. And no."

"Why did you give her a napkin?"

"Um…see, I wrote a note on it and added a tip."

"How much did you tip her?"

"Twenty."

"You tipped her a *twenty*?" Yasmin shouted. People around us stopped talking and *blarked.* Was I a total fool? In any case, they all knew of my good deed.

Yasmin didn't speak again until we were out in the parking lot, drinks in hand. She unlocked the Honda and I went to open the door, only I caused a *knoblidge.* Then another *knoblidge.* Then another until Yasmin shouted, "Stop!" and I held still while she got the door unlocked. When I climbed in, we put our drinks in the cup holders. The ice sat there melting all the way home.

For days I *isolized* in my room, wondering where I'd gone wrong. I had loaned out every pen I owned (now I needed to borrow one); let dumb-as-a-doorknob Dylan copy my homework (did that count as heroic?); told the cafeteria ladies their lunch tasted great (it did not); gave sympathy nods to the few other kids Sean and Keith teased (they just seemed spooked); and helped my teachers by moving desks, passing out tests, wiping Smart Boards, and feeding crickets to the Homeroom 201 chameleons even though it grossed me out. But for all of these efforts, I wasn't any closer to becoming a local hero and gaining adoration. I was, however, inventing new words at an alarming rate. Maybe the JFD was my sole reason for existing.

blark (verb) – to stare at a stranger because you are judging them

knoblidge (noun) – when a person tries to open the passenger door at the exact same time the driver tries to unlock it, but it doesn't open because you're out of sync

oopsy doo (noun) – a bad hair/clothes/face day you can't fix

isolize (verb) – to think excessively all alone, without saying or doing anything else

By Friday I was too pooped to even do much *isolizing*. Junior high was exhausting, especially since I'd been spending so much time trying to save someone. I plopped down on the living room couch and blindly watched *America's Funniest Home Videos* while scooping peanut butter from a jar. It was the kind of thing girls did in movies after getting dumped, which felt appropriate.

A portly lady climbed a ladder, waved to the camera, and grabbed hold of a rope swing. I wished I could swoop through the TV and stop her. Just as I feared, she landed smack on the dirt, splat like a bug. I hoped there was a video of Sean and Keith doing something stupid. They deserved to be laughed at.

The screen door banged shut and in walked Cammy and Annabel. Either they didn't see me or ignored me on purpose as they moved into the kitchen, opened and closed cabinets, climbed the stairs, and made their way to Cammy's bedroom, chatting like hyper cockatoos the whole time. I seethed with envy. I wanted to join them, or at least make my presence known, but I forced myself to watch a few more videos that were much more pathetic than funny. They should rename the show *America's Most Pathetic...America's Saddest...*they needed a new word! I rolled ideas around in my mind, then switched off the TV.

Tiptoeing toward Cammy's slightly opened door, I peered into the chaos of her room. She and Annabel were sitting cross-legged on the bed, phones in hand and snacks splayed around them. Annabel had spent the whole summer at sleepaway, so I hadn't seen her since June. Her hair was shorter and a big chunk of it was purple, like a misshapen lightning bolt about to strike her shoulder. She still wore braces, but somehow they looked cool on her. I imagined the three of us munching popcorn and binge-watching *Batman*, though I would have settled for munching popcorn and playing truth or dare if that's what they wanted to do.

All of a sudden Annabel squealed. "I can't even!"

"I know!"

"Like, Matt's officially your bae now."

What did that mean? Were they inventing words too?

"I know," Cammy repeated, though this time her *o* stretched like periwinkle taffy.

"'In a relationship with Cameron Elizabeth.' Here, for everyone to see!" Annabel waved her phone in the air. "Like, sorry bitches, I'm in a *relationship*."

"And I didn't even ask him to do that!"

"Which makes it so much better, obvi."

I couldn't stop myself from interjecting: "Who's Matt?"

All eyes turned to me. The grin fell off Cammy's face. Annabel smirked.

"None of your business!" Cammy shouted. "God, can't I talk to my friend in peace?"

Annabel gave me a sorry look as Cammy ran over and slammed the door. *Cameron,* that is...that was definitely Cameron's doing. I stood there in a daze, then slinked back to my room and quickly opened the JFD on my laptop. I spent several minutes creating my new word and said it aloud to test its strength.

piticarious (adjective) – intended to be funny, but actually sad and/or pathetic

America's Piticarious Home Videos. That sounded okay. I felt a bit better.

I wanted to read a book or play a game or help Yasmin in the garden, anything to get away from the giggly girls behind the slammed door, but before I knew it my fingers were typing, "What does bae mean?" into the trusty Google rectangle.

"Before Anyone Else," "a shortened version of baby or babe," or "poop" in Danish

Okay. The only logical explanation was that my sister had a boyfriend. And that boyfriend's name was Matt. Matt who? Before I could stop myself, I pulled up Cammy's Facebook page. I had never joined Facebook so I couldn't see much. I doubted she'd accept me as a friend anyway.

Cameron Elizabeth's profile picture was the definition of "selfie" (yes, I knew that word). There she was in our bathroom—I spied the edge of my Superman towel—giving doe eyes, pouty lips, and a peace sign. When I clicked the picture it had 62 Likes and several comments containing hearts, smiley faces, and phrases like "omg stop it cam, why u so preeeetty!?!!" In the next picture, she wore a stringy bikini and tinted sunglasses under a sky that looked unnaturally blue—"#sexygirl," "legit stacked," "holy hawt bod mmhm," and "dam! thx for this, gorge!" all from different boys.

I quickly exited the picture and searched her page until I hit the jackpot: "In a relationship with Matt Danger Donahue." I clicked his name. He looked older than Cammy, maybe sixteen. His profile picture was a four-image montage that showed him gradually consuming a slice of pizza. He was sitting on a rooftop wearing bright red headphones and a beanie that said "Whatever." 101 Likes. A guy named PJ Swag wrote, "killer beats." A girl named Zoe Katz wrote, "I'm jelly of that pizza LOL."

I turned off my laptop. My forehead hurt. I felt like I'd invaded a secret society I'd never belong in, though I was pretty sure I didn't want to anyhow. But now that I'd encountered this strange new world with strange new words, I knew I had to do something. Did Dad care about Cammy posing in a bikini? Or getting praise from different boys? Or dating a guy with the middle name Danger? And what would Mom have to say about it?

I lingered on that word: *Danger*. It was a hint like none other. A superhero's call to arms. A sure sign from somewhere above.

I wanted gadgets like Batman—I'd envisioned hanging upside down and using grapple hooks on rooftops—but I had to do things the old-fashioned way. So I pressed my ear (the left one was better) to Cammy's door whenever Dad and Yasmin weren't around. There wasn't much to hear though, since the wood was thick and most of her chats seemed to happen via text. I tried different methods of snatching her phone, like scanning her room while she was downstairs, but that phone was always with her, even on the toilet.

Meanwhile, I kept Googling Matt Danger Donahue and returning to his Facebook page. I figured out that he'd started high school two years ago, which made him a junior. A few more pictures revealed that he owned a beagle, or at least hung out with one, and rode a skateboard. Like Cammy, he also had a beach photo: his skin was tanned and his abs were stacked like cinderblocks. He wore different color hoodies and different color sneakers and had a cocky grin like he was saying, "I know you're looking at me, Jacob." But I couldn't tell if he robbed banks or kidnapped ladies or did weed. I thought it best to assume that he did.

On a Wednesday after school, Yasmin roped Cammy into doing a dance workout video; she was always getting free stuff to review for her healthy living website. Sharp beats pumped from the speakers—the frequency hurt my ears—as the two of them boogied all over the living room. I made a beeline for Cammy's bedroom; this time, her phone was sitting face up on the desk, waiting for me. I lunged for it, banged my knee, *splimped* into the bathroom, and locked the door. It didn't take long to find what I was looking for.

Matt (bae)

so your still coming to my place friday night, right?

Yeppp!

r u excited?

Of course!!!

me too

😊

so its 216 MacArthur Lane
how u getting here?

My dad or stepmom will prob take me.

ok cuz my parents won't be home so I don't want them to freak
do they need to meet me?

Not sure...I'll figure something out.

sweet, its gonna be lit

Totally!
I luv you

luv u too 

This was really happening—my sister was going to a boy's house alone. A boy she apparently *luved.* A boy she had probably kissed. No parents, no protectors. My Spidey sense had been right after all: *Danger danger danger*! I managed to put the phone back on the desk before Cammy, tomato-red and sweaty, plodded up the stairs. My knee throbbed for hours.

Matt appeared in my dream that night. He was dressed like Spiderman except his face was uncovered and he wore bright red headphones. He scuttled nimbly up the side of the house and slipped through Cammy's window, where he found her asleep. I knew he was going to do something bad and I wanted to stop him but my feet were stuck to the carpet in the hall. I watched helplessly as SpiderMatt swung around the room and crushed Cammy in bed.

The only way to defeat Matt—or Sean and Keith, for that matter—was to know his strengths and weaknesses, but all I had at my disposal were a few useless photos: Matt with a dog, Matt on a skateboard, Matt eating pizza without pepperoni. I didn't even have to open Facebook to see his knowing smile, the angular swoop of his goldeny hair, the hard ridges of his torso, and those bright eyes that were bluer than mine. I felt like someone was wringing my appendix dry.

When I got home from school that day, Dad was already home. He announced that he was cooking "an honest-to-goodness, no-bones-about-it, stick-a-fork-in-it-I'm-done family dinner!" Yasmin kissed his cheek and said, "It's about time." I agreed, although Dad wasn't what anyone would call a good cook. After Mom died, we had to stomach his dry cutlets, gluey mac and cheese, and spongy hamburgers for an entire year until he met Yasmin. Now Cammy and I scarfed down whatever Yasmin made before Dad even got home, and Cammy was always playing on her phone. I knew Dad wouldn't stand for that at "family dinner."

Sure enough, he told Cammy to "give the horn a rest" as soon as he passed his soggy mashed potatoes around the kitchen table.

"The horn, Dad? Really?"

Somewhere in the world, it was taco night.

Yasmin told a story about visiting a healer who placed crystals on her "chakras" and made a bowl sing, whatever that meant. "I'm definitely giving her a rave write-up; I've never felt so invigorated." She dipped a biscuit into the potatoes as if they were soup. Then Dad explained some "computer simulations" that were supposed to test "real world probabilities." His hair had turned grayer in the past few months, probably because he'd been working so much. Then he turned his attention to me.

"How's the junior high life, Jacob?"

"It's...okay."

"Have you joined any clubs or teams? Any afterschool what-ya-ma-call-its?"

"Extracurriculars," I replied. "Not yet."

"Well what about the math team? It's a great fit for you. Didn't you say you were going to join?"

Dad did math all day every day and adored making graphs: pies and spikes, slopes and arrows, he couldn't get enough of them. I was an A+ math student too, but I liked words better. Numbers were like soil—rigid and elemental—while words were like clouds. Endless rolling clouds.

"I've had a lot of homework," I explained. "And I've been reading library books and stuff." I wasn't sure if I should mention the JFD just yet, but as Cammy talked about auditioning for a play, I revisited the newest words in my mind.

splimp (verb) – to run with a limp from a sudden injury

boo-nilch (noun) – a messed up high-five because one person misses the other person's hand

wamore (adjective) – feeling sure of yourself while admitting that you have no reason to feel sure of yourself

unsibler (noun) – an older sibling who isn't nice to his or her younger sibling(s)

"Any big plans this weekend?" Dad asked. "Cam, Jacob?"

"Annabel invited me over tomorrow night and said I could sleep there if I wanted. That cool with you guys?"

My stomach did an Irish jig as my mouth literally fell open. Was this what Cammy had meant by *I'll figure something out*?

"I hope you're planning to factor some schoolwork into the equation."

"Oh yeah, definitely."

"Dad, she's lying!"

Dad laughed. "I'm aware of that, pal. Schoolwork on a Friday!" He grinned at Yasmin and winked at Cammy like the three of them shared some big secret.

"Not about that! Tell him the truth."

Cammy gave me a death stare, her eyes like ice cubes. "What are you talking about?"

"You know."

"No I freaking don't."

"Tell them about...your boyfriend!" There. I'd said it! I hadn't planned to tattle and it didn't feel heroic, but at least it would keep her safe and sound.

"Now what's this about?" I could tell our spat was riling up Dad. It was all over now for Cameron Elizabeth and her bae.

"She's going to his house," I said. "He's a junior, about sixteen." I was on a roll. "And his middle name is Danger!" Let the grounding begin.

"Oh my god, stalker much?" Cammy picked up a piece of chicken and squeezed it so hard the juice ran down her wrist. "Are you trying to ruin my life?"

"It's not my fault you're an *unsibler*!" I pounded the table, which sent my spoon flying.

Yasmin gasped and said "*In bimani ast*!" in what I could only assume was Farsi. I hoped I hadn't any triggered any trauma from her past.

"You're legit mental!" Cammy shouted.

"Stop this, I can't understand anyone!" Dad cried out. "What's happening here? Jacob, are you spying on your sister?"

"No," I squeaked. "Aren't you going to stop her?" *Do something,* I begged him. Cammy was still squeezing her chicken.

Dad crossed his arms, which everyone knew meant serious

business. "Are you really going to Annabel's tomorrow?"

"Of course I am, ask her if you want," Cammy replied, surprisingly calm. "Jacob doesn't know what he's talking about. He's, like, jealous of me or something!"

"No, but, I saw these messages, Dad, and I'm not *wamore* about this, I mean I really know for sure that—"

"You've been acting strange lately," Dad interrupted, glancing at Yasmin and uncrossing his arms. "We think you've been spending too much time alone."

"But...but," my tongue was tripping all over itself, "but danger."

"Cameron is in high school now." He exhaled loudly. "We need to give her some space."

I couldn't believe it. Even if he didn't care about Cammy's half-shirts or eye gunk or Facebook comments or door slamming, shouldn't he care about *this*? Why didn't he believe me?

"She needs to start making decisions on her own," he continued. "*Smart* decisions, right Cam?"

"Absolutely," she said, nodding like a teacher's pet.

"And Jacob," Dad said gently, "Yasmin and I want you to start seeing Dr. Novak again. It's been awhile, but she really helped you, remember? She helped all of us."

I lowered my gaze to the swamps and streams of gravy. We all sat in silence for another minute until Yasmin started yakking about a new type of broccoli she was planting in her garden. I pretended to listen but all I could see was a pale blue couch in a pale gray room with a ten-year-old Cammy holding my hand as Dr. Novak let us cry.

I couldn't focus on anything at school the next day. I didn't blink when Sean and Keith called me "faggy" (I vowed to look that up later) so they just yawned loudly and walked away. At lunch I kept my eyes locked on *The Hobbit*, but I couldn't stop replaying our "family dinner" conversation. Dad cared more about giving Cammy space than protecting her from all the terrible things Matt might do, like tie her to a pipe and blow up the house or carry her to a bridge and toss her out to sea.

For the first time in my life, I realized that Dad was just a regular person...just a math-lover named Bradley Farrow who'd grown up, got a job, married a woman named Phoebe, had two kids, buried Phoebe, married a woman named Yasmin who'd never had kids, and together with her tried to raise a teenage girl and almost-teen boy. It dawned on me that Dad didn't really know what he was doing. Maybe, just maybe, I knew better than he did this time.

At home after school, Cammy gave me another ice-cold glare as we passed each other in the hall. If she met a tragic fate at Matt's, she'd deserve it. And if she lived to tell the tale, she'd probably regret all the mean things she'd done, like calling me mental! But I couldn't take that risk—no matter what Cammy did, she was still my best friend. I'd do anything to save her. So I turned to my most trusted gadget: Google Maps.

On street-view, Matt's house looked surprisingly peaceful, with trimmed hedges, stone siding, and a footpath leading to a side-yard gate. I studied it closely from every possible angle. The house was 6.4 miles from here, but only one mile from Annabel's. Cammy could easily walk from her place after Dad dropped her off. I longed for an earthquake to keep her home.

"Dinner's ready!" Yasmin said just outside my door. It was only 5:30. I closed my computer and trudged downstairs.

A single plate holding garden greens and tricolor pasta sat on the kitchen table. Yasmin poured a glass of juice and set it down in front of me.

"What about Cammy's plate?" I asked.

"She said she's eating at Annabel's, and Teresa just called to invite your Dad and me to a dinner party. So it's dinner for one tonight!" She giggled softly. My stomach felt like I had swallowed silly putty.

Yasmin winced and sat down in Cammy's chair. "Are you going to be okay here tonight? We're not staying late...or hey, you could come with us! I'll call Teresa now, I'm sure she won't mind."

I looked into Yasmin's eyes, full of confusion and compassion. She had no idea what was going on. If she and Dad weren't home, I wouldn't have to sneak out behind their backs. It was a golden opportunity.

"I'll be fine," I told her. "I just want to keep reading my book and go to bed early." I couldn't believe I had lied to Yasmin's face, and she didn't suspect a thing! Maybe Cammy had poisoned me.

"Alright kiddo, but if you change your mind let me know in the next twenty minutes. I'm going to jump in the shower now. Enjoy!" She ruffled my hair and pranced off. I poked my kernels of corn and they stuck out their little tongues at me.

On the way back to my room, I caught sight of Cammy through a crack in her door. She was brushing her hair in front of the mirror decked with photos and stickers and funny postcards. It looked like her closet had thrown up on the carpet. I remembered Dad's words—"Cameron is in high school now"—as I watched her watch herself, and I couldn't help wondering what it must have felt like to be a teenager with 391 Facebook friends and a handsome new boyfriend. My heart twitched like a mouse in a trap. What if she needed Matt more than me? What if Matt was her hero and *I* was the evil villain? No, I couldn't think that way! He didn't know her favorite crayon (seafoam green) or animal (snow leopard) or dessert (Dixie Cup) or Disney movie (Tangled, last I checked). Plus, he was obviously dangerous and couldn't be trusted.

Once Dad got home, the house buzzed with *frinze*. I grabbed the extra bookbag I'd packed for the mall two weekends ago: Shield-binder, check! Mini baseball bat, check! Deadly scissors, check! I added a small flashlight, then held my Captain America piggy bank and shook out everything I'd saved since buying Minecraft and Infinifactory, which was 52 dollars and 67 cents. Seeing the money made my skin feel clammy.

"Five minute warning!" I heard Dad shout.

"I need ten minutes!" Cammy shouted back.

"Seven then!"

I rummaged through my closet until I found my black cape. The Halloween I'd dressed up as Batman was also the last Halloween I'd spent with Mom. I wrapped the cape around my shoulders and pressed its silky fabric to my cheek. I tried to imagine Mom standing beside me, but a patch of fog obscured her face.

I stuffed myself inside my closet and turned off the light. I wanted to practice being alone in the dark, the way I used to practice holding my breath underwater. But standing in my closet made me feel like Helen Keller, and then I thought of spending my entire life trapped in silence and darkness, and I felt so sorry for Helen Keller that I wanted to cry.

I took a deep breath, counted to ten like Dr. Novak once taught me, and gently packed the cape in my bag. I needed it to be strong.

"Can you drop me off on the next block instead?"

The cab driver had a Mario mustache and a Chihuahua nodding *yes* on the dashboard. "I thought you said 216? This is 216."

"I did, but uhh, I want to just go another block. Please. I'll pay extra!" I ducked down in the backseat. The man snorted and drove on.

I'd decided to give Cammy a long enough head start so she'd already be settled in at Matt's but not so long that she'd be maimed or killed by the time I arrived. I'd felt very *bi-fluxy* while waiting for my first cab, so very *bi-fluxy* that I had to take several more deep breaths, using my Iron Man watch to count each second. It also helped to repeat my newest words like a magic spell.

bi-fluxy (adjective) – anxious to leave the house yet absolutely dreading it

frinze (noun) – frantic Friday energy

yolp (verb) – to abbreviate a word or create an acronym out of laziness and/or the need to follow a trend

synthamum (noun) – a plastic bag caught in a tree

To be honest, I felt like the autistic boy in *Curious Incident of the Dog in the Night-time*, who goes on a journey to visit the mother he'd presumed dead. Unlike him, my Mom was actually dead and I wasn't autistic, or at least I didn't think I was.

"How's right here?" the driver asked.

I pulled myself up and looked out the window. Darkness gathered like a massive murder of crows.

"You okay back there?"

"I'm fine."

"You don't look fine." He had turned around in his seat and clicked on the overhead light.

"Please stop *blarking*, sir."

"What's *blarking*?"

"Staring at someone because you are judging them." I put a hand over my mouth.

"*Blarking*, huh? Never heard that one. You must be smart."

"I made it up actually."

"Even smarter."

I paid him and calculated the tip in my head, but I didn't overdo it this time, even though he was nice.

"Have a good one!" His words felt ominous, like several shiny knives aimed in my direction. Maybe he'd be the last innocent bystander to see me alive.

"By the way," I said, halfway out the car, "my name's Jacob Farrow. Just in case."

"Just in case of what?" I heard him say as I shut the door.

I walked quickly, but not too quickly, past two-story houses, basketball hoops, and mailboxes with their red arms at rest. I looked both ways, crossed the street, and then hid behind a tree in front of Matt's house. Three windows flickered like spastic lightning; otherwise, the windows were black and there were no cars in the driveway. My heart swelled like a balloon. I wished I had a sidekick—a Robin so to speak, or at least a loyal dog—but I had to do this on my own.

I unzipped my bag, took out my Batman cape, and tied it around my neck. I said a little prayer to anyone or anything that might have been listening and counted under my breath—*three, two, one!*—then bolted across the damp grass to the side-gate, opening and closing it in a flash.

Gusts of air seemed to lift my sneakers as I followed the path around the house and onto a cobblestone patio. A giant barbecue in a black hood guarded the back door. I marched past it, then silently cursed myself: I hadn't brought anything to pick a lock! Not that I really knew how to pick one; I should have watched a few YouTube videos. Hoping against hope, I reached out and palmed the doorknob. It turned as smoothly as a pinwheel and emitted a delightful click. Open Sesame! Matt sure was trusting for someone so dangerous.

The dark kitchen smelled like delivery pizza and freshly popped popcorn. Revved engines, tribal drums, and strained shouts filled my ears, causing my neck hairs to stand on end. With my cape draped over my backpack, I pressed my chest flat against the wall. I had to be invisible. I had to disappear.

Light on my feet, I baby-stepped across the kitchen, then crouched behind an archway that fed into the room full of lightning. A TV was to blame for the bright flashes and loud sounds; on screen, bald demonic guys raced flaming vehicles across a desert, and a man in a metal muzzle was chained upright to the front of one car. I tried to figure out who was chasing whom when one of the demon-men threw a missile at a porcupine mobile, which caused an explosion. The muzzled man yelled, "Watch my head!" and then a silhouetted fist reached up from the back of the couch to punch the air. It could only be Matt's fist, Matt's arm, Matt on the couch with my sister. My balloon-heart threatened to burst.

I scanned the living room in search of a better spot. The couch met the wall on its right, but there was much more room on its left, where a small table stood between the couch and a large recliner sitting at a diagonal. On hands and knees I spider-crawled, moving in a wide arc along the floorboards until landing behind the recliner. I sat up, sucked in my breath, and peered over the plush armrest. I hoped my head looked like nothing more than a shadowy blur, simply part of the chair.

The front of the couch was now in full view: Matt and Cammy were spread across it, illuminated by the screen. A candle burned on a low coffee table, which also held a bowl of popcorn and two glass bottles. I couldn't read the labels, but they looked like the bottles Dad drank on Fourth of July. Cammy and I stole a few sips once. Tart, tangy, and terribly disgusting.

With their heads resting on a pillow, Matt lay behind Cammy, his arm across her hip. She was wearing an entirely different outfit—patterned skirt, knee socks, and one of her tight half-shirts—and from the position of her body, I could tell she was uncomfortable.

I tuned out the movie and watched Matt slide his fingertips along Cammy's bare shoulder. Goosebumps rose on my arm.

He tucked Cammy's hair behind her ear and leaned down to kiss her neck. A chill ran down my spine.

He leaned farther and turned Cammy's face toward his, their heads so close they looked cross-eyed and cuckoo. Now none of us were watching the on-screen action.

I braced myself, waiting for Matt to strangle, punch, or shake Cammy 'til she screamed, but he said a few words I couldn't hear, made a fishy face, and kissed her sweetly on the lips. There was that wringing again: a washcloth jammed in my intestines.

I remembered how I used to make out with my knees in the bathtub. I didn't pretend they were anyone specific, but I did pretend they weren't my knees. I thought I was pretty good at it, but so far I hadn't met a single person I wanted to kiss. I didn't want to watch Matt smooch Cammy either, but I couldn't look away—

like rubbernecking an accident, or watching a violent scene in a movie, or witnessing Sean and Keith pick on other kids. Why did we love to see such horror?

Matt's lips released Cammy's and they both returned to the film. I ducked behind the recliner, counted fifteen seconds, and poked back up. Matt was partially sitting now, grabbing a handful of popcorn and washing it down with a swig of his beer. He wore a plain white t-shirt, jeans, and a belt. Aside from his hair, which fell in a perfect wave across his forehead, he looked like he'd spent a whole two minutes getting dressed, unlike Cammy.

He stared at the TV, momentarily forgetting her. I wondered if he liked superheroes. Maybe he'd want to watch a movie with *me* someday.

Wait, what was I thinking? Matt was the villain, the big bad boss, the not-bald demon! A word Cammy had used at dinner appeared in my mind: "jealous." I'd thought she'd just said it to defend herself in front of Dad, but now I had to wonder if there was any truth to the statement. Maybe she did think I was jealous of her. Hadn't I felt that way when she and Annabel girl-talked in her room? And every time her eyes lit up as she checked her phone? And now, watching her kiss Matt…didn't that make me feel…well…

I had to face the facts.

I hadn't wanted to be a hero for the same reasons Batman and Spiderman and the muzzled-man (I could tell already) became heroes. What I'd really wanted was for kids at school to like me; for Sean and Keith to back off; for Cammy to be my best friend again and take me to Annabel's; and for my good deeds to hit the airwaves so everyone would know and appreciate *the* Jacob Farrow. Somewhere along the way, my priorities changed; now I wanted to save Cammy and only Cammy, whether or not anyone else knew. I'd already lost Mom; I couldn't lose her too.

But the word wasn't *jealous*. I needed to create a much better word.

revless (adjective) – feeling like nothing will ever be the same because things you once had no longer exist, or because you aren't the person you once thought you could be

Tears sprang to my eyes and I clamped them tight. This was no time to cry. I rubbed my cape against my cheek and directed my gaze back to the couch.

They were kissing again, only Matt's hand now crawled all over

Cammy's stomach. My gut burned, hot as a glue gun.

His hand moved down to her hip and her thigh, over the fabric. He played with the hem of her skirt. Then his hand touched her bare leg and started moving up. The burning in me spread, a wildfire scorching my bones.

Cammy's body stiffened like a corpse. Enough was enough! Who did Matt think he was?

What would Batman do?

Matt was lean, but he had twice my muscle mass and an extra eight or nine inches of height, so I didn't think attacking him at close range was wise. If only I had a stun gun, a lasso, a flamethrower, a bow and arrow, a ninja star to fling into his face. I did have my bat and scissors...the bat was my safest bet, especially if I knocked him unconscious. Movies made that look pretty easy.

I ducked back down and slipped off my bookbag, balancing on the balls of my feet. I unzipped the main pouch when I smelled something foul. Every muscle froze. I knew that smell.

Slowly turning, I came face-to-face with a pair of radioactive eyes. It was the beagle from the photo! I'd completely forgotten.

I put up both palms and gave the dog a weak grin, but I knew that it knew I didn't belong there. I sat perfectly still as it dragged its wet nose along my clothes and skin, sniffing me fully. Then it reared its head, opened its jaw, and did the unthinkable. One loud bark.

"Please stop," I whispered, but the dog barked again, sending shockwaves through the room.

"Chill out, Coco!" Matt shouted.

Coco grabbed my cape and tugged with her canines. Maybe she was hungry. I plunged my hand into my bookbag, found the Sour Patch Kids, and ripped open the bag. The multicolor kids catapulted like acrobats, scattering across the floor. I dusted one off and held it out to Coco.

"Here, eat this instead," I whispered. Releasing a toxic cloud of stink-breath, Coco lapped up the kid. "Good dog."

She spat it on the floor. Sour sugar was probably an acquired taste. Coco tugged my cape again; I was afraid she would tear it. Maybe she wanted to play. I reached out to pet her floppy ears, but she howled as if on the hunt.

"Shut the hell up, girl!" Matt yelled louder.

Matt didn't deserve a dog, and he certainly didn't deserve my sister. Beads of sweat trickled down my forehead. I had to think of something. Coco continued barking, engines rumbled from the speakers, and Matt was starting to get up from the couch. I gripped my sixteen-inch bat, raised it high above my head. One good swing, that was all it would take.

A battle cry escaped my lips as I sprung from my hiding place like a stealthy warrior, running around the recliner with Coco at my heels. Cammy screamed "Oh my God, no!" as I swung at Matt, aiming for his head. The bat connected with his shoulder and produced a hollow *thwack*. "Ow! Holy fuckin' shit!" Matt held his shoulder and crumpled to the floor. I had done it!

Dizzy with rage, I raised the bat again and took two steps forward, but my knee hit the coffee table and I flew across it, spilling popcorn, toppling bottles, and landing atop Cammy with her knees in my ribs. She screamed again, breathing hard and fast like she'd swum twenty laps. Was I giving her a heart attack? The next thing I knew she was crying out, "It's Jacob! What is *wrong* with you?" and pushing me to the floor.

"Who the fuck is Jacob?" Matt roared.

Before I could think, speak, or raise my hands in self-defense, Matt grabbed the back of my neck and lifted me with him. He wrapped those muscular arms around my throat so my feet dangled a good foot above the ground. I could feel his heart pump against my spine.

"He's my dumbass brother, I told you that!" Cammy shouted above Coco's barks and the movie's sounds. She stood on the couch, towering over Matt and me. "Stop, put him down!"

His body heat, leathery aftershave, and headlocking skills made the earth spin way too fast. After holding me up for an eternity or more, Matt released my windpipe and tossed me like a piece of trash. For a split-second I was airborne, just like Superman, until I face-planted in the recliner. Luckily there was so much adrenaline in my veins that I didn't feel much pain.

"Cameron!" Matt hollered, like Dad on a very bad day. "What is your little brother doing in my house?"

"I don't know, I guess he followed me here."

"He followed you from Annabel's? Or did she rat on you?"

"I said I don't know! He's been spying on me, okay? He's a legit mental case. I'm gonna kill you, Jacob! You are *so* dead!"

"Coco, shut up!" Matt did something to the dog and she hightailed it out of the room, then he picked up the remote and pressed pause. I could hear Coco's nails scrape the kitchen's linoleum as I buried my face in the seat. My body shook like a maraca even though I was overheating. In my peripheral vision, I watched red-cheeked Matt and Cammy stare each other down, the three of us frozen in the TV's milky light. There were so many things I wanted to say, but the words rattled like spare change in my skull.

"I want your crazy-ass brother out of here," Matt said, pointing to me. "Right now."

Cammy huffed. "Yeah, no shit."

I took that as my cue to stand, secure my hearing aids, and grab my bookbag. The bat had probably rolled beneath the couch, but I didn't dare search for it. I backed away slowly, careful not to trip or faint or cause another scene.

"I'll text you tomorrow," Matt said.

"Uh huh."

They didn't kiss. They didn't even touch.

Cammy grabbed her own bag, slipped on her shoes and jean jacket, and marched toward me like an angry teacher. Clasping my wrist, she dragged me to the front door. Before I knew it we were back outside stomping across the lawn, and before I could ask what she wanted to do now, I noticed a gray taxi idling at the curb, coughing up exhaust.

The front window rolled down and a bushy mustache appeared. "Need a lift, Jacob Farrow? It's on me."

Had he really remembered my name? I struggled to find my voice and make sense of my good fortune. "Oh okay," I stuttered, then turned to Cammy. "I, I know him. It's safe."

She raised her eyebrows in disbelief, but I opened the backdoor and she reluctantly entered my getaway car. I scrambled in after her, buckling my seatbelt.

"Why'd you come back?"

The driver tapped his bobblehead Chihuahua. "It sounded like you might need some help, and I had time to spare. Also, I felt bad for... *blarking* was it?"

He clicked off the overhead light and started to drive; he already knew the way to our house. Hearing him say my word made me smile, but the grin vanished as soon as Cammy crossed her arms and inhaled loudly, a sign that tears were on the way.

I untied my cape and held it in my hands; one side was full of teeth marks, tattered at the edge. "I'm sorry," I whispered to Cammy, to Mom, to Batman, to Dad and Yasmin, and even to Matt.

I could tell she didn't want to look at me. I needed her to say something, *anything*, even mean words, but minutes ticked by and she didn't say a thing. I had ruined everything. Cammy would never speak to me again, let alone be my friend. I was doomed to spend the rest of my life *isolizing* in a *revless* state, with a pounding headache to boot. In a few years, Cammy would forget she ever had a brother.

Finally she spoke, still staring straight ahead. "You know what you did was wrong, right? On, like, so many levels."

"I know."

"You can't *do* things like this! You can't try to control my life, and you definitely can't hit someone with a bat. You're not five years old; I shouldn't have to tell you that."

"I wasn't trying to control your life...I was trying to, um...save you."

I balled up my cape—so childish, I realized—and swallowed back tears. A single one slipped down Cammy's cheek; she sniffled and wiped it off.

"Is it because you still feel guilty?" she asked.

"Guilty about what?"

"About Mom."

"What do you mean?"

Another tear careened down her cheek. She let that one dry.

"You don't remember, do you? We were sitting in Dr. Novak's office and you told her you thought it was *your* fault...because Mom went downtown to buy you a new controller for your Xbox or whatever, since you'd thrown yours across the room and broke it." Cammy paused, her eyes glazed over. "Of course that wasn't the only reason she went shopping that day, and it wasn't the reason it happened...but that's when the construction crane collapsed."

A memory appeared in my mind: a clear blue sky, a falling crane, and an older, stronger, black-caped me soaring in to catch it. To save her. To save *us*. It wasn't a memory, but a memory of a daydream.

"So I'm guessing that's why you did this. To be the hero?"

I couldn't contain my tears any longer. They broke free with a vengeance, two cascading waterfalls. The driver didn't say anything, but I could tell he was listening. Not judging, only listening. I wiped my face with the silky fabric still bunched in my fists.

"You said I was a dumbass, a mental case," I blubbered. "You, you said you were gonna, gonna kill me."

Cammy sighed and turned to face me. "I was mad. Duh."

She placed her hand on my wrist, gentle this time, and leaned in. "Jacob," she whispered, "thank you."

My body jerked in shock. "Huh? For what?"

"With Matt, things felt...well, he was being too...don't worry about it, okay? Just, thanks."

A warm sensation enveloped me, like sunshine in my blood. A hug from a happy ghost. A baby in a mother's arms.

"By the way," Cammy said, "his middle name isn't Danger."

"It's not?"

"Nope. It's Herman."

"Herman!?"

We looked at each other for half a second and then cracked up laughing, nearly bumping heads as we bounced up and down in bubbly hysterics. I even heard the driver chuckle.

I started to think of a new word for this feeling. Then I stopped myself. A perfect word already existed. That word was love.

Underneath Orion

When she couldn't find a parking spot, Erica rejoiced. Arriving late was far less awkward than her unfortunate habit of showing up early. She praised herself for changing outfits three times, finally settling on a pinstripe pencil skirt, silky teal blouse, and chunky high heels that already hurt her feet. She'd even applied the under-eye concealer her mother had considered an excellent stocking stuffer. Erica dreaded what she might receive this year.

She drove up and down the block, finding a spot a little too close to somebody's driveway. *Whatever*, she thought, checking the mirror—mostly to ensure that the under-eye stick was properly concealing—before stepping out of her car. She didn't know why any of this mattered tonight: what clothes she wore, how radiant her skin appeared, and whether or not her hair fell straight. Usually she didn't give a damn if her hair was brushed or her eyebrows tweezed, and she waited several months to wash a pair of jeans. Still, it was her first time attending the McCourt family Christmas party, and the prospect of being surrounded by someone else's family, friends, and family friends had prompted the desire to "dress to impress." *It's only Paige's family*, she reminded herself.

Gold lights twinkled on the bushes and green ones marched along the gutter. Through the bay window she saw people passing in front of a Christmas tree, which stood at the very back of the living room. She thought of planets orbiting distant stars, their faint shadows detected light years away. Walking into someone else's house, brimming with childhood photos and family recipes, must be a little like finding yourself on one of those faraway planets.

She took a deep breath and rang the bell, hoping no one would hear it and she could slip inside an unlocked door and find Paige without any fuss. But the door soon opened and Paige's mother, Lynn, stood on the threshold with outstretched arms.

"Erica! I'm so glad you could make it this year!"

Before she knew it she was deep in Lynn's embrace. Erica remembered the nature walks Lynn would lead them on in sixth grade; one time, Lynn had let the girls wander alone while she sat on a rock to meditate. "Your Mom is *such* a hippie," Erica had whispered as they watched Lynn's long skirt catch the breeze. Seeing her now in a crisp black dress—her wavy hair clipped back and a string of pearls around her neck—came as both a shock and a comfort. Even Lynn had dressed to impress.

"Let me take your coat," Lynn said. "It'll be in the hall closet if you need to step outside. I think I saw Paige in the kitchen. Drink and eat anything!"

Erica nodded and made her way through the dining room, which connected to the kitchen. She had been in Paige's grandparents' house a few times before and had a decent memory of its layout. Bypassing the goodies on the table, she entered the kitchen and scanned the room for Paige. A smaller table by the backdoor acted as a makeshift bar, with one of Paige's alcoholic uncles manning drinks. She kicked herself for not bringing champagne or wine or at least some treats—being cordial didn't come naturally—but there seemed to be enough of everything, and Lynn hadn't noticed.

"Eri!" Two arms enclosed her from behind, squeezing her stomach. Erica swung around and pecked Paige on her cheeks. Like her mother, she had dressed the part of classy hostess, wearing a deep maroon dress with quarter-length sleeves. Her usual heap of curls had been carefully upswept, revealing dangly earrings that brought out the gold flecks in her green eyes. Just a few of her curls framed her freckles, nearly hidden beneath a coat of foundation.

"*Bonjour, ça va?*" Paige said, putting one hand on her hip.

"*Ca va bien, et toi?*" Erica responded, giggling. The only time she ever spoke French, or what little she remembered from high school, was with Paige.

"Ehh, *come ci comme ça.*"

"What, sick of the party already?"

"No, no, it's all good, I'm just kidding." Paige let out her signature laugh: a crescendo of chuckles like skipping stones.

"Although I do feel a little disgusting after eating god knows how many cookies. *Please* have some."

"Don't worry, I'll get to that."

"I hope you do," Paige said sincerely. She took a step back to look Erica up and down. "You're getting a little too skinny again."

"Oh, please!" Erica retorted, waving her hand. "It's an illusion."

Paige frowned and Erica felt as if her outfit had melted away. She didn't know why Paige had to bring up this kind of thing so frequently; after all, she hadn't given her cause for concern in quite some time. Paige had always been maternal, even though Erica was seven months older. Back in high school, she'd relied on Paige most out of their tight circle of friends, since Paige was undoubtedly dependable; unlike Erica and the other girls, she never suffered any teenage drama—she didn't cut or starve or throw things at her mom or let a boy fuck with her.

Erica and Paige both came from broken homes: single mothers and absent fathers. They met on the playground, rubbing sticks together in a futile attempt to make fire. They attended Catholic school from kindergarten through twelfth, received Communion wafers on their tongues, confessed their sins to a priest with a glass eye, and chose Confirmation names they thought sounded cool. They ate the same square pizza in the same cafeteria, collected Lisa Frank school supplies, rolled down hills in their skirts, recorded songs off the radio, wrote epic plays about the Greek gods, and stayed up all night conducting Ouija Board séances. They were the first person the other called when they got their periods (Paige first), kissed a boy (Paige first), and lost their virginity (Erica, regrettably, first). They dyed their hair with Manic Panic, got their cartilages pierced without permission, smoked cigarettes behind the gym, watched from the sidelines at the skate park, blasted music in a black-lit basement, and trespassed into the reservoir on hot summer days. And yet, Paige had risen above so many of the things to which Erica had fallen prey. Even at twenty-six, Erica couldn't help feeling like a poor excuse for an adult next to her oldest friend.

"Well, you do look fantastic, I'm glad you dressed up," Paige said, adjusting the single wing pendant on Erica's necklace: a bird that flies between the stars. "I need to make the rounds and stuff; I told you my mom and I are in charge this year, right?"

"Yeah, I'm guessing she's on door duty. Go do your thing."

"Mingle and drink and eat and be merry, then come find me." Paige squeezed Erica's hand and started to walk away before rushing back to her side. "Oh, I forgot! Don't be obvious, but my cousin and his friend are standing in the doorway over there...do you think he's cute?"

Erica glanced past Paige to the boys at the other end of the spacious kitchen. They both had freckly skin and short gingery hair, both wore button-down shirts and what appeared to be loafers. The kind of shoes her stepdad wore.

"Which one? They look the same."

"Not my cousin! Thc guy on the right, in the striped shirt. His name is Mark and he's in his second year of law school. Want me to introduce you?"

Erica gave Mark another subtle glance; he looked like the epitome of a frat boy, but maybe the red plastic cup was to blame. Either way, nothing about him was appealing, and she wondered why Paige had picked him out for her. Did she really think he was her type? Or was she trying to sway Erica from the boys she typically dated or pursued; the ones who chose writing or music or sculpting giant scorpions in their parents' garage over something as practical as law school. Paige had found her current boyfriend in medical school, though Erica knew that wasn't going as well as Paige had hoped. Erica had yet to meet him anyway, since Paige had been so overwhelmed with schoolwork. Almost every time Erica called, Paige would whisper, "I'm in the library, call you later," but then she rarely did. Finally, Erica called her out on it: "I'm at a new school too, you know, and I still make time to talk to you," to which Paige replied, "But you're in grad school and I'm in *medical* school. It's not the same." After that conversation, Erica didn't phone for a week, but the next time they spoke neither of them mentioned it.

"No, that's okay," Erica said.

"Fine, but you should talk to them; there aren't many people here our age. See you in a bit." She pinched Erica's cheek before she walked away for good, leaving Erica feeling naked again.

She decided to approach the makeshift bar before the inevitability of speaking with the button-down boys, or anyone else. Parties were always more bearable with a glass in hand.

"What'll it be?" The mustached uncle behind the table waved his fingers across various bottles in buckets of ice. "We've got just about everything, but most ladies are drinking the Sauvignon blanc."

"Sure, I'll have that."

He took a glass from the countertop, tilted it slightly, and began to pour. Erica watched the silky liquid swirl; it reminded her of spiral galaxies, or of stars falling toward a black hole...she imagined herself on the lip of an event horizon, her face frozen in a frightened smile that would last for all time, or no time, or however that phenomenon played out. Transfixed, she felt adrift in the outermost reaches of space, like a planet that had veered out of orbit.

A moment later, there was a tap on her arm: Paige's uncle reminding her to take the wine he had just poured. Her cheeks burned and she mumbled "thanks" before dodging the button-downs and finding herself in the living room, where the star-topped Christmas tree stood proud. It looked less magical than it had from outside, but it was still a beautiful sight.

She inspected the ornaments one by one, lingering so she wouldn't have to interact with the well-dressed people flooding the room. She poked the googly eye of a clothespin reindeer (*did Paige and I make these?*) and listened to the ebb and flow of intersecting conversations. Laughter rose to a pitch in her left ear, while the smooth jazz of Nat King Cole entered the other.

She turned the corner of the tree and held a "Baby's First Christmas" Nativity scene inside a glass rattle. Her mother had a similar ornament on her tree: one for Erica's first Christmas and one for her younger brother's. She'd been gung-ho about attending mass as a family every Sunday, until Erica's outfits and incessant eye rolling embarrassed her so fully that she decided to go alone.

With one eye still on Jesus in the rattle, Erica watched two middle-aged women nod profusely while a little girl in a poofy dress twirled in front of them, singing to herself. She wore sparkly silver shoes that Erica would have loved as a child.

"I have to give you the number of Dr. Ferguson," the blonder woman said to the other, "he's absolutely marvelous, and not bad to look at either."

"Did he take out both ovaries or just one?"

"Oh honey, you have to do two if you're going to get it done. It's just not worth going back in again when the other one goes the way of the first."

Erica recoiled—was this what she and Paige would be casually discussing at a holiday party in thirty years' time? One ovary or two? She shuddered at the thought.

The little girl, probably too little to belong to either of these women, was still twirling away, oblivious. As her red dress billowed, she resembled a whirling dervish, deep in kinetic prayer. Erica remembered herself at that age, and how comfortable she'd felt in almost any situation. At eleven and twelve, she and Paige would dress up in tutus and wigs and berets, pick flowers from the side of the road, and go from door to door in Paige's neighborhood. "Free daisies, free daisies!" they would chant, trying to make the neighbors smile. Somehow, just a year or so later, Erica's self-consciousness crept in like a weed and the free daisies decayed.

"Isn't that one just beautiful?" an accented voice said behind her.

"Uh, what?"

"The icicle ornament...do you know, it's from Ireland. The homeland."

Erica hadn't realized she was holding onto a glass icicle; it was a miracle she hadn't broken it. Releasing her grip, she turned toward the elderly lady with close-cropped white hair and the kind of knitted Christmas sweater she'd never be caught dead in, even at this lady's ripe old age. She studied the three snowmen prancing across the sweater and thought of Orion hovering above the house.

"Oh, Ireland." Erica took a sip from her glass and tried not to sound bored.

"What's your name, dear? You look familiar."

"Erica."

"Erica what?"

"Pakulski."

"Pakulski," she said, tapping her finger to her sagging chin, "is that a Jewish name?"

"No, it's Polish."

"I see, a Polack girl! Not many Polacks in this town."

"My dad is Polish, my mom's Italian."

"How interesting. Similar cultures, yes, I can see how that works just fine."

"They're divorced."

The woman's lips puckered, wrinkles gathering on either side. She put her hand on the middle snowman, who was dancing with his hat off, and snorted good-naturedly. Erica felt like a teenager again, the past ten years of her life slipping off like snakeskin. In those teenage years of suburban rebellion, she'd loved to make adults feel uncomfortable. A deadpan voice, a jarring comment, a controversial pin—one of those would do the trick. But now she was much too old for such antics, especially in front of Paige's great-aunt, or whoever this lady was.

"Sinead, I see you've met Erica."

Erica locked eyes with a slim man in his fifties, who possessed the kind of angular jaw, high cheekbones, and deep smile lines that tended to look better on older men. Clad in a fitted blazer, his wire-rimmed glasses gave him the look of a hip professor. His skin was caramel, his hair jet-black. And those eyes...they were cat-like, green, flecked with bits of gold, just like Paige's. *Paige's dad!*

"Erica and Paige have been friends since...kindergarten is it?" He smiled at Erica and his eyes twinkled in the golden glow of the Christmas tree lights.

"Yeah, that's right," she said quietly, taking another sip.

Sinead clasped Erica's hand. "I knew I recognized you. Of course, you probably would have been wearing that cute little school uniform. Or a graduation gown. Say, were you in the high school play...what was that one called? The one with the fairies, and Paige wore a silver dress, I remember that, and there was that boy with the megaphone, no not a megaphone, Ray what do you call it, not exactly a bugle either—"

"Sinead," he interrupted, "Winnie just got in from Maryland and she was in the dining room asking for you."

"Is that so? My, how delightful." Sinead's papery hand slowly released Erica's. "It was so nice to meet you, dear. We'll talk more later."

Erica released her breath, which she hadn't realized she'd been holding, and stepped toward the window to give Sinead enough room to leave. Ray smiled again and stood facing Erica with one shoulder against the windowpane.

"Thanks for that," Erica said, smiling a bit. She took another sip.

Ray laughed and swigged from his square glass. *Scotch?* she wondered.

"Don't mention it. How are you doing? I haven't seen you in...how many years now?"

"I'm not sure."

Erica tried to recall their last encounter. He lived several hours away in Boston and worked as an administrator at a progressive high school. She had seen him sporadically throughout the twenty-one years of her and Paige's friendship, though nowhere near as often as she'd seen Lynn or even a couple of the alcoholic uncles, who never said much but always seemed to hang around. Then she remembered: she and Paige had driven to Boston for a long weekend, more to visit a mutual friend and less for the sake of Paige's dad, but they'd slept in his guest room during their last night in town. In the morning, Ray had set out muffins and tea as he launched into an open-ended conversation about race, class, and education. It was the lengthiest conversation Erica had ever had with him or with *any* of her friends' parents, since attempting to talk to them always put her on edge. *When was that?* The four years of undergrad and the four years since had flown by faster than the speed of light.

"I'm doing okay," Erica said, shrugging.

"Just okay? Not marvelous, enlightened, stupendous, or resplendent?" Ray's eyes twinkled again, as iridescent as Jupiter's moons.

Erica laughed. "I wouldn't go that far."

"That's too bad. But you do *look* stupendous, so that's a start."

"Thanks," Erica said, feeling simultaneously delighted and embarrassed.

"This attire suits you better than all the black clothing and skull shirts I recall from the high school days."

"Oh, those." Erica laughed again, her embarrassment turning into a sense of pride that was hard to place. Maybe she'd reached a stage where she could joke about and even appreciate her younger self, despite the feeling that not much had changed.

"Yes, those," Ray said, still smiling. "I liked them just fine at the time, they suited you then, but I know Lynn said a word or two about reintroducing color to your wardrobe. Glad to see it's working out."

He gulped the last of his drink and set the cup on the windowsill between them. Erica looked down at her skirt; she felt like an imposter. She wondered if she'd spent all that time dressing for this moment with Ray, unknowingly of course.

"So tell me then what you've been doing. Tell me what is happening in the world of Erica Pakulski."

She could feel her cheeks turn pink again and quickly swallowed the last of her drink. For the first time in awhile, she was going to need more wine.

"I'm in grad school now," she started slowly, wondering what Ray wanted to know and how much she should reveal. Should she mention that she hadn't kept a boyfriend for more than six months, and that the last one dumped her via text? Should she admit that she'd been a terrible roommate and hardly ever did dishes? Should she divulge that Paige had to remind her to place her napkin on her lap whenever they went out to dinner? Should she tell him about her endless procrastination, even when she loved her work, or how little she got paid as a part-time copyeditor? How about the fact that the only poem she'd penned in the past two years had been for Paige's birthday in October, and how she'd actually written a line about him...*some words, now / for the smoke we swallowed as one; some words for the men / who carried us home; some more for the fathers / who left us to rust...*

"Remind me what you're in school for," she heard him say, though she was lost in the cadence of her own lines, this last little poem, floating where only nebulae roam.

"I'm getting a Ph.D. in comparative literature, but I just started this year."

"How perfect for you," he said in the same sincere tone Paige often used. "I remember you, as a little girl, with a book under your arm; it was always there in case you got bored. I thought Paige tore through books, but I suspect you were even more voracious."

How does he remember that? And was it even true? Did she always have a book under her arm? She did have a prized collection of books about outer space, and she'd often carried one to school.

"I assume you're working toward a dissertation. Do you have a focus?"

She couldn't get over the familiar intensity of his eyes. Of course they were wiser than Paige's, since he'd lived twice as long, but it was more than that...it was as if his eyes could see more of her than Paige ever could.

Erica fumbled as she placed her glass next to his, then pushed her dark brown hair behind her ear. The right side of her body was cold from the window, but her face felt flushed. Someone had changed the music from Nat King Cole to a lilting Celtic melody. The whole room felt fuller, laughter gaining momentum, but she kept her eyes on Ray. The pin on his lapel read *Liberal and Proud.*

"I have one, yes," she began. "I want to focus on authors who weave cosmology, or theoretical science, into their fiction, though I'm leaning toward focusing on cosmology as symbolism."

She paused to make sure he was still interested, since so many people weren't. His gaze could not have been steadier. Had he inched closer too?

She went on. "I hope to find different examples in modern and classic world literature, but I'm not really sure how it will go since I've just been focusing on my classes this semester. So far I only found a couple books that might work and they're all American."

"Nothing wrong with American literature. I find all of this very interesting."

Ray had the same lips as Paige too, though a shade darker. Everything about him, save for those eyes, was darker. He was a multiracial Dominican, which made Paige half-Dominican, although no one ever believed her when she said that. Ray seemed to be the only other person in the house, besides herself, without a drop of Irish blood.

"What makes you want to explore this topic?" he continued. "Knowing you, I was expecting to hear something about the Beat writers, or something tied to aberrant subculture. Why cosmology?"

Knowing you...did he really know her? Did he remember when her collarbones poked out like knobby spikes? Gravity was slipping from under her feet.

"I've always been interested in astronomy, well in any natural science, I'm just not great at applying it...not like Paige. Otherwise I might have chosen a different path, something more hands-on."

Ray shook his head to the rhythm of the Celtic violin. "You and Paige are similar enough to be as close as you are, but you are very different people. There's no reason to compare yourself to her."

"But she's going to save lives while I'll be, you know, teaching college kids how to analyze books." She looked down at the floor. This thought had been plaguing her since starting her program, yet she hadn't said it aloud until now.

"Medical school, or any science-based program that doesn't

allow for a creative, academic process, is simply not the right fit for Erica Pakulski. What you're undertaking is very impressive and very much needed."

In her peripheral vision, the little girl was performing a song in sign language; her hands formed graceful shapes as her lips mouthed unspoken words. Erica thought of Ray watching her twirl in a poofy dress, graduate kindergarten, sing in the spring recital, and attempt to play basketball while Paige and the other kids towered above her. But had he been there for such trivial events, or had he been as absent as her own father? She felt dizzy again, trying to account for all the time that had elapsed between then and now. And here she was having an adult conversation about her future dissertation.

Glancing away from the little girl, Erica noticed Paige by the fireplace. Erica smiled, but Paige returned it with an exaggerated gesture of *what are you doing*, elbows bent and palms up. Erica glanced looked back at Ray, unsure of what to do. His eyes were still fixed on her as if she were some incredible creature he'd never seen before. Maybe he was comparing six-year-old Erica or sixteen-year-old Erica to the twenty-six-year-old woman who stood before him tonight. Did he really think she looked "stupendous"—even beautiful—or was he just trying to cheer her up, the way dads sometimes did?

"It dawns on me that you've never been to one of these parties before, in all of the years," he said, oblivious to Paige's stare burning into them. "Why is that?"

"I don't know..." Erica let her sentence trail like the tail of a comet.

"Is there a Pakulski family party in the same orbit?"

He's flirting. The realization took her by surprise. Or maybe he wasn't flirting exactly...maybe he just understood how anxious she felt in exactly these scenarios, and he was giving her the chance to blame her avoidance on something tangible.

She'd just started to whisper, "No, not really," when a hand grabbed the back of her arm.

"Dad, I need to borrow Erica right now," Paige said. Erica glanced from father to daughter, feeling something stir in the air between them. She thought of a rapid polar shift, the earth's axis in sudden disarray.

"Okay, sure, how's everything going?" Ray asked coolly.

"Fine, fine."

Paige didn't waste any time pulling Erica through the nearest archway and into a den that reeked of potpourri and perfume. Several women were seated on the couch, but Paige faced Erica away from them, placing both hands on her shoulders.

"What was that about?" Paige kept her voice low, even though the couch conversation—*I took the kids skating there just last weekend, but it gets so crowded right around the holidays!*—was loud enough to mask theirs at any volume.

"What was *what* about?"

"You and my dad having a private chat. Don't play dumb."

"Um, we were in the living room…not so private."

"Why don't you go talk to Mark like I suggested, since you obviously feel the need to flirt tonight."

"What is your deal?" Erica could feel herself getting angry, but tried not to show it. "I wasn't flirting, I was just talking. I don't even know how to flirt. Why are you making this a big thing?"

Paige closed her eyes and took a deep breath. When she opened them again, they flashed with anger. "He's like that with everyone, just so you know."

"What are you talking about?"

"He makes you feel so special, like you're the only person in the room, like he actually cares. He's good at making an instant connection with people, with *women,* but it's not real, okay? He just wants you to feel like he cares because it makes him feel better about himself."

"Paige…" Erica started, but she didn't know what to say.

"Don't fall for it, okay? None of it is real."

"You're getting really worked up for no reason. Are you drunk?"

"No, I'm not fucking drunk," Paige spat back, though Erica sensed that wasn't the case. Any minor event took on great significance whenever Paige was drunk, sleep-deprived, or both.

"Okay," Erica said, "on that note, I think *I* need another drink."

Paige sighed deeply and pushed the curls out of her face. She squeezed Erica's shoulder harder than usual and let her hand travel the length of her arm.

"Look, I know I'm being weird," Paige said, sounding slightly calmer. "Go get your drink and we'll talk about this later."

"Are you sure?"

"Yes, just go."

Erica lingered for a second longer, then took the opportunity to exit. She walked past the women—*Can you believe how expensive it is just for the day? I told the kids that if they really wanted to go, they'd better*—to the other archway, which fed back into the foyer. She wanted to avoid Ray, avoid the Christmas tree, avoid the little girl and her little dance, avoid the ridiculous conversations floating like space junk throughout the house, and she definitely wanted to avoid Paige, who was also being ridiculous. Erica looped back through the dining room and into the kitchen, revisiting the mustached uncle at the makeshift bar for her second glass of Sauvignon blanc. To her relief, the button-downs were no longer in the kitchen and Sinead was heartily chatting with a woman who looked like a Winnie.

She stood idly in the corner and sipped her drink, feeling it glide down her throat like liquid nitrogen. An image of Paige's eyes appeared before her—what could have possibly caused such hostility? Maybe Paige was just upset about the pitfalls of her relationship and was projecting them onto Erica; after all, her medical school boyfriend hadn't come to the party. Erica knew better than to dismiss Paige's concern, or anger, or jealousy—though why she would be *jealous* Erica didn't know—but she also felt unfairly accused. She had finally mustered enough courage to attend Paige's party and now Paige was blaming her for doing exactly what she'd suggested: *Mingle and drink and eat and be merry.* Besides, Ray was the one who'd approached her! And if it hadn't been for him, she'd still be stuck with chatty-chat Sinead.

Fuck Paige, Erica thought boldly, the wine going down faster than she'd planned, turning her insides luminescent. She stopped herself before finishing it and crept back to the living room. From the open doorway, she glanced at the window where she and Ray had been standing, but only their empty glasses remained. She scanned the rest of the room, but Ray had vanished. She thought about going outside for a smoke, but figured that was what Paige, or Ray, or both of them were doing. The safest course of action was to stay out of the way.

It didn't take long for the scene to change. Without any announcement, Lynn and two other ladies began moving the coffee table and rolling up the rug to reveal a hardwood floor. Meanwhile, a different mustached uncle carried in a hefty crate of records, which everyone flocked to like a keg. Records were lifted and passed around, inciting *oohs* and *aahs* as they made their way to the player.

Erica watched Lynn free her long hair and kick off her heels as "Uptown Girl" sprang to life. She grabbed the hands of a slightly older lady, wearing a sweater almost as silly as Sinead's, and the two began trotting in a circle. Erica smiled to herself, clutching her near-empty glass. More and more people, most of them around Lynn's age, slipped off their shoes and jumped onto the dance floor, spinning and tripping and swinging. Erica thought about impromptu dance parties she'd attended in college, but even when drunk or high, she was still too uncomfortable to give in completely.

As Lynn's long hair swayed to the beat, *Your Mom is such a hippie* replayed in Erica's head. Perhaps, all of that time, she had wished her mother were more like Paige's...and, quite possibly, she'd wished her father were more like Paige's, too.

She retreated into the hall so she was even less visible to the people on the dance floor, since Lynn was clearly on a mission to get every guest involved. Erica prayed she wouldn't be noticed. Refusing to join the hostess of the party would be almost as terrible as trying to dance to Billy Joel.

"*Cloud Atlas.*"

The voice in her ear was just above a whisper.

"Huh?" Erica turned around to find shiny-eyed Ray with another glass of Scotch in hand. Of course he had found her again; she'd had a feeling he would.

"For your dissertation," he continued softly. "I read it last year, and I do recall cosmology symbolism. Subtle, but it's there. And the author is British, so that's a start."

Erica inhaled sharply and leaned against the wall. She could still view most of the frenzied dancing, though it seemed to belong to another world. *The hallway is hyperspace*! Just then she spotted Paige: Paige who loved to dance, Paige who lived for moments like these and always sought to create them for herself. For years, Erica realized, she'd been the black hole in their friendship, draining Paige's light.

Bruce Springsteen's "Dancing in the Dark" came on next, the volume cranked up, and Erica watched Lynn take her daughter's hands and drag her into the circle. Paige resisted at first, but then laughed and gave in easily, spinning her mother under her arm. Erica envied them...hated them, even. She didn't know where this new feeling came from. Normally she adored Lynn, she adored her own mother, and she adored Paige, yet *Fuck Paige* came back to taunt her. Fuck Paige's beauty and confidence and ability to know the right thing to do in any situation.

"Now, what were you saying before my lovely daughter interrupted us?" Ray was inching closer, no question about it.

Springsteen crooned, *I ain't nothing but tired, man I'm just tired and bored with myself. Hey there baby, I could use just a little help.*

"I don't know," she said, looking up at Ray who was looking down at her.

"If I remember correctly, I was asking why you hadn't attended one of these parties before."

"Oh." There'd been a litany of excuses, year after year, and yet here she was in the hallway with Ray. This year, she was trying.

I check my look in the mirror, wanna change my clothes, my hair, my face.

"I feel out of place," she admitted. "I suppose I always do."

"You have no reason to feel that way," he said. "If anyone should feel like that, I should, yet I refuse to. You're wanted here just as much as I am."

The history began to fall into place—stories Paige had told her and then immediately tried to bury. Lynn and Ray had never married, and they'd only lived together until Paige was five. But for years Ray would still spend weekends at Paige's house, sleeping in Lynn's bed and cooking breakfast in the kitchen, and Paige never knew what to make of it. He would stay for several weekends in a row, then disappear for months on end.

You can't start a fire, worryin' about your little world falling apart.

"It's getting crazy in there, isn't it?" He gestured toward Paige in mid-twirl, her dress billowing like the little girl's.

Above the scent of sugar cookies and old lady perfume and the Christmas tree in its prime, Erica detected Ray's cologne. Woody and smoky, he smelled like a perfect autumn evening and nothing like the boys she dated. He wore a sly smile now, like a fairy tale wolf. He wasn't much taller than Paige, and Erica remembered how she'd once stood on tiptoes to kiss her when they were sad and drunk and lonely. *Why am I thinking like this?* But she had to admit the truth: she found Ray attractive. That was it, wasn't it? She reminded herself that they were *both* adults, and this wasn't some Lolita fantasy. She was allowed to feel attracted. He was too. The two of them were extrasolar planets tonight.

"Do you want to take a run upstairs? I'm willing to bet it's quieter there. We can discuss your work more peacefully."

The song changed again: "Please Mr. Postman." Paige was bumping hips with the teenage cousin who used to follow them around the park. At any moment, Paige's eyes would land on Erica and then her anger would turn to rage. *Fuck Paige.* Erica could make this decision if she wanted...if she dared.

"Sure," she heard herself say, tasting the wine on her tongue as she drained the glass. Ray took it from her and placed it on an end table that held statues of angels.

Erica followed his lead up the carpeted steps. Along the way, family photographs appeared on the walls. She tried not to look, but noticed a tiny version of Paige—eyes wider, curls curlier—tucked into Lynn's arms.

You gotta wait a minute, wait a minute...

The lower half of the house receded as they reached the second floor landing. Ray ushered her into the study, closing the door halfway and pointing to a lumpy leather couch across from a wooden desk. Erica didn't remember this room. She wondered who usually sat at the desk and what important business they'd conducted. Then she focused on a framed map of Ireland, trying to remember the city from which the McCourt clan hailed. Dublin, Cork, Limerick? She didn't know anything about Ireland; nor did she know much about Poland or Italy. There were no maps in her grandmothers' houses, neither of whom had even been to Poland or Italy themselves. Erica was third and fourth generation American, as distant from her genetic homelands as she was from phonographs. But Italy and Poland were only superficial origins; a map of the solar system, the Milky Way, the Local Galactic Group, and the universe at large would have provided a much better sense of time, place, and purpose. Still, this map of Ireland must have been a nice reminder for the McCourts. A map on her wall might have made all the difference.

She knew she was distracting herself from the inevitable—Ray joining her on the couch—because she feared what would happen once he finally did. He approached the couch slowly, movements calculated. Lamplight pooled around their feet and Erica imagined the Andromeda galaxy, a lake of stars. Otherwise, the ceiling light stayed off.

"In *Cloud Atlas,* there was a birthmark shaped like a comet…I won't explain the significance, but a comet counts, doesn't it?"

He sat with his back against the cushion and body angled toward hers. She couldn't help searching for signs of an erection. The shadows made it hard to tell.

"Yeah, that counts. I want to read that book, too; it has amazing reviews. I hear a movie is coming out soon, so I better read it fast because I hate to see the movie before I read the book."

She squeezed the webbing of her hand. It felt like a lid on her head had opened, letting in too much air. Her heart bobbed up and down in her chest. She recalled a dream about a tree of souls that could change the weather and another about a memoir she'd written only to realize it wasn't true.

"I completely agree," Ray said, grinning slightly.

She imagined the two of them as binary stars orbiting a dark center.

Her mind backtracked to the woods, to a crooked trail where two twelve-year-old girls tried to uncover what made their fathers want to leave, or, in Paige's case, sometimes want to stay. They had picked them apart, analyzed them from a hundred different angles, and then decided they didn't deserve their attention. *some more words for that one winding road, the forest where we / buried our fears and forsook our fathers / this poem is for your unending smile / that won't quit shining, that look in your eye / when I'm making a fuss…*

"I am trying to uncover the symbolism of my life," Erica blurted.

She covered her mouth and began to turn away—to look back at Ireland safe behind glass—but Ray's hand was traveling. That hand stroked her hair, turned her chin, held her cheek, and pushed her lips against his. So soft and simple, as natural as dreaming. And yet, her cells began to thrash—the calcium and carbon that had once belonged to stars now threatened to tear themselves apart. Ray's hand moved up and down her face, his fingers grazing the under-eye concealer that had probably been her mother's way of saying, *You're an adult now, just like me.*

As their tongues touched, she tasted the Scotch, smelled his cologne, and felt his stubble rough against her skin. She wanted to lose herself, to forget who was downstairs, to leave her past in the dust, but her blood was slowing and her heart was cramping and she had to wonder why. Why like this?

None of it is real.

Her mind returned to the breakfast table in Boston, when the rain had tapped the window like a tiny persistent hand. She had talked with Ray so easily then, pouring a second and third cup of tea, secretly hoping their discussion would never end and she could stay in her pajamas all day, with Ray paying her so much attention. Paige's eyes had flashed across the table then too, eyebrows arched and lips tight. Something had been set in motion that morning, something she and Ray were finishing tonight, and Erica didn't understand what it meant for Paige, but she understood one thing: she didn't know Paige as well as she'd thought, and that was enough to make her stop.

"We shouldn't do this," she said, out of breath.

"Erica," he whispered, holding on.

"No. We can't." She stood on shaky legs, trying to find balance on the gravity in the room. "I need to go. Now."

She flew out of the study, into the hall, back down the carpeted stairs, and straight past the photo of Paige in Lynn's arms.

The music was still blaring, the guests still dancing. Erica entered the hall closet, pushing aside black peacoat after black peacoat until she found hers. She slipped it on, darted into the foyer, and paused.

The Christmas tree's star burned bright, like the fire she and five-year-old Paige had tried so hard to light. She decided to wish on it, that plastic star beneath the constellations she knew by heart. But she didn't know what to wish for. So she confessed her sin, as fresh as a newborn pearl. She begged the star to forgive.

Paige spun around, cheeks red, hair mussed, a silly smile slapped on her face. She looked across the room—across a sea of dancing aunts and cousins and uncles and friends—and held Erica's gaze inside of hers. Did she know? Could she tell?

Je t'aime, I love you, Paige mouthed. Her hands made a heart, thumbs pressed tight.

Je t'aime aussi. I love you too.

Blue Velvet

SHE WORE A BLUE VELVET DRESS when she took out the trash. I watched her from the window, hovering above my semi-girlfriend.

"What the hell are you looking at?" she asked, all breathy.

"Just that woman across the street. She always dresses like she's going to the prom twenty years late."

The blue was a stark contrast to her pale skin, the velvet to her trash bag, tightly gripped.

"Who the hell cares," said my semi-girlfriend, placing me back inside her.

I could have told her I didn't care, but that wasn't true. Even with my general lack of self-awareness, I knew I had a sixth sense for this woman; every time she stepped out of her house, I'd sprint to the window in the nick of time. It was almost like I was reverse-stalking her.

She was nearly as old as my mother and certainly no beauty queen, but there was something about her that screamed a sense of dignity no one could touch. She wore blue velvet (like the movie, like the song) to take out the trash for god's sake, and to walk her ugly dog, retrieve her mail, and water her tiny patch of sun-bleached grass. I took out the trash in dirty underwear.

It was July then: 85 degrees on a good day. The semi-girlfriend and I had been spending a lot of time naked. She didn't live with me, but she was always around. I didn't mind for two good reasons: free sex and free crank. Who could complain? I knew I did not and would not ever love her, but that didn't matter. We were mid-twenty-somethings, and neither of us on the lookout for love.

I lived on the second floor of a sagging three-story house and worked the nightshift as a tollbooth operator, or tollbooth monkey was more like it. The semi worked nights too, pouring booze for the down-and-out and carrying home the occasional twenty in her bra strap. On these hot summer days, recovering from our shifts, we'd lie on my floor to fuck and make splatter paintings until we decided to snort our heavenly powder and go out to do regretful things. We were proud of our childlike art but had resigned to waste away like dazed corpses with miraculously still-beating hearts. No one dared or cared to stop us.

Mine wasn't the type of neighborhood where you were likely to find women dressed like Ms. Velvet, in case you were wondering. Semi aside (she preferred plaid skirts), most women wore Disney shirts or maternity pants or too-short sundresses hoping to impress the deliveryman. It wasn't a gardener and recycle bin kind of town. My street was a shitty cul-de-sac just beyond the downtown of a town south of the Midwest and north of the South. The neighborhood, if you could call it that, was white and trashy. People scrounged and bought Wonder bread and left their kids' bikes to rust in the rain. But then, of course, there was Ms. Velvet.

One night, too tweaked to sleep, I decided to come up with explanations for her fancy pearls, curly up-dos, red nails, and unforgivable blue velvet in the summer heat. What if she was a mob boss's former wife...maybe she even killed the guy? Or better yet, she was a high-class hooker, the madam type. Maybe my lady (the semi) was working for her and Ms. Velvet kept sending her over to spy. But despite all possibilities, I couldn't wrap my head around this older woman's grace, her unshakable pride in the midst of so much shame. She consumed my every thought, drug-induced or otherwise. My only reprieve was sleep, and even then she peered into the dusty window behind my eyes.

I was shoving popcorn down my parched throat the next morning (and by morning I meant afternoon) when I saw her again, my personal hummingbird. I rushed downstairs, thinking this the perfect chance to say hello. I knew I needed to get a grip on the situation before it turned me psycho.

She was standing on the sidewalk across from my house, usual trash bag in hand. Sweat poured down my bare chest. What would I say to her? Something neighborly? Should I offer sugar? A barrage of cartoony images (me and her simmering in Elmer Fudd's pot) pummeled my brain as I watched her place the trash bag in the can, stare longingly at the crisp blue sky, and turn around. The slamming of her door rattled my ribcage. I couldn't help but bring a fist to my forehead, shouting "Stupid shit" and punching my face.

The next day I decided to stake her out. The semi didn't notice when I positioned myself at the front window, blinds drawn, and waited for Ms. Velvet to emerge on her own, no binoculars needed. I had fully prepared: drugs busying themselves in my arteries. I'd never have the guts to approach her sober, so it was a necessary part of my plan to not be such a fucking coward.

After an hour of waiting, jumping like a skittish cat at every sound, I spotted her on the doorstep. This was it! I pulled on mesh shorts and raced down the stairs, stepping my bare feet onto hot concrete and blinking against the sun's harsh glare.

There she was: ruby lipstick, blue velvet dress. What was she doing? What was I doing? I coughed up phlegm and hacked it to the curb. She didn't have the leashed dog or mail in her hands or even a trash bag; she was just standing on the sidewalk, staring at the sky and then staring at me, the slightest inkling of wrinkles beneath a smooth mask of powder.

"Hello," I offered, choking on what might have been my very first word, except that my first word was "Mama" and I'd said it with delight.

She raised her dark eyebrows and nodded. Maybe she couldn't speak. We entered a sort of staring contest.

"What's your name?" was about to spill from my lips, but the look in her eyes (hazel and catching bits of sun) kept any more words from seeing the light of day. I couldn't gauge the emotion behind her glare, but I knew I needed her to know me, to touch me, to heal me. For some reason, I wanted her to be the one person I could possibly love. The one person who might possibly love *me*. I wanted her to be something, anything, besides a voiceless blue velvet bird out the window. The bastard sun bore down as she looked at me with her all-seeing eyes.

My words finally came out: "What's your name?" in barely a whisper.

She's a mirage, I thought, *I can see through her*, but I was not on acid and this was no hallucination. Then I remembered the dream I'd had that very morning, trying to untangle myself from twisted sleep and the semi's grasp. In the dream, the Great Lakes were a fifth of the size of the sun—geography distorted, stretching at its seams. The world was aching and splitting apart.

What was the significance? Did I have a fever? Why wouldn't this woman fucking speak?

But then it happened. She said her name. Only the birds in the sunlit trees were hollering, drivers down the street were honking, and the semi-girlfriend was calling from inside my house. Sweat pooled in my ear canals and every dream I'd ever dreamt gushed into the empty spaces between my thoughts, and I could hear my mother screaming from far away and my father cursing from the grave and my whole life flashing like a violent strobe light.

When I came to, Blue Velvet was gone. I was the only one on the street.

MAY DAY

SOPHIE MADE SURE she was the first to arrive.

She showed up in a black skirt and black shirt because only black seemed fitting for an evening with Skiff. Before ringing his doorbell, she buckled a leather collar around her neck and tightened the laces of her 20-hole Docs.

Skiff answered the door wearing an apron over a plaid kilt and old-man slippers. Sophie laughed.

"Nice outfit."

"I'm making borscht. Did you bring a mask for the ceremony?"

"I made myself mouse ears. I can paint my face too."

"Come in."

Sophie tiptoed into Skiff's house like stepping into forbidden territory. She already felt closer to him, just knowing where he lived.

The living room was filled with children's toys and smelled like yellowed paper. Skiff's mother, whom Sophie had yet to meet, ran a daycare there. Most of the toys were decades old, with missing parts. A row of dolls sat on one long shelf. Messy-haired, stone-faced, and pale-skinned, they looked like orphans waiting for someone to swoop in and adopt them. They also reminded her of Skiff's exgirlfriend, Dasha.

"This island of misfit toys has taken over your living space," Sophie told Skiff in the kitchen, hoping to impress him with a film reference.

"I never go in there. Want tea?"

"All right."

Skiff poured barley tea into matching mugs and led Sophie to the second floor. Two of the four rooms were gutted, with slates of sheetrock stacked against the walls and tarp covering holes in the floor. Sophie hadn't been inside a suburban home in quite some time, and she'd never been to Staten Island. She wondered if every house in the neglected borough looked like this.

They climbed a ladder to the attic, most of which functioned as practice space for Skiff's band, with his bedroom crammed into a sectioned-off corner. The wood-paneled walls of his room rose to a sharp point and a measly slant of light entered a half-covered window by his bed. Candleholders had been drilled into the paneling and hardened clumps of black wax caked the floor. A draft blew in from overhead, swaying an upside down doll. She'd expected to find a vintage *Wicker Man* poster, but supposed it wasn't Skiff's style.

Skiff turned off his Virgin Prunes album, sat on the bed, and crossed his ankles. He hadn't expected Sophie so soon; the others wouldn't arrive for hours. What was he supposed to do with her? It was Sunday in the daytime, in his bedroom no less. He found it easier to talk when they were working in the video store or watching movies at her place. Things felt different now—stripped too bare.

"I love this," Sophie said, pointing to the table taking up most of the room's floor space. On it, two swan-like statues—wiry necks and exposed chests revealing clay organs—faced one another, their legs intertwined. One had green feathers, the other purple. They each had one marble eye and stared back and forth indefinitely.

"I made that years ago. I only brought it out because I want to add real feathers. I dyed pigeon feathers last week."

"It's beautiful. Do you still make art like this?" Sophie knew he was an art school dropout, but the only art she'd seen were cartoon caricatures of the other employees at the store. She fished out the receipt paper sketches he'd toss in the trash.

"Not anymore."

"Why not? You should get back into it, or go back to school." He was twenty-one, a year older than her. If she possessed a talent like his, she'd like to think she would have done something with it. Something more than they were doing now.

"Eh. I don't care much," Skiff said, though he knew he was lying. He cared more than anything else, but that side of him was soiled. He couldn't figure out a way to keep art in his life without

Dasha.

"Where's your mask?" Sophie asked.

"You'll see it later."

"What should we do now?"

"Whatever."

Tentatively, Sophie sat beside Skiff and stroked his mangled stuffed dog, which had two missing eyes. She stared at the safety pin poking through Skiff's ear. An ear with extra notches, six holes aligned. She wanted to touch his rough cheeks. The gaps between his teeth. She wanted to pull his dyed red hair. She craved his collarbones, his wrists, his ever-present frown.

"I could show you an old video I made."

"I'd love that."

Skiff set his mug on the table and shuffled to a shelf, where stacks of videotapes and records collected dust. Most of the videos were unlabeled and he shook them to make sure they weren't broken.

Sophie fixed her hair while Skiff bent down. She tried to see herself in the reflection of the television.

"I don't know what these are, but they might be good." He shoved one tape into the VCR and sat back down on the bed, somewhat closer to Sophie.

The unmarked tape was a series of short films he'd made in high school. The first showed animated clay figures. The second, a visual montage of flesh-eating diseases and bacteria. The third, a teenage Skiff wandering his school's hallways, covered in butcher's blood and carrying a cross, as other kids looked on confused.

Sophie wished she had been this daring. Skiff was embarrassed.

The next tape was only a year old. His older brother wore a tutu and feathered wings, prancing around their half-gutted bathroom, where a freestanding tub sat on a concrete floor surrounded by wayward pipes, broken tiles, and piles of plaster. Skiff lay in the tub filled with leaves, rocks, and dirty water. He emerged naked—shivering, skinnier, if that were possible. Fade to black. Then he and Dasha wandered through woods that opened to a cemetery. Holding hands, the two looked like genderless twins, perfectly symmetrical. In the final scene, Skiff shaved one side of his head. His hair was black then, reaching his shoulders like Dasha's.

"Enough of this garbage," Skiff said. He lay down with his head where his feet should have been, and Sophie did too. They faced one another. An invisible division of empty space prevented them from touching.

He looked at her, so close.

Whenever his work shift ended at midnight, rather than wait for the R, ride the train, wait for the ferry, ride the boat, wait for the bus, ride in back, walk ten minutes in the cold to this dark room, where he downed pills to fall asleep, Skiff often chose more convenient shelter. Sometimes he stayed at Vile and Zuzu's rent-controlled place on 8th Street, where the only available floor space was an inch-thick pad amid the ceiling-high clutter that epitomized Zuzu, like the bracelets stacked to her elbows. On those mornings, Skiff's lungs would ache from the couple's dual chain-smoking. Other times, he went to Astoria to drink beer and crash on his drummer's floor. For the past few months, he'd walk home with Sophie or buzz her building if she didn't work his shift. The apartment she shared with her older stepsister didn't pollute his body with smoke.

At Sophie's, they would drink detox tea and watch videos from the store. His favorites were psychological horror and German Expressionist. Hers were surrealist fantasy and Czech New Wave. At three or four in the morning, Skiff would watch Sophie brush her teeth, and she would change while he looked away, and the two would lie side by side listening to the cold glimmer of Cocteau Twins as he told stories about seeing ghosts in Siberia, or eating from a dumpster, or building a raft like Huckleberry Finn and riding down the East River. Sophie always listened and rarely spoke of herself.

She had a Cabbage Patch face: round and cute and young. Her body was shaped like a fat girl who'd lost weight or a thin girl who'd gotten a little chubby; he couldn't tell. She had blondish hair and eyebrows to match. She smiled too often. She asked a lot of questions. There was always a moment when Skiff felt like something ought to happen. Not that he necessarily *wanted* it to happen, not that she was his type, not that he found her attractive, not that he felt attached, not that he wanted to taste her, but still.

Sophie knew something was bound to happen soon, though they fell asleep in separate worlds and he always wore his clothes to bed. Peter at work said: Skiff is shy, Skiff is passive, Skiff is insecure. In the morning, he'd tickle her awake, violently pinching her hips until bluish marks appeared the next day.

"Are you sleepy?" she asked.

"A bit."

She thought about kissing him. She thought about grabbing him and biting his lip. She wasn't sure she could be that kind of girl.

They heard footsteps on the staircase and Dmitry bounded in, wearing a black eye patch.

"Yar!" he shouted, waving his arms. Skiff and Sophie bolted upright and moved apart. Dmitry hopped onto the bed between them and placed a scrawny, scarred arm around Sophie's shoulder.

"Pavel, you like? I'm a pirate, thieving your girl." His smile was eerily large.

Sophie blushed. Skiff sighed. He hated that Dmitry refused to call him Skiff.

"Right," Skiff said. "And it's the May Day ceremony so you have to wear an animal mask, not a poor excuse for a pirate costume. You've seen *The Wicker Man*."

Dmitry always made a mockery of everything. Skiff had told Sophie about "babysitting" Dmitry when he was strung out, though Dmitry was older by nine years. Skiff had pried knives from his hands, tossed syringes to the trash, searched for him in alleyways, and lied to their parents on his behalf.

"I'm not planning to partake in your paganism, Pavel. I'll be filming it." Dmitry's hair was faded purple, stringy and breaking, and his gaunt face had caved in. His eyes were deep wounds. Crevices formed at both sides of his awkward mouth. Sophie knew he had to ask permission to even leave the house.

He started rambling to Sophie about the Aztecs; she had no idea why, but she nodded and pretended to listen.

Skiff stood, adjusting his apron. "I'm going to check on my stew."

Dmitry, still babbling, and Sophie, still nodding, followed Skiff down the ladder. "When it comes to making precise astronomical calculations, the Aztecs were infinitely more intelligent than the Druids."

"The Druids were the most intellectually advanced group of ancient people, more so than even the Egyptians," Skiff retorted.

"Yes yes," Dmitry said to Sophie, "and they burned people alive in effigies like our dear Pavel made outside."

"Dmitry, the Aztecs sacrificed millions of people. They cooked their limbs and ate them."

"It's all a matter of perspective, little brother."

Time passed unnoticeably in the kitchen. The table was crowded with bakery breads, half-empty mugs, and idle hand tools. An audible hum emerged from the dying overhead light. Skiff's soup was a liquid bruise. He sang Celtic songs softly as he stirred, layering a Scottish accent atop his Russian one and trying to drown out Dmitry's rambling. Sophie nibbled a piece of babka and watched Skiff stir.

Kneeling on a chair, Dmitry drummed his thumbs on the table. "They believed that gods and goddesses sacrificed themselves for humanity, so the Aztecs sacrifice *themselves* to Huitzilopochtli and the other gods every day. They didn't think, oh the sun comes up and the sun goes down, they think, the sun is a warrior, and it fought bravely with the moon and the stars for the Aztecs, and they have to help the sun win all of its battles, so they offer it blood...human blood, animal blood."

"That's kind of sad, though," Sophie said, cupping her chin in her palm.

"Sad? The Aztecs believed in life! They needed life, they cherished life, and killed for life. They had reasons, deep spiritual reasons like you and me in this modern world will never understand, and it's that element of ritual and sacrifice that made them strong. Gave them purpose and meaning."

"The Druids had celebrations *and* rituals," said Skiff in his normal accent. "During the day they had parties, elaborate and mystical, and then at night they would perform spiritual ceremonies, lighting fires and jumping over them naked to purify themselves. And their May Day ceremony celebrates life returning to earth, so it's just like worshipping the sun god or whatever you said."

"Little Pavel takes everything seriously," Dmitry whispered to Sophie.

"I want my crops to grow this year. My precious apples." Skiff winked at Sophie. Sometimes she thought his whole life could be boiled down to a curated collection of film references.

Just last week they'd heard rumors of the store's imminent closure due to outrageous rents in the East Village and the rise of online streaming. Sure their rental system was archaic, and fewer and fewer people were buying DVDs these days, let alone the vast array of VHS tapes Sophie and Skiff took home, but she liked to think the cinephile community was just as vibrant now as it had been when the store opened in the '80s. Sophie wanted to rewind time as easily as a videotape. None of them really belonged in this century.

Dmitry wandered back upstairs and Skiff, still in his apron and slippers, covered the soup. He took Sophie through a backdoor and into the yard. On the stone patio sat two rusted tricycles, a few toy wagons, and a dirty picnic table for the daycare toddlers. The yard was an overgrown uphill slope, with chicken wire fencing at the top of the hill. A narrow path had been trampled through weeds and wild leaves all the way to that fence, where piles of dead branches and brush surrounded an upturned wheelbarrow. Several skinny trees remained bare. The air remembered winter and stung at the fingertips.

They approached the wicker man, sticking out of the dirt. It was four feet tall, made from bone-like branches Skiff had zip-tied together. Its arms were outstretched and its legs came down from a sexless torso, equally proportioned like any person. It loosely resembled the hulking figure from the film, except far less formidable.

Sophie was impressed with Skiff's dedication to reenacting a cult classic, which she'd only watched after he'd invited her to celebrate May Day on Staten Island. Of course she'd pretended she'd seen the film dozens of times, just like he had. And she'd only just realized, during his and Dmitry's conversation, that the ceremony went back centuries. The irony wasn't lost on her—they were going to make a film of a reenactment of a film that had reenacted a pagan ritual in which people acted like animals. She wondered if Skiff was aware of this.

"I need to add more to the head and shoulders," he said, gently touching his creation as if trying not to hurt it. "I wanted it to be huge, gigantic, at least ten feet tall, but I don't have enough branches. I made him this morning."

"Looks great to me," Sophie said.

"Find tiny branches for the face."

Sophie did as he asked, crouching in her skirt and sifting through the dirt. Skiff whistled as he pulled out more zip-ties. After ten minutes, Sophie had collected two handfuls of baby twigs. Skiff licked his finger and threw it up to the graying sky.

"It better not rain tonight."

"I won't let it," she said, offering her gatherings. He set to work fixing his progeny as Sophie picked dirt out of her nails.

"What's with the borscht, by the way?" She always wanted to keep Skiff talking. It made things feel less prickly between them.

"For after the ceremony. Beets cleanse the blood."

"Who else did you invite?"

"Vile and Zuzu, this girl Ricki, and Dasha and Peter."

"Dasha? She's coming?"

"Maybe."

Sophie thought back to her last Dasha encounter, two weeks prior. Everyone had trekked to a bar in Bed-Stuy to see Skiff's band, since they hardly ever played. Peter had worked that night's shift so Skiff and Sophie could both take off from the store. Skiff played guitar with bandages electrical-taped to his sinewy torso for a goth-punk effect. His band played five originals and one cover: "Pagan Lovesong" by his favorite, the Virgin Prunes, who'd disbanded in '86. *I want to steal your heart, your heart.* Sophie swooned and couldn't help wondering if he'd chosen the love song for her. But then Dasha pulled a stool to the middle of the floor and sat with her newly shaved head down, soaking up his attention. Sophie watched Skiff watch her from the stage; *I want to eat, eat your heart.* With her long limbs, jagged bones, and pout that never quit, Dasha posed for Dmitry's camera and lifted up her dress. She threw her bare legs onto Dmitry's shoulder as he squatted in front of her, and she kicked a stranger with her thick-soled boots. She crawled onto the stage to inhale the smoke-machine's reverb and then scampered off to hide, waiting for Skiff to find her.

Peter had stolen Dasha from Skiff, but Skiff said he didn't mind; Dasha had been his for four years, but he said he didn't care. Now Dasha, Peter, and Dasha's lizard Nosferatu lived out by Coney Island. The lizard turned brown when it was stressed; she bred crickets for him and fed him blood from her fingerprints. Dasha claimed to be suffering from acetaldehyde poisoning and underwent ritualistic detoxification. She and Peter ate nuts and seeds and dried fruit like rodents. They lived like two hospital patients: reading medical textbooks, furiously scrubbing their hands, and dressing each other's self-inflicted wounds. Sometimes Peter showed up at the video store with scratches down his neck. Skiff would ask, "What'd she do to you this time?" but Peter never answered and Skiff didn't really want to know. He kept Dasha's drawings on his closet floor. The penciled faces were always her own.

By the time Skiff stepped back to admire his work, the sky had deepened and the wind picked up. The two turned around and went inside. Vile was standing in the center of the kitchen. He was tall, broad-shouldered, and wearing a black hood that covered most of his head.

"Hi baby!" he shouted at Skiff, who slid across the floor to greet him. Vile extended a large hand with chipped nail polish and Skiff bent down to kiss it. They had been friends since they were seventeen, but Vile was also a regular at the video store, browsing the used bins at least once a week.

"We were outside, I didn't hear you come in."

"We just got here." Vile's eyes darted to Sophie, who stood timidly by the backdoor. As much as she liked being part of Skiff's world, part of her hoped that his friends would bail, leaving the two of them alone.

"Oh hi Sophie," Vile said. "Zuzu, you remember Sophie, right?"

Zuzu lingered in the hallway and slowly entered the kitchen. They had met at the Bed-Stuy show, but Sophie saw her now as if for the first time. She'd woven flowers through the thick curls of a tousled black wig, which sat clumsily on her head. Rows of chunky, colorful bracelets decorated her arms, well above the elbows.

"Zuzu, don't be rude, take off your sunglasses," Vile told her.

She removed her oversized shades and blinked twice. She was nearing forty and had lived a life marked by excessive drug use and seclusion, evidenced by worn-weary eyes. Sparkles and glitter adorned her eyelids and cheekbones, and she offered a tight-mouthed grin that revealed smoker's teeth, slightly protruding.

"Hi, so good to see you both," she said in a low rasp. "Sorry we're so late, we missed the 5:00 boat and had to wait for the next one, and then, oh Vi, you tell them what happened."

"They don't care."

"This guy tried to pick a fight with Vile. Why do people always try to fight you? It's like they can smell you from miles away or something."

"Because you lost my brass knuckles and they won't sell them to me anymore," Vile said, his voice peaking.

"That wasn't my fault, Vi. You left them in that guy's car."

"Actually Zu, *you* left them in that guy's car."

"Well you're here," Skiff interrupted forcefully, untying his apron. "Did you bring masks?"

"We have great masks, you're going to fucking love them." Vile pointed to the shopping bag dangling from Zuzu's jeweled hand. A metal ball poked through the flesh of his right cheek. His smile stretched wide and the piercing looked like a dimple. "And you're wearing Scottish garb," he said to Skiff.

"I had to. You know, May Day. Did you bring anyone?"

"Oh yeah, Ricki met us at the ferry. I don't know where she went though." Vile's eyes darted wildly as he spoke. He could never look anyone dead on from a combination of generalized anxiety and over-medication. He and Zuzu rarely ventured far from her chaotic apartment.

Vile popped his head into the living and shouted, "Ricki?"

"Seems like that girl is always running off," Zuzu said to Sophie.

They found her curled up in the corner of the living room, hugging a grubby stuffed bear to her chest.

Sophie glanced at Skiff, but he didn't seem to notice her. His more important friends had swallowed her up.

"Ricki baby," Vile said, "nap time is over." In one fluid motion she leapt nimbly to her feet.

"Have you meet Sophie?" Vile asked Ricki. She shook her head. Pin-straight, jet-black hair cascaded to her hips. Her body was nearly as small as a child's, though a doctor once said she was aging faster physiologically due to insomnia and dehydration. Her torso was lost, as always, under the fabric of a thick sweater. She despised femininity and had been wearing extra-large shirts since the year she grew breasts. She kept her hair long only as a testament to her distant Inuit ancestors, who believed that hair was the physical manifestation of their thoughts.

Sophie wondered what Skiff had told them about her. Vile and Zuzu probably knew that nothing had *happened*, but maybe Ricki assumed she was his girlfriend. She'd never been anyone's girlfriend. Not seriously.

"Hi," Sophie said, feeling intimated by Skiff's eccentric friends, who were far more interesting than she could ever hope to be.

They, more than anyone else, might chip and chip away until they found the bruised little soul beneath her ordinary skin.

Ricki glanced curiously at Sophie. "Hi," she said finally, flashing a nanosecond smile.

"I have to get everything ready," said Skiff in a serious tone. "Can someone grab the bag of supplies I left by the drums? And tell Dmitry to come back down if he wants to film this."

"Remember the first time I met him?" Vile said. "And he was carving some hieroglyphics shit into his arm and pouring rubbing alcohol all over it? Ha ha!"

"He's very backward and forward with himself, isn't he?" Zuzu rasped. "It's like destructive habits really *define* him. It's self-devotion, in this primal way."

"Self-devotion and self-destruction, every man is both savior and destroyer," Vile declared.

"I mean he puts thought into everything," Zuzu continued. "There's something to be said for such personally meaningful destructiveness."

"Dmitry has died a million and a half times," Skiff said. "He's immune to anything else."

"Darling, we die a little more every day," Vile said, with hands on his hips. "We all unravel. We're all looking for our own ways out. I'm mad, you're mad, we're all fucking mad, meow."

"I have to go outside and smoke," Zuzu croaked.

Ricki shot up the stairs like a cannonball. Skiff returned to the kitchen with Vile and Zuzu arguing at his heels. Sophie grabbed her messenger bag and crept away to find a bathroom.

It was the room from Skiff's film, but even more decrepit. The light didn't work. Melted candles sat on what remained of the sink. With the door cracked, she found matches to light two of them, then shut herself inside. An ornate mirror clung to the damaged wall and she found herself there, dimly reflected, lit from an upward angle so shadows danced upon her face. *Like a ghost,* she thought.

Sophie leaned closer, eye-to-eye with her reflection, and painted three black whiskers across each cheek. She found ruby red lipstick at the bottom of her bag and smeared that on too, then took out her ears made of blue and purple felt attached to a cheap headband. She'd stuck a safety pin through one ear, just like Skiff.

Backing away from the mirror, she approached the stained tub.

Slowly, she stepped in. Lying with knees bent and arms behind her head, Sophie closed her eyes and tried to imagine Skiff lying naked and cold among leaves. She wanted to know what he knew, feel what he felt. She wanted to leave herself and become someone else.

After a minute or two, she got up. Her birthday was in sixteen days, so she pretended the sink's candles were the ones on a cake, which meant that she got to make a wish. *Let him love me.* She blew out the flames, and left to find the others.

Naked trees shook. Darkened clouds swung low to the ground. Everyone stood on the patio, preparing for the procession.

Skiff was the wolf. His handmade papier-mâché mask had large holes for eyes and an exaggerated muzzle. He'd traded his slippers for boots, tied a pouch to his kilt, and flung a velveteen cloak over his shoulders.

Sophie was the mouse, with her homemade ears and painted whiskers. She hoped no one noticed that she hadn't made a tail.

Vile was the tiger, in a striped, store-bought mask held on by an elastic band. He smoked a black clove through the slit of its mouth.

Zuzu was the zebra, but the mask's elastic wouldn't stretch enough to fit over her wig. Skiff gave her feathers and deemed her a peacock; she stuck them in her wild curls and behind her ears, carrying more in her cigarette-free hand.

Ricki was the rabbit, wearing a fuzzy hat with floppy ears. Velcro closed the hat around her chin, and her long hair stuck out from the bottom.

Dmitry was the raven. He wore the wings from his and Skiff's film, though most of the feathers had since fallen off, exposing an overlain network of wire.

Skiff distributed props as Dmitry switched on his camera.

"Sophie, you hold Punch. Vile, you take the mandolin. Ricki, you bang the drum. Zuzu, you play flute."

Punch was supposed to be the ceremony's jester. A clown doll made of ruffled cloth, it had a porcelain face and dunce cap sewn onto its head. Sophie held Punch tightly; he smelled like Skiff's living room. She felt special just holding him.

"Now line up," Skiff commanded.

In a deep voice, he sang a folkloric tune, leading them slowly up the small hill. Sophie, behind him, giggled softly. Vile, behind her, violently plucked the mandolin. Zuzu, behind him, exhaled a puffy cloud of smoke and blew harshly into the wooden flute. Ricki, at the end, pounded the hand drum. Dmitry ran alongside the parade, stumbling through thick weeds, tripping and laughing with the camera pressed to his eye.

Skiff sang louder. Vile chanted. Ricki screeched. Sophie laughed. Zuzu lowered the flute for another long drag of her unfiltered cigarette.

They reached the top. Phantom clouds sunk even lower and the house appeared shrunken behind them. Wind shook the trees, undid the sky's gauze, numbed their skin, and grazed the wicker man's body. He stood proud, withstanding the breeze. Waiting.

They formed a half-circle around him. Zuzu leaned against the wheelbarrow. Ricki crouched to the dirt. Sophie clutched Punch to her chest. Vile hacked up phlegm. Dmitry moved in circles as Skiff faced his creation.

She hadn't shown up; she hadn't even called.

Skiff imagined Dasha on the patio, running up the hill and shouting, "Wait for me!" They used to hide in his attic for days, skipping art school, drawing each other, fucking and singing and speaking in code, shining flashlights to watch their eyes contract, watching Christopher Lee films and blasting Dead Can Dance. They'd film themselves cracking eggs on the floor and beheading his mother's dolls. They'd climb onto the roof to spy on Dmitry in his room. In the dead of night, they'd sneak out to the yard, crawl in the grass, roll in the dirt, and pin each other flat against the earth. Dasha used to kneel on his chest, digging her pointed kneecaps into his ribs, choking him until he tasted death. With her long nails, she would chisel his chest and his back. After that, Skiff had tried scratching his skin, but the pain was never real enough.

"Here we go," he said to the group. Removing a lighter from his pouch, he bent down. Blue sparks flew as he offered his flame to the wicker man's femur.

Nothing happened. He wouldn't ignite. Vile squatted with his lighter and tried to burn the other leg. Again, nothing happened.

"Ah fuck," Skiff said.

"Zuzu, give Sophie your lighter," Vile instructed.

"At least no's one inside of it, right?" Zuzu muttered. "The anticipation might kill him before *you* could." She handed her lighter to Sophie, who kneeled on the dirt beside Skiff.

On the ground, Skiff leaned near Sophie and whispered, "I think the branches are too damp. Did it rain last night?"

Sophie could have kissed him then. She realized she had made the wrong wish in the bathroom; she would have done anything to take it back and wish instead for Skiff's dream to come true, for his progeny to burn, for his heart to mend and love to return. Or maybe for the courage to grab his face and bite his tongue.

"This isn't looking good on film." Dmitry zoomed in on his brother's furrowed brow.

"We'll get it, we'll get it," Skiff said.

"Can someone can find newspaper or something?" Vile asked.

The three of them moved their arms up and down, wielding the small flames. Skiff's hand grazed Sophie's. She smiled shyly and pulled away.

Dmitry filmed from atop the wheelbarrow. Ricki did a handstand. Zuzu fished another cigarette from her boot and lit the new one with her last.

A strong gust of wind carried a ghostly cry from the house. Skiff spun around quickly, his heart screaming *Dasha*.

It was only his mother.

"What are you doing?" she yelled in an accent even thicker than his or Dmitry's. She scooted up the hill, with Skiff's father lumbering in the rear. Sophie froze, worried they were in trouble.

Skiff removed his mask. "It's May Day, Ma, I told you about this. We're trying to burn the goddamn wicker man."

His mother was short and squat with a full head of curls that rivaled Zuzu's wig. She argued with Skiff in Russian. Meanwhile, his father thrust armfuls of brush and dead leaves around the wicker man's ankles.

"We'll get this thing," he told them.

Soon, Vile's and Sophie's lighters caught onto the dry shrubbery. Tall orange flames leapt at the wicker man's legs, twisting around him like loose ribbons.

Sophie watched Skiff's face break into the purest smile she had ever seen—an echo of a forgotten childhood. She imagined Skiff, or rather Pavel, scampering around some backyard in Russia, believing he was magic.

"Woo woo!" Skiff's mother shouted, patting her palm to her open mouth. She ran in a circle, whooping and shrieking, reliving a moment from the primeval past.

Ricki emphatically banged her drum. Zuzu tossed her cigarette to the blaze and shook her bracelet-ridden arms. Vile grabbed Sophie for a dance. She let him twirl her in front of Skiff. Dmitry belted ancient verse and shot a close-up of the fire that was growing larger still. Skiff reached into his pouch, clutched a handful of dried flowers, and sprinkled them onto his creation.

It looked like the earth had swallowed the sun. Wind knocked feathers and flowers from Zuzu's hair, drawing them to the flames. Tiny embers leapt around Sophie as she danced. Her skirt fanned out as she swayed her hips.

This was no longer about some '70s cult classic or some ancient celebration or even about Skiff. In the brilliant glow, as she kicked her legs and flung her arms, Sophie caught Skiff's gaze. She watched him watch her. He was smiling at *her* now...was he falling in love? She closed her eyes. Something told her to keep them closed, to let the world fade to black. Nothing could ever hurt her this way.

Skiff watched Sophie and his other misfit toys, who had lost or removed their masks. His heart ached with gratitude; he loved them all for giving in to this ritual, for trusting his vision and fulfilling his fantasy. He wanted to tell them: You are all my Pagan Lovesong. *I reach for the sky but never, never can touch.*

Ricki threw her heavy sweater to the ground and raised her arms high above her head, baring her stomach and shouting unintelligible words. Vile hugged Zuzu and Skiff heard her say, "I've never seen anything like this before" as the two stood transfixed. Dmitry jumped up and down with their mother. Their father threw on more and more twigs, feeding the wicker man's hunger to keep them all alive.

They are forgetting themselves, Skiff thought. They were shedding their desires, shunning their egos, spurning expectations of what it meant to be human. He too wanted to forget.

He tossed his cloak to the dirt and spun madly, shifting his gaze and rolling his head, allowing the warm waves of light to invade his body and reel him in. The revolving faces of his clan blurred as they pranced around the fire, changing shape before the wicker man's eyes. Souls whirl-pooled, lifting higher and higher. The past was almost gone, the pain was almost dead. His bones were the glue that held them all together, and he was melting now, evaporating into the pool of souls swirling overhead. He would never forget this, and never forget them.

It was then that his mother shouted, "Look look!" and everyone stopped, following her gaze to the moon that poked its head between vaporous clouds. The moon was full, haloed, gold, heralding spring and summer and everything thereafter. The light. The harvest. The future they would share. Their eyes turned up as the wicker man fell.

The moon looked down and laughed.

GLOW

MY WRIST LOOKS LIKE MOLD.

"Tye, see this?" I thrust my arm in his face as he exhales smoke into my eyes.

"Yeah, that's disgusting," he mumbles, pushing me away.

"You're the one who did it."

He butts his cigarette on the coffee table and flicks it across the room. It misses the trashcan by a mile. "What are you babbling about?"

"Nevermind," I sigh. Of course he doesn't remember. It wasn't even while we were having sex. It was during an argument over his hair collecting dirt and dust and grime because he hasn't washed it in months. Apparently "dreads don't need washing," but the dankness of unclean hair has started to seep into the pillows. I remember saying, "You're as white as a picket fence and they look ridiculous on you anyway," to which he grabbed my arm, twisted it back, and bit me as if thirsting for blood. I enjoyed the feeling of canines digging deep, but then my skin turned carmine red, purplish-blue, lavender, and finally green. Moldy-green. He's right: it's disgusting.

"What are we doing tonight?" I ask. "There's that show at the TLA. You said Jesse could get us in free."

He huffs like an old man, even though he's twenty-four, and walks across the room. Maybe he's going to pick up that cigarette? No. He scratches his head and lowers the blinds. It's about time for his across-the-way neighbor to start getting nosey and we've always got something to hide.

"I'm staying in."

"On a Friday night? Since when do you do that?"

He stares at me hard. It's the look my mother gave me when I'd tell her something true and she'd say, "Too many goddamn fairy tales, this girl has some imagination," while drinking coffee and motioning wildly to whichever boyfriend was keeping her sane.

"Does everything have to be your business?"

"I was just wondering." I pick up the pack of Newports on the table, but he's smoked the upside-down lucky. Just when I could use some luck. I watch a baby cockroach dart across the floor. "What's going on with you?"

"Nothing," he says, peeking through the blinds. His fingers dance along the aluminum panels. "Ryan's coming over...I'm nervous about it, that's all."

"Oh." The refrigerator starts breathing, reminding me I haven't eaten all day. I fold my knees and press my chin to them. "You can talk about it, Tye. You don't have to hide it like some big secret."

He turns to lean against the wall, near our favorite tapestry. Whenever we're on acid, we lie on the floor with a flashlight shining up against the fabric of this tapestry. Its tie-dye swirls slip out of place and dance midair. I can almost see it now...the walls become water-colored, curious and new, and every particle of dust that drifts through the air is alight with a substance I cannot name. It makes me forget the dirty plates collecting fruit flies, the ninety-nine-bottles-of-beer we never recycle, the flea-ridden bitch of a cat that hates me, and the fact that his sheets sting and his pillowcase stinks. I forget the miniscule clouds Ryan forms when he does lines off Tye's table—the only surface-area in this one-room hide-away.

Sometimes it's too much. I'll hold my breath, afraid that every swirl escaped from the walls will infect me. Afraid they'll sit in my gut and manifest a beauty I could never keep down.

"Morgan, stop kidding yourself," he says. "I can't talk about it with you because you'll either make some 'Ry and Tye' joke or burst out crying. I hate to kick you out and all, but this is *my* apartment. I want Ryan here tonight, not you."

I'd like to say his words pinch or bite or otherwise hurt, but they don't. They settle into a dull ache, collecting their own breed of dust in the empty lining of me.

"Whatever, okay? I'll just go."

I unfold my legs and stand barefoot on the floor. Chills scurry through my veins even though it's August. I fumble through the pile of clothes at the foot of his bed. Amid his and mine and probably

Ry's, I find my tired pants that need a patching. I pull them on as he places one soft hand, dainty like a girl's, on the back of my neck. I let him linger there and leave my pants unbuttoned, hoping he'll slide his palm along my shoulder, over my nothing-breasts, down the rickety steps of my ribcage, all the way to my underwear. Maybe he'll breathe into my ear and bend me over and tell me I need to stay for at least another hour.

Instead, he pulls away. "I'm worried about you."

I button, then zipper, and push stray hair from my eyes. "Why?"

"For one thing, you're becoming skeletal."

Straight-lined like the boy I wish I were, you wouldn't have it any other way. *You like it,* I want to say. "What are you, my mother?"

"No, your friend."

The word sticks in my ear like a trapped bee. I want to shake my head and scream, *You're my friend today, my lover the next, and my dick older brother the week before.*

"I've had a stomach ache for weeks."

"So go to the fucking doctor. It might be serious."

"I'm fine. It's not like I've ever had an appetite."

"Morgan, you're impossible."

He plops down on the couch and flattens the empty pack of Newports. He's probably got another one stashed with his goods: hash in little plastic bags, marijuana plants I water twice a day because I like to watch things grow, dancing Dead bears to lick and peace-sign pills to swallow. Everything's in the toolbox under the sink, though the plants grow in halves of two-liter soda bottles in the only functional kitchen cabinet; he installed florescent bulbs to give them artificial sun.

Zeppelin, the bitch-cat, is hoarding my flip-flop. I wrestle it away as she claws my hands.

"When *was* the last time you went home? Honestly, I can't remember."

"Well *that* doesn't surprise me," I say, avoiding his gaze.

Hoisting my bag over my shoulder, I survey the clutter of the room. On the windowsill sits my bottle of pills—I forget which kind. Near the kitchen sink is my waterproof watch. On the bookcase, middle-shelf, there's my copy of *The Lion, the Witch and the Wardrobe*, a present from my father for my tenth birthday. It waits like an abandoned child between *The Cannabis Grow Bible* and a bathroom-reader of puzzles. I leave everything in place.

"Just do me a favor." I grip the doorknob like I might fall through the floor. "Don't fuck him while you're tripping."

Everyone fights to get the last word.

★

A thirty-minute train ride from downtown Philly to its northwest suburb, and another ten walking from the station to my block. Here it is. Home.

On the stone path, I stand rigid like a corpse. My house stares me down. I can almost see ghosts in the windows. I know they're just smudges on the glass but they mock me, each window a gaping black hole sucking me inside. Gravity drags my bones.

Like Tye, I can't recall the last time I was here. High school ended in early June and already I've lost my diploma. It's been nine months since I met Tye and nearly two since I started waitressing at the diner on Chestnut downtown. I can afford to pay utilities and chip in for food so his studio apartment's basically half mine, except when he kicks me to the curb for a private night with his pseudo-boyfriend.

I stare harder; it's like seeing a friend after years have passed, though I haven't many friends so I wouldn't really know. The hedges need trimming, the ivy's grown tall, and the unused chimney's missing most of its bricks. Detailed moldings border the windows and columns connect the awning to the porch's railings. This wraparound porch, dating back to the Victorian era, was one of the main selling points of the house, aside from its oddly affordable price.

I give my old enemy a defiant glare and stride quickly up its steps, onto the porch's tattered welcome mat. Luckily, no one's here. The staircase creaks as I climb to the second floor, bypassing my bedroom and locking myself in the bathroom.

The tub still has its golden claws. The cabinets don't close. The overhead light fixture's painted pink. Salmon-colored tiles are cool against my knees, exposed through my jeans, as I empty the contents of my bag on the floor. Coins roll under the old-fashioned radiator and chapstick finds a hiding spot behind the pull-chain toilet. I've got a few tank tops, dirty underwear, and a coupon for the drug store. Out of habit, I look through my wallet and find two measly bucks after train fare and spotting Tye for lunch. Not that it matters.

It takes a few minutes for the water to warm. I try to avoid the mirror with its baroque frame, but I catch a glimpse of a second bruise and must inspect. Tiny teeth marks, not yet green, on the tip of one shoulder. Another lovely treat from Tye. I sneer at the glass. My skin is dry, my gray eyes duller than ever. They aren't the windows to any sort of soul.

★★★

It was one of those cold November evenings where the sun slinks low around the earth and you're left shivering in sudden dusk. I hadn't worn a coat because I hadn't wanted to stop home; on that particular day, and on most days prior, all I'd wanted to do after school was head into Philly and get myself lost. Usually I'd wander South Street, lusting over albums I couldn't afford. I'd add my green gum to the vibrant collection on the gum tree and dart in and out of shops.

That night, I bought tea with the dollar and change I had to spare and chain-smoked half a pack of cigarettes in quick succession, never needing to relight, right down to the upside-down lucky, though I forgot to make a wish. Balancing the near-empty cup on my kneecap, I spotted a boy sitting on the curb across the street. He wore a large knit hat and fingerless gloves. For a moment his face shone in the glow of a match. We locked eyes and he smirked, which hardly meant "come here" but I picked myself up and sat beside him.

"Can I bum one from you? I just ran out."

He raised an eyebrow. "They're rollies. Unfiltered."

"That's fine, quicker death."

His eyes smiled. "What's your name?" he asked, smoothing a flimsy piece of rolling paper with his thumbs.

"Morgan."

"I used to know a dude named Morgan." He looked wistfully at the absent stars, then scrutinized my face. "But you're not him."

"Um, no."

"Tye." He extended his partially gloved hand. "You look cold."

"Kind of."

"You look young, too."

"How old do you think I am?"

He rubbed his chin and cocked his head. "Fifteen, sixteen?"

"I'm seventeen."

"My bad." He offered a lit match, another short-lived orange glow, and we slipped into a rhythmic silence: short inhales and long exhales, ashing on our shoes. I took to glaring at a group of kids wearing studded belts and collars. They looked like they were in the middle of making a memory.

Beneath our little cloud of smoke, Tye wrapped his palm around my knee.

"Hey Morgan, do you get high?"

"Occasionally." *Only if you count my mother's sedatives.*

"I sell, you know. Want to buy?"

"I don't have any cash. At all."

"Man, that's all right, you look like you need a good time. You can owe me later. Is that cool?"

"Sure," I said, trying to sound like I didn't care.

"Okay, let's go to Addison."

"What's over there?"

"My apartment. Dirty, but it works."

"Let's go." We walked at a clipped pace, and the air that slapped my cheeks felt clean, certain, no longer cold.

★

I told him he wasn't my first and he believed me.

"Tell me something about yourself," he whispered in the fragile afterglow, our bodies parallel like two half-moons. It was January. His body was naked and I was still wearing my shirt.

"Like what?"

"Whatever, be creative." Steam hissed from his radiator and we lay exposed as if under the sun.

"So," I started, searching the ceiling, "I don't believe in anything I can't see."

"What? How does *that* work?"

"What do you mean?"

"I mean, how does it work? Like not believing in atoms?"

"No, more like not believing in abstractions."

"Because you know we can *see* atoms, right?" He lifted his arm and pointed to nowhere.

"I never said I didn't believe in atoms. Atoms aren't abstract, they're tiny."

"All right, then god?"

"Really it's just that I don't trust anything unless it can be scientifically explained. And god fits into that category, but I don't trust people either."

"You trust me. You came home with me the first day we met."

"It's not that I trusted you, it's that I gave you a chance because I had nothing to lose."

"Aren't you a little young to be this cynical? You sound like a nihilist." He said the word *nihilist* as if it meant Nazi.

"But nihilists believe in nothing. They think life has no meaning whatsoever, that it contains no real truth."

"Yeah..."

"See, I look for the truth. I don't believe that something created or controls us, but I *do* think there's a fabric that ties everything together. The universe exists because events have occurred, unconnected, throughout history for no apparent reason, but actually, everything could be explained if you looked for the underlying connections between them, using science that is." I paused to take a breath, sneaking him a sideways glance to see if he was paying attention. "We can only explain the present by analyzing past events, but even if we discover those underlying connections, it doesn't stop the world from exploding. It never hands you the reins or gives you control over what happens next. It doesn't stop your life from going off the rails."

"So, you think everything is a potential disaster? But somehow it all makes sense?"

"Something like that." I needed a better way to explain myself. "Okay like, in Earth Science, we learned that the moon broke off from the earth billions of years ago and went into its own orbit. It made me think…we see the moon as this territory that needs to be explored and even colonized, but it's *not* a separate entity, it's been part of us all along. Conquering the moon would be like christening your breath." I tried to imagine myself floating, but I was too aware of my bones on the bed. "Everything happens both by accident and for a 'reason.' A never-ending cycle that affects everything and nothing."

"What about love?" he asked, opening and closing his fist.

"Love is suicide."

"That's a song lyric."

"I know."

"Seriously Morgan, have you ever been in love?"

"No." *You don't get it,* I wanted to say, *I don't believe in love.* "Have you?"

"I'm in love with everything...and everyone."

He turned to face me, his forehead glistening. His lower eyelids still bore black smudges from when he'd asked me to do his makeup earlier. He took the hand that had been open-and-shutting and ran its fingers, delicately, across my bottom lip. "Anything you need," he whispered, "you come to me. I'm here for you, understand?" His finger traveled to my head and he pet me as if I were Zeppelin.

Sitting on the pinkish tiles of my bathroom floor the day before, I'd cut seven long inches off my hair. Dirty-blond fish lying dead and detached, everywhere.

I knew what he wanted. I knew it wasn't me.

★★★

In the tub at home, water laps my ankles. My face is reflected in the faucet: golden-hued, elongated. My eyes are bugs trying to crawl out of their holes.

I try to concentrate on the way the water collides with the cells of my skin, but I can't feel a thing. It's tingly like when limbs fall asleep, only I can't shake it off, can't circulate my blood and make it stop. It's a knot you can't untie, a secret you can't tell, a perpetual paradox, like a liar telling the truth: two mirrors face-to-face and me in the middle times infinity.

I am swollen, perhaps water-logged. A crater on the surface of the moon. I wrap my arms around my knees and collect myself, all of my self, into a silent shell. A half-life.

★★★

We moved when I was five, just my mother and I. The house was quite a find, I'd hear her say. Severely underpriced and vacant for two decades.

The floorboards creaked and the heat moaned. The basement flooded in the rain and smelled of mold; it was unfinished—cold and dark with indoor-outdoor carpeting partially covering mulch-ridden cement. We never left anything there. We never went down there at all except to do laundry, and even then we only walked two feet from the stairs. Monsters lurked silently in the darkness, waiting to snatch me if I ventured too far.

My bedroom was at one end of the second floor, the pink

bathroom at the other, and my mother's room in between. She had a private toilet and the front balcony. None of the doors fit correctly in their frames, and the walls were thin as ghosts.

My walls were plastered with fleur-de-lis paper, misaligned where it met the ceiling. My furniture came with the house: a dresser, bookshelf, night table, and armoire—all antique rosewood with dull brass knobs. I would stare into each surface, measuring the dark rings in the reddish-brown. A tall window over my bed faced the wraparound porch and backyard. The air snuck through the window and I'd wake with a chill.

★

The first time it happened was one year after the move.

Sleep had always been difficult. It wasn't just the new house and its unexplained sounds that invaded my dreams—the floorboards "settling," my mother said, as if becoming accustomed to us. Sleep was a strip of gauze wrapped over my eyes; I was aware of the gauze as it pushed me further and further inside my mind. I found it nearly impossible to give in, to let go.

When I did sleep, I dreamt lucidly. I'd rise from my bed and fling my body at the window, passing through its glass unharmed. A warm gust would lift my weightless bones to the rooftop, where I'd perch bird-like, watching ribbons of light unfurl in the midnight sky. I could jump into the atmosphere, swim mid-air over chimneys and streetlights. As dawn set in, I would sink and solidify, dream-air sticking to every pore. The sleeping-me would scream, trying to force my body awake before the dream-me crashed to the street.

But the night it happened I was sitting up in bed, staring out the window.

For a week I had been waking abruptly, drenched in sweat. So I sat up instead, reading fairy tales by book-light and waiting for the whoops of morning birds. I happened to glance out the window just as a person appeared on the porch, where the backdoor let out. At first I thought it was my mother, but a match was struck and a man's face shone in the momentary glow: a scraggly beard, long unkempt hair, and a tattoo on his neck.

He shuffled around the porch as if he owned the place, trailing his palm along the sanded railing, exhaling clouds I could almost smell through my window's invisible crack. Eventually he butted the cigarette on his boot and flicked it to the grass. He ambled around the house's curve and disappeared. I bolted out of bed, flung open my door, and scampered downstairs to the front window. I watched him dart from one streetlamp to the next, racing his own impermanent shadow.

The next morning, I found my mother in the kitchen with her boyfriend and her coffee. I climbed onto the whitewood chair, resting my elbows on the table. Beams of sunlight snuck into my vision, forming prisms when I blinked. I bit my thumb.

"Mom?" I said, as she exhaled smoke. "There was a man outside the house last night."

"What are you talking about?" she asked, ashing into a ceramic bowl.

"She said she saw a man outside," Richard said. He licked a finger and turned a page of *Newsweek*.

"I did, Mom, I saw a man outside my window and then he ran away down the street."

"You were dreaming," she said calmly, sucking her cigarette dry.

"But I wasn't asleep."

"Don't be stupid. Why would a man have been outside your window?"

"Wait a second, maybe someone robbed us." Richard raised his head and widened his deep-set eyes.

"Nobody robbed us. Don't you think that would be pretty apparent?" She waved her arm as if to illustrate the non-disarray of the room.

"Is anything missing?" he asked, glancing at the counter.

"Of course nothing's missing! Morgan was dreaming, that's all."

"But I wasn't, I really wasn't," I protested. "I saw a man on the porch and he had long hair and a beard."

"Sounds like Jesus," Richard muttered, refilling his mug.

"Too many goddamn fairy tales," my mother said. "This girl has some imagination."

⋆

The next year, I started stealing coffee from the kitchen. Night after night, I'd keep watch by the window until my legs fell asleep. The cloudy dimness of my bedroom bred new beings, strange shadows. I stopped reading fairy tales and switched to books on science: dinosaurs and anatomy, evolution and astronomy. Those were things I could believe in.

On my tenth birthday, my father appeared at the house. He wore a denim jacket with cuffed sleeves and carried a package wrapped in shiny paper. I heard my mother tell him "five minutes" and watched through my window as she paced across the porch, creating temporary clouds.

He came into my room and sat in my desk chair. He watched me unwrap a box set of books: *The Chronicles of Narnia.*

"I used to read these when I was your age. They always fascinated me."

It was strange; he looked younger than the last time I'd seen him, five years before. He no longer wore glasses and his hair had grown curly to his collar. He smiled at me and curved his hand around my coffee-stained mug. "A little young to be a coffee drinker, aren't we?" he asked, laughing.

"Um." I bit my nails and tried to inhale my mother's smoke through the glass.

"Morgan," he said, in a serious tone. "I'm sorry. I'm sorry for everything. I hope that you're doing okay."

I fumbled with my ponytail, tossing it from shoulder to shoulder. His eyes were gray and dreary like mine. "I'm fine."

He kissed the top of my head. "Enjoy the books," he said, and never came back.

★

It happened twice more.

The second time, I was twelve years old. My mother was dating Derek—a nondescript man who took photographs for magazines, reeked of stale cologne, and tried to teach me chess. Some nights, I'd steal one of his cameras and wait to capture proof. When it finally happened, I was too afraid to use the flash and the photos came out underexposed. This second man was tall and dark and he stood on the back porch for what felt like forever before jumping over the wooden fence into the neighbor's yard.

The next time, six or seven months later, I watched a shorter, stubbier man wearing a flannel shirt and grimy bandanna lean his elbows on the porch railing. I snatched Derek's digital camera, took a deep breath, and pressed the button for the flash: the two of us connected in a burst of artificial lightning. He snapped his head toward the house and raised a hand above his eyes. I flattened myself against my covers, ducking out of sight. A few seconds later, I peered through the glass again; he was still there, staring, under the dim porch light. Our eyes met. He gave me a stiff bow and sped off.

Instinctively, I leapt from my bed and dashed downstairs to the living room window. I watched as he landed, with forceful precision, on each flat stone of our front path. His back glowed under the streetlights' florescence until he disappeared into the hazy dark. I checked my digital photos: bursts of light and streaks of shadow. Nothing more.

I didn't bother telling my mother. She'd become possessed by a certain type of illness. She called them "hell-aches" instead of headaches and would lock herself in her bathroom for hours at a time. From any room in the house, I could hear her wail. Her bathroom shelves were stacked with prescription bottles and aromatherapy rubs that smelled like flu season. Sometimes she'd wander into my room wearing only a towel. She'd collapse on my bed and proclaim that she was thinking of "ending the pain for good." She'd make the motion of slashing her wrists or wringing her neck with an invisible noose and then laugh, clutching one side of her face.

We developed a system for her attacks so she wouldn't have to move. When she rattled a plastic maraca we bought for ninety-nine cents, I came with bags of ice and whichever pill she most desired.

When she started injecting herself, I'd watch as she held the plastic "pen" to her skin for exactly ten seconds. Her shoulders were speckled with splashes of blue-violet. I could tell the oldest bruises from the new by their greenish outer rings.

⋆

By the time I was thirteen, the basement no longer held monsters, only mold, and I gave up my night-watch duties for temporary escape among its underground shadows, oddly shaped boiler, and overhead pipes. Everything above ceased to exist: the bedroom where I didn't sleep, the bathroom I would lock myself inside, and my mother and Derek's room with its pills and remnants of pain. I'd tell myself that nothing up there mattered, and I'd steal my mother's cigarettes, one by one so she couldn't tell, on my way downstairs. I wove the cigarettes through the flames of votive candles, taking long, deep drags and coughing up creations of breath. Tiny ghosts.

One night, I wandered to the far end of the basement, no longer fearing its distance to the stairs. I tripped over a crack in the floor and fell hard on my bare knees. Turning around, I discovered the outline of a circle where the dingy carpet ended and the cement lay bare. I ran my fingers along its perimeter and found two small holes with rough edges. Sticking my fingers inside, I lifted the flat chunk of floor like the cover of a manhole; it was heavy but moved easily.

Inside was a void. A gaping hole. A bottomless pit. Our own private crater. It had been there all this time.

I found my way to the stairs, the candles still burning in their glass cribs. Like a seasoned spy, I crept along the creaky living room floorboards and retrieved a flashlight from the kitchen. Shining the beam two steps ahead, I returned to the trench—the basement's black hole—and gave light to its darkness. Rusted iron rungs protruded from concrete walls and the bottom looked to be about fifteen feet down, into the darkest depths of the earth. With one hand holding the flashlight and the other gripping the ladder, I eased myself down, rung by rung. I held my breath the entire time.

A wave of vertigo knocked me off balance as soon as I sunk to the ground. I waved my flashlight and the beam illuminated a pitch-black opening. This wasn't just a hole, but a tunnel! A tunnel stretching before me like an endless road to somewhere new. My mind was reeling. What kind of secret passage was this? Where did it lead? Was it a wormhole? Did a place like Narnia exist on the other side?

When I calmed my frenzied lungs, I decided to be logical. There was no such thing as fairy tales or Narnia, or possibly even wormholes. Searching for an acceptable answer, I recalled the string of men who had appeared outside my window. *Yes!* The tunnel must have started in a place from which people needed to escape, ending in relative safety at our house. But what kind of place might that be? A prison? *Maybe whenever a convict breaks out, he uses the tunnel to slip out of sight and travel underground until he's far enough away! Maybe it's been used for hundreds of years, before this house was even built! Maybe the people who lived here thought the house was haunted! Maybe I'm the only outsider who knows.*

I stared into the pitch-black tunnel, stared until my beam of light lost itself amid the dark, but I couldn't make my legs walk through. I couldn't lose myself, too. I wished so badly for a sibling or close friend, someone with whom to explore these depths, to embark on this quest, to discover this treasure and keep this secret. But it was only me, so I turned back.

Rung by rung, I climbed up and slid the lid into place. For fear that I'd meet a confused criminal face-to-face, I stopped hiding in the basement. I continued to keep watch at my window, but nobody else appeared on the porch.

★★★

I turn the faucet off.

Goose bumps travel the lengths of my arms, but my legs are anesthetized with dense heat. I tell myself: life is never linear because time is cyclical. Moments never coalesce or make much sense; our lives are fragmentary, disjointed—the present moment is nonexistent, breathed second by second, evaporating before we can hope to hang on. We make mistakes, pick ourselves up, dust ourselves off and fall again. My jaw is tired of hitting dirt. My voice is barren, my heart weak. This ache in my gut is a permanent bug, a gravitational tugging in the pit of me.

Everything that ever existed is buried under layers of skin, tucked numbly into the fibers between muscle and bone. My blood feels pale, my oxygen stale. I lean into the tub. Her curvature embraces me. Entombed, I am embryonic, alone. She holds me as if I were hers, not yet born.

I want to wilt and wither until I am infinitely halved. I want to lose any semblance of self until I am a decaying star, a shard of glass, a slivered memory too far gone to feel.

★★★

He came years after Richard and just before Derek. Ed—I hated his name. It felt ugly and cruel. Dead meat on my tongue. Granite rocks or rotten eggs.

He wore ties each day as if his head might fall off, and smoked cigars on the porch, shooting streams of discolored saliva. He'd take my mother to fancy restaurants, leaving me alone to wander the house: its shadowy corners and clamoring pipes, its threat of apparitions only I might see. I would hide under the covers and read until they returned.

Sitting on her fluffy bed, with its wooden posts and lacy canopy, I'd watch my mother prep for their dates. She'd sit at the vanity desk, combing her hair and applying pink to her cheeks, green to her lids, and red to her lips.

"Morgan," she said once, inviting me to sit beside her on the bench, as the oval mirror reflected us. "Would you like some too? Perhaps the red is too strong, let's try mauve."

She hardly ever touched me. But that day, she swirled cosmetic chemicals and splattered pinkish colors up and down my angular face. In the mirror of my bathroom, I studied my newly made self and felt silly, ashamed.

Ed started to notice something. He'd stare straight through. I never understood what it was he was looking for.

*

The first time it happened I was drifting with outstretched arms, surrounded on all sides by vast nothingness, where time stands still. There was no beginning or end to this darkness, yet it was comforting. I felt protected. It enveloped my floating body and my head rose like a balloon.

A sudden weight on the bed sent my eyelids ajar. My head was still inflated, slowly rising to the ceiling; I was becoming fuzzier, fainter, composed of static electricity and empty atoms. I tried to move, tried to speak, but a thick hand covered my mouth: *Shhh*, it said in a tarry voice. I pictured the man from outside my window, the one with the tattoo, but as soon as he said, "It's only me," I knew it was Ed.

The scent of cigars was everywhere. He pulled down the floral quilt and touched me through my nightshirt. I couldn't make him stop, couldn't do anything as he poked and prodded like a disobedient doctor. My head flew all over the room.

The next morning, I found my mother in the kitchen with her cigarettes and coffee after Ed had gone to work. Perching myself on the edge of the whitewood chair, I blocked my eyes from the glaring sun and bit my finger as hard as I could.

"Mom?" I started, watching her exhales coil and disperse.

"What?" she asked. Dark circles hung like half-moons beneath her eyes. Perhaps they were mascara remains. Perhaps hell-ache wounds.

"Ed came into my room last night."

"What are you talking about?"

"He came into my room and touched me." I tried to swallow but my mouth felt chalky.

She gave me a look as if we were enemies: a deep, scathing stare.

"Don't you ever start that shit with me. We all know your stories and your lies and this is one thing I will not stand to hear. Do you understand me? I never want to hear this again."

She left behind an empty mug and whispers of smoke.

★

The second time it happened I was already awake. I told him no. I thought vocalizing might solve the problem, but he only seemed to want it more.

My bedroom door didn't lock. I tried to block it with my desk chair, but the doorknob was old and it didn't take much for Ed to knock it down while my mother swam the black sleep of sedatives.

Sometimes I would try to fall into a dream world, propel my body to the ceiling and slip, like a wispy cloud or beam of light, through the invisible crack of my window. I wanted to float under streetlamps, glowing proud.

When that didn't work, the fourth or fifth time, I started to picture my own private Narnia. Ed's bulky hands and heavy breath sent chills along my spine, but I imagined my bones as strong blue icicles, my body hoarding an eternal winter that would soon become spring. Someday, violets and poppies would bloom in my marrow. Someday, sunlight would shine from every pore. My eyes no longer sad, no longer cold, would turn bluer than the bluest sky.

After the tenth time, and without a word from my mother, I started sleeping in the bathtub. It was the only room in the house that locked. I would run the tub until midnight, when my mother would bang on the door and yell, "Knock it off!" I would sit alone in the soapy water, studying skin that felt foreign to me, bruises from where he'd held on too tight. I'd let the water turn cold, afraid of waking my sedated mother. Eventually, I would drift into a lucid dream, my head on the tub's curve, my shoulder tucked into her loving porcelain.

★

With Tye I usually left on my shirt. It was better this way, for both of us. Our toothbrushes kissed more often than we did.

He liked to slide his fingertips up and down my ribcage. He didn't touch much else. He liked the boyish parts of me best—my hair (once it was cut), angled jaw, square hands, and figureless hips. Mostly we fucked on the floor or the couch. Facing him, I stared at the wall or the ceiling or the mutable shapes behind my eyes, but never into his. I didn't want to imagine what they saw.

He made me a copy of his key so I could slip in whenever I wanted. I'd sleep on his chest, imagining his breaths as ocean waves rising and falling, carrying me across vast distances.

When Ryan the coke dealer came by, Tye stuck a yellow Post-it on the doorknob—a not-so-subtle code meaning "Morgan, go away."

On those nights, I climbed three more flights to his apartment's rooftop entrance: a small landing with no windows. In the corner there, I curled knees to chest using my bag as a pillow, though I never fell asleep. Sometimes incalculable amounts of time would pass, empty moments I couldn't put a finger on.

★

One night, we lay on Tye's floor with a flashlight shining up against our favorite tapestry. Suddenly, my body froze—a solid chunk of ice. Tears emerged like icicles dripping down my cheeks.

"What's wrong?" he asked, rubbing the water away.

Ice cracked at the corners of my mouth. "I'm cold."

"It's July," he whispered, "but I'll warm you up." His arms enveloped me, but I couldn't feel a thing.

Then a watercolor lion—my oldest, dearest friend—floated ghost-like above my head. I pointed to his shape: "There's my lion!" He was as golden as sunshine, taking up half the room's space. My blood began to flow again, hot lava in my veins.

"I don't see it."

"But he's there. Look Tye, he's right there!" I pointed again, every which way, as he grew even larger.

"That's nice," he said, stroking my arm.

"Please Tye, please…just tell me you can see him."

"But I can't."

Who knew what Tye could see? Who knew how to jump between realities?

He was growing, expanding, coloring the walls and the ceiling and the window. He was phosphorescent, iridescent.

"I need you to tell me. Please," I sobbed into Tye's ribs. The lion's golden yellow was too strong; the sunlight in his skin threatened to melt mine to oblivion. Soon I would evaporate. Soon there would be nothing left.

Tye smoothed my short hair and whispered, "You're fine, you're fine, don't freak out. This is a potent batch, but you'll be okay."

"Please tell me. I need you to tell me!"

The lion's fiery breath invaded my pores. He was strangling me, forcing me down beneath the wooden floor.

"I see it, Morgan. I see it. All right?"

★★★

My pulse pounds hard in my ears.

I used to imagine that my legs had gills. I wanted to be self-contained, wanted to sink into the tub and never reemerge. I wanted to inhale each breath as it floated to the surface. But fishes live second by second, while I remember everything. I hold too much weight. Gravity gets heavier the older we grow.

Two floors below me, down in the basement, the tunnel still promises eternal escape. It has taunted me since the day I discovered it, reminding me that I have a choice. A choice I couldn't make. A choice that came too late. The damage had been done.

One floor below, the front door opens and forcefully shuts. I hear high-heeled footsteps enter the kitchen.

She must be turning on the coffee pot, searching for a clean mug. She's probably tapping her fingernails on the counter, reaching for her pack of smokes, bowing her head to the stove and lighting a cigarette from the blue flame. Now she's waiting, legs crossed, on the kitchen's whitewood chair. I see her bruised shoulders, her weary eyes. She's holding her head in her palm, leaning her elbow on the table's smooth edge, staring at nothing. Maybe she's thinking of me in that chair—the things I tried to tell her—and asking herself what she could have done. Maybe she's wondering why I don't come home…maybe she's hoping I can forgive her. Maybe she even discovered the tunnel. Maybe she knows the truth.

She probably smells of cheap perfume, synthetic spring. She's probably worn out from too many hell-aches and impermanent loves.

I miss her. I remember her laughing the first time she found coffee in my room. Perhaps she thought I was trying to be grown up, trying to be like her. Perhaps she thought doing my makeup would make me smile; it was something a mother and daughter could share. After all, I am her moon.

I envision grabbing a towel from the rack, wrapping it around me, unlocking the bathroom door and stepping into the hall, the floorboards cool beneath my feet. Suddenly I'm not walking heel-to-toe but floating, following an invisible pull towards the past or the future or one breathless moment in this quickly fleeting point in time.

I do climb out, I do rise. Reaching my arm into the tub, I pull the plug and watch the water swirl around. A tiny black hole gulps everything down.

Skills

STARE AT THE CARPET. Don't blink. Watch it mutate. Brown fibers will expand and contract, ripple and undulate. Sink, breathe. Think Mindfulness. In, out. Free-floating thoughts, like harmless clouds. Wise mind. There it is. Easy does it.

Fuck, you don't belong here. Not like awkward Gracie in the blue armchair who somehow sewed her fingers together. At least that's what's been circulating campus like a cold. She hasn't mentioned it, but it's probably true. Not like Monet either, who fights with Stephen every session and arrives late, holding coffee. Whoever's in charge of these things on campus requires her to be here, or else she's expelled. And not like the girl next to Monet, who has "Blessed" (bless-*ed* she said, not *blessed*) tattooed over the scars on her wrist. She also bears a colorful Krishna on her shoulder and always offers advice about how *she* copes and *she* meditates and *she* tries to help people listen to their inner selves. Now that girl definitely belongs here.

If you're even the least bit depressed and too obvious about it, or if your RA tells the Dean of Whatever that he or she is concerned about how you're holding up, you can bet your wallowing ass you'll be plopped into one of Health Service's many "free" and "confidential" mental health groups: Eating Disorder, Substance Abuse, Stress Management, Bereavement, Minority Identity Process, Queer Support, Smoking Cessation, Survivors of Sexual Assault, Mastering Your Moods, Dialectical Behavioral Therapy Skills. That's where you landed. Skills, for short. Or as Stephen says: DBT.

One of your friends took you to Health Services after you showed him your scratches and Bic-razor triple cuts. What were you thinking? You shouldn't have shown him. Always use the cat excuse, even though you've never had a cat.

They set you up with a counselor named Janis who sat with you for nine private sessions. She tried to convince you to throw out the monogrammed pocketknife your uncle once gave you for Christmas. You shouldn't have told her about the knife, but at least you failed to mention the X-acto blades in an empty Altoid tin. You didn't tell her: tiny cuts bleed enough to compensate for one good cry or wave of rage. Lick your wounds, cover the scabs with bracelets and wristbands, then break open the seals, again and again. Year in, year out.

Janis wanted you to throw out the knife (not even give it away!) because she said it was like an alcoholic keeping drinks in the house or a drug addict keeping his dealer's number, and you nodded and said, "I know, I know," but didn't toss it. Then you said, "It's not because I feel like I can't stop, but because I can't throw anything away!" She didn't buy that. But Janis wasn't a good therapist. She made you draw pictures with your left hand. One night, manically to music, you drew yourself as a demon. Janis also said that your ulcer was metaphorical and then she cried. Therapists should never cry. Perhaps you'd make a good one.

Keep your eyes on the carpet. An otherworldly terrain, like the surface of the moon. The rest of the room will recede, fade away. Breathe. The carpet will mimic your breath. In, out. Slow heart. Steady lungs. Loose mind.

Listen for other students on the crisscrossing paths below the window, laughing and flirting and swinging their hair. They have just as many problems as you do but their overly emotional on-campus therapist didn't beg them to join an ineffectual group to replace self-destructive coping mechanisms with new Skills, where one must stare blindly and breathe Mindfully for ten long minutes of each session.

Hell, you're not even that destructive. You don't write suicide notes. You don't drink excessively or do hard drugs. You've never had an abortion or emergency room fiasco. All you do is cut yourself now and then, drag your fingernails across your skin, smear your blood into notebooks, lie awake until four a.m., create irrational rituals to deal with a lifelong phobia about which hardly anyone knows, and fuck a few "emotionally unavailable" guys who "use you." So what?

Drew and Caroline are in the same boat, although Caroline's scars are much more visible. You've always been an inner/under wrist kind of girl, but she's the bicep/forearm type. Bold. Both of you are righties, so the left arm gets the brunt of self-defeat. She digs deeper, you can tell. Dark circles decorate her eyes and perpetual knots mimic dreadlocks in her hair. She freaks out when papers are due and hides under the table in the library, and you know she does coke at parties. Wonder if she uses the same razorblade to slice her skin? Maybe Caroline needs Skills more than you do, but she's your friend, sort of, so the two of you analyze awkward Gracie and talk shit about Stephen, mocking the foofy way he speaks and all his guru nonsense. Drew gets in on that sometimes when you're walking back to the dorms feeling sticky and deflated. For a performance artist who would probably be bullied at any other school, Drew is one of the most popular guys on campus. And for you, the most alluring.

Don't tell anyone you stay up reading his blog late at night. He feels guilty. Ugly. Unloved. Unhealthy. He was diagnosed with Borderline Personality Disorder and takes Prozac. Or actually, borderline-Borderline. All he wants is to be talked about in the third-person, to be thought of when he's not around. He overheard someone say, "Bones mend, wounds heal, and chicks dig scars," but called it cliché. His thing is bruising. He calls himself a bruise. He punches himself hard in the arms, legs, stomach, wherever he can reach. You've never seen the bruises even though he wears booty shorts when he dances in the coffee house, sing-reading his song-poetry to monotonous beats. Oh well.

Keep that breathing even. Five slow-moving, ever-expanding,

mind-numbing minutes to go. In, out. Don't glance up at Stephen across the room, hands folded prayer-like in his khaki lap. Don't slip your gaze sideways to Caroline with her knees up, or Monet with her arms crossed, or Bless-*ed* with her eyes closed.

Visualize, briefly, the green rectangular Skills card in your bookbag and try to remember what it asks of you. You'll have to turn this in to Stephen like you do at the end of every single session. Wonder what he does with his stacks. Maybe he whacks off to your teeny handwriting, maybe all of this is some sick perversion: coaxing college girls out of their private miseries, imagining how profusely they bleed. Bet he'd like to lick that.

Every day for eight weeks: Have you self-injured; if so, how; if not, how strong was the urge? Have you taken illicit drugs; if so, which? Have you taken OTC drugs; if so, which? Have you taken prescription drugs; if so, which? Have you lied; if so, how many times? Did you feel joy; if so, how much? Did you feel anger; if so, how much? Did you use any skills; if so, which ones? How low was your self-esteem? How did you cope with the day, with the week, with the year, with the weather, with your childhood, with your parents, with your classes, with your art, with your job, with your friends, with your fuck-buddies, with food, with the mirror, with your doctors, with your dreams, with your genes, with your skin, with your fears, with the silence and the noise, with girls and with boys, with sunsets and sunrise, with your impending demise? Just how crazy are you?

Dialectical. Behavioral. Techniques. What the fuck? Recall Stephen's petal-soft, lily-white, laundry-scented voice. Sit back and observe your emotion. Describe *it* in words. Allow yourself to feel *it*. Let *it* be whatever *it* is. Do not judge *it*, yourself, or others. Don't concentrate on the past or the future. Be here, in *it*. Focus on the positive. Delve into the acronyms. Be gentle. Interested. Validate. Easy manner. No apologies. Truthful. Balance. Sleep. Eat. Exercise. Express. Avoid mood-altering drugs. Self-soothe, improve moments, make lists, accept *it* and your various selves. And always be Mindful.

Well how about saying "fuck you" when you mean it? How about distracting yourself from your *self* when you need to? How about always bringing a condom to parties? Now there's some good advice. Write this on your next card.

At the end of each session, before completed cards get passed to Stephen and blank ones redistributed, before he reads a meditative poem that should last you the week, he opens the group to discussion. That's when Bless-*ed* brags about all her new coping strategies and her success in reaching others. That's when Monet gets into a fight with Stephen by rolling her eyes and saying, "This is stupid." That's when you hope Gracie will tell the story about sewing her fingers because you really want to it to be true. That's when you'll look at Drew and wonder if you should tell him that people *do* talk about him in the third-person, or at least you do. That's when you want to grab Caroline's arm and touch her perfect pearly scars.

Suddenly you're struck by the burning desire to tear off your skin, to release it from its soil. You can already feel the cool metal blade gliding like a swan as it stings the pale underside of your wrist. You can feel the endorphins begin to dance. You can see the blood slip out like acid rain. You can taste it on your tongue, rusted and rich. You wear your scars like armor. Like a red badge of courage. Like a goddamn Purple Heart.

Slow your heart rate, it's getting up there. All this internal thinking when you're supposed to be *Mindful*! Concentrate. Present moment. Calm seas. Let the barrage of interlinking thoughts, anxieties, and memories pass through. Watch them float away, like pink fluffy clouds.

What would it take to become a happy-go-lucky person who isn't afraid of herself? These kinds of people exist, don't they? But you're not any closer to discovering how to do this than you were before Skills, before Stephen, before Janis, before college, before the fucks you keep fucking, before the scars piling up like a car wreck. You have to wonder: why is it so intensely difficult to love yourself? And does anyone ever really *love* themselves? Certainly none of these other self-destructors emerging from their Mindful comas, or coffins, as Stephen rings the little bell near his chair to signal the end of ten minutes. Finally.

His dainty voice drifts into the silent space as Stephen asks everyone if they used any skills this week. Don't look at him, he might call on you. Concentrate on your hands. Think of what these hands have done. Think of how they act on their own sometimes, tearing through skin cells, ripping flesh, gripping the body that grew them, trying to claw you out. Now imagine your hands balled up inside your mother's womb, powerless to fight you, or her, or anyone. Sneak a glance at Drew's hands lying limp and imagine how they connect with his thighs in the bathroom: at night, alone. Think of everyone here: at night, alone. Imagine Gracie's hands sewn together, unable to destroy her.

Stare back at the brown carpet. Let Stephen's voice dissipate. Feel your heart speed up, but try to stare yourself into inner peace. Self-aware. There, the carpet is melting. The room is fading. Remember that you are who you are. You won't ever be anyone else. *It* is only you. Be *it*. Love *it*? The carpet is quicksand. Now, leap off the folding chair. In one fluid motion, jump in.

DREAMACHINE

WE'RE DOING A WHOLE LOT OF NOTHING in this place. The five of us sit in a circle, allowing patterns of colored light from a cardboard Dreamachine to polka-dot our skin and stimulate our optic nerves.

Everything in this room is makeshift or duct-taped and sporadically falls apart. The table is a horizontal door unhinged from the alcove. The centerpiece is a hookah, and ashtrays, empty jars, marked cards, guitar picks, torn loose-leaf, the tail-end of a candle, and neon magnetic fish are scattered around it. The couch, shuffled between prior living spaces, with god-knows-what trapped mercilessly between its cushions, leans against the wall. Odd pieces of furniture and décor abandoned by previous occupants (cat light fixture, musical lampshade, and China cabinet acting as bookcase) populate the rest of our living room.

We are quiet as mice, except for the occasional smoker's hack or self-referential sigh. It is late February; we've lost feeling in our fingertips and toes, the cold turning us pale and asthmatic. The heat's busted and we ran out of firewood and marijuana. Tonight, we aren't blasting music or biased newscasts, aren't making papier-mâché planets or doing anything art-kid-clichéd. Tonight, we've (regretfully) abandoned drugs and more active forms of procrastination to embrace the restless boredom that strikes everyone in the pit of winter's belly. Tonight, we've embarked on a new mission: total silence (except for these damn coughs) and an around-the-room staring contest. At my request, we're seeking something deeper than conversation; telepathy like sound waves, call it what you will, but I want to see everyone's soul. I want to find my self in the whole.

Yet I have to wonder, *Is such a thing even possible (without drugs)? What Would Ken Kesey Do? Can anyone "hear" me. Hey room: if you can hear me* (a manifestation of my physical voice resounding in my head) *please raise your hand.* Nobody? *Hello?*

There's something creepy about silence. It tears a hole, like a cloudless day that allows the sun to run amok without a raincoat. An extra stratum, a miniscule fiber, a tiny tear in the fabric of time or space or both...you can hear the underlying layer, the "quantum foam" bubbling and frothing like hydrogen peroxide. You can hear your heart pump itself silly like the little engine that could. You can almost hear the splashes of blood cells slip-sliding through your veins, or the synapses click-clacking as they electrify and polarize. We're encased in air that reeks of trial-and-error existence, but we cannot detect the scent anymore.

Tommy to my left is scruffy and dazed, weighed down by politics and overtime. He's a long ways from his real home and this city's becoming a drag. I know he prefers eye contact to staring at people's shoes—a problem on the long subway commute. He was born of green-green grass and saltwater baths, no grimy curbs or slushy paths. I can hear him now; his raspy voice narrates quicker-than-lightning thoughts (the synapses at work) that flutter like an invisible bird in his head. He's wishing he were home in forever-summer-land, he's wishing our cannabis wasn't gone and the dealer wasn't nowhere-to-be-found, and he's wanting, badly wanting, one of us to hold him. Not necessarily because he needs the love, but because he's cold. Californians have thinner bones.

Tommy, do you want me? I'll come and wrap myself inside you. I'll sneak into your room tonight and we'll braid ourselves until warm. He stares at Ella and rubs his palms like cricket legs.

I remember when we moved here in June. That first week was a dizzy one—none of us had beds, jobs, or local friends. Lion duct-taped a recorder to his wrist and talked to himself in funny accents, extending his arm outside the shower. Ella was "queen of margaritas" and created odd concoctions that tasted rubbery. Jed traced our shadows on the walls and hung empty bottles from the ceiling. Tommy and I, newly aquatinted, slept side-by-side on a mattress pad in the vacancy of my room. He asked me to kiss him everywhere and told me to be gentle on his ticklish hip. He said, "You can hurt me if you want," and begged me to tell him when I came. A week later, our beds arrived like brides and we never spoke of that again.

Ella doesn't notice Tommy's eyes. She's studying the Dreamachine and biting her lip. She wears carved bone earrings and a ribboned gypsy scarf. She doesn't drive cars or buy new clothes or use store-bought toothpaste. What remains: an addiction to blowing pills, a notepad beside her bed for catching dreams, and a sewing machine, more often than not, sitting smack in the middle of our kitchen table. She's remodeling her past to fit the future, pretending she was once *that kid* who spread anarchy like wildfire and caught everyone's attention. I can hear her rattling off names sometimes, trying them on for size, wondering who she might become. Now she can feel Tommy's gaze, but stares into the fireplace, where we sometimes burn pictures and race ice cubes.

Ella, I want to be as tar-lunged and scar-lined as you are. I lend her my debit card to divvy up lines of cutesy-blue Adderall or powdery Oxycodone and peek at the markings on her inner arms—evenly raised, pristine artifacts.

I remember our first playdate in the big city. We counted the coins in a nickel-couch on Prince and waved hello to passengers on big red buses. We lost our silhouettes somewhere in Chinatown and scored a batch of drugs in Tompkins Square. We floated on the ferry, shouting obscenities at prophetic Miss Liberty. Back home, Tommy was rewiring his electric guitar. Lion was brewing mushroom tea and combing Jed's cat with a toothbrush. Jed was sculpting skull candles for each new roommate, using wax he'd found at the base of a tombstone. They gathered round Ella and me as we sat on the table and spun stories of shimmering sidewalks, trees that bloomed plastic, and a man who told us we were prophetesses. This, of course, was back before the "big city" lost its charm.

Jed, with eyes shut, smiles vaguely to himself. He's Native American, rebelling against a Social Security number or proper ID. On account of this choice, he can't find real work, pay taxes, earn a license, get into school, or even vote, but "no one's worth voting for anyhow" and Jed makes do selling objects from dumpsters, tag sales, and bargain bins. Like some fabled cowboy or Beatnik poet, he hitchhiked out here from Arizona (a little-more-than-the-clothes-on-his-back kind of trek), where he worked on a cactus farm and grew peyote. I can see his jaw muscles tense as he thinks about everyone he's left. He's thinking, too, about the very center of the Earth, where the Equator meets the Prime Meridian...the ocean must be deep and wise and magical there. Once, he was standing in a field alone at night and a full moon floated overhead—a lit balloon just out of reach. This is how he imagines it to be, that place where the earth's X and Y axes finally meet.

Jed, I can see what you saw then, twisted in hallucinogenic euphoria, and I feel the loneliness that glues your bones. I water his pet mushroom and feed his skinny cat, which Lion has taken to calling a completely different name. I piece together his visions like patchwork: a quilt I can't create because it'd contain colors unseeable and strange.

I remember one morning when Jed and I were the only two not sleeping or badly hung over. We crawled onto the slanted rooftop and lay outstretched, our bellies to the sun. He told me, in hushed tones, about a girl with mismatched eyes who'd let him tattoo a salamander on her shoulder. He said they used to do it in the grass, taking turns staring into the sun's sultry eye, and her hair smelled of dirt and flowers. One night this past August, Tommy lit firecrackers down the road, Ella somersaulted down the stairs, Lion took one-too-many tequila shots and passed out in the backyard's hammock, and I'd had too much of this or that and scurried away like a mouse, crying behind the house. Past Lion, past Ella, and up the stairs to my room, Jed carried me like a child and kept watch 'til I calmed down.

Lion's consulting the ceiling's snakelike cracks. I wonder, can he concentrate without typewriter at hand? With Lion, it's always type-type-type everything everyone says. He reads aloud as if projecting reality back upon itself: a big joke, slapstick comedy, a one-act play starring *us* as incongruous actors. Lion's just like that: a typewriter-writer and crayon-colorer and he burns pages off books, spills coffee stains on unlined paper, hangs cigarettes from soda cans, and hides marijuana in a hollowed out encyclopedia like they do in the movies. He doesn't yet know it, but he cannot be alone. It's either the typewriter (and its incessant tap-tap) or some other contraption extended from his flesh, or one of us he plants in his room to read poems to or draw portraits of. He even coerces Jed's cat to come sleep in the crooks of his arms at night. And, yes, he's entirely renamed him.

Lion, I can hear you calling out for someone, anyone, in dog-whistle undertones...hoping they'll hear you above the songs in their heads. He was the kind of kid who collected bugs in empty jars and pulled pranks on teachers. He would have been my own personal bully and I would have relished the attention.

I remember the day I gave Lion his name. First, we called each other Cat and Mouse because he'd chase me round the house and scoop me into his arms on the couch (really, I was more his cat than anything). A week later came the day that we—still becoming acquainted with one another's breathing patterns, sleep cycles, and peculiar quirks (Ella's soundless laugh and Tommy's stacks of vitamins, Lion's aversion to socks and my notes-to-self taped all over the mirror, and the way Jed never eats what he cooks)—made up our own games with Frisbees in Central Park. I sank to the grass and watched the four of them transform. He became the not-too-cowardly Lion, Tommy the lanky Scarecrow, Jed the rusty Tin Man, and Ella homesick Dorothy. Me? Pay no attention, I watched from behind the curtain.

Tommy breaks the silence. "Can we move the Dreamachine to the middle of the room?"

The rest of us, having perfected the art of eye-speech, nod in stillness like sanctified monks. Yes, we are monks in a circle, perhaps demi-gods, perhaps peace-abiding superheroes. Each of us possesses a great and necessary power. Each of us, with otherworldly insight and enlightened perception, controls different parts of the world, subconsciously. We are the chosen ones. Here, in a forsaken land, during the coldest of winters, we meet in this sacred chamber to prepare Earth for her untimely end. Master Jed gets up to move our giver of light (whose mystical life began as a record player my mother bought in 1974) and extend its umbilical cord across the holy floor. Goddess Ella raises her hand and Lord Lion calls on her.

"I have to pee," she says, completely throwing my vision out the window.

Lion turns to me and cocks his head like Jed's cat: "Let's play Questions!"

I sigh. "We're supposed to be meditating...talking without words, you know. That's the whole reason Jed and I made the Dreamachine."

"We can go back to that when we're finished playing Questions," he whines.

"That game is more fun when we're high," Tommy intervenes.

"I'm always high," he responds.

Ella returns and sits cross-legged on the floor, fraying the stray ends of her jeans.

"We're playing Questions," Lion informs her.

Ella asks, "Can I start?"

Lion winks. "You just did."

Ella: "Okay, we'll start counterclockwise. What...what do blind people dream?"

Jed: "Shades of light and dark. Shadows. Or possibly sounds. What do you do when you're sad?"

Lion: "Jumping jacks and drugs. Or wait, jumping jacks *on* drugs. Ha. What color underwear are you wearing?"

Tommy checks: "Navy blue. What is your favorite song to sing in the shower?"

Me: "'Wish You Were Here.' Especially the fishbowl part. What is the difference between zero and one?"

Ella: "Zero is invisible and isn't divisible."

"One isn't divisible either," I answer, breaking the rules.

"If you have one of something, you can most likely break it in two," she responds.

"I guess so...Jed, your turn."

Jed: "Okay, clockwise...why. Why does everyone wear Converse these days?"

Ella: "Because of collective unconscious. Why do people say, 'Because Y is a crooked letter?'"

Me: "Because they think they're clever. Why do people bother getting married anymore?"

Tommy: "Because they think they're clever? Or because they think they can beat the odds. Why do jumping jacks make you feel better?"

Lion: "I don't know, they're funny. Maybe it has something to do with the adrenaline. Or maybe because I'm so bad at them."

"Or maybe because you're on drugs when you do them," I interrupt.

Lion: "Ahh yes...why can we fly to Mars but we can't cure cancer?"

Jed: "Because the body is the most mysterious terrain of all. And because cancer, like everything else, is big business. Lion, you go."

Lion: "Mmmk...how. How many licks does it take to get to the center of a Tootsie Roll pop?"

Tommy: "Uh one uh two uh three. How did Kurt Cobain really die?"

Me: "Bullet to the brain instigated by psychological abuse from Miss Love, plus lots of heroin, stomach pain, and hyper-celebrated depression. He pulled the trigger with his toe...well, with the tip of his sneaker. How fast do you have to go in order to free yourself from gravity?"

Ella: "I have no idea...pretty fast. 1000 mph, does that sound right? How do you define axinomancy?"

Jed laughs: "A romance with an ax? Or an ex? I don't know, man. How do you brush your teeth?"

Lion: "Left to right, top to bottom, and then I spit a lot. Tommy's turn, right?"

Tommy: "I think so. Counterclockwise again...Um, where. Where did god live before the first day of creation?"

Lion: "Nowhere, nowhere before mankind. Where should we plant hemp seeds in this place?"

Jed: "Nowhere until springtime. Where is your favorite place in the world?"

Ella: "I don't think I've found it yet. Where in the world is Carmen Sandiego?"

Me: "Nowhere, she's a figment of our imagination. Where did you lose your virginity?"

Tommy: "Don't you know this already? In a closet at a party." He coughs. "Your turn now."

Me: "Whoopty fuckin' doo. Do! Clockwise...do you think we can define something into existence? Like, create an object or color or person in our brain and then introduce it to the world as a living, breathing entity?"

Tommy: "I'm going to go with no. Do you ever wish you'd been born female?"

Lion: "Hell no! Does your face hurt?"

Jed: "No."

"It's killing me!"

Jed: "Ha ha. Do you believe in the afterlife?"

Ella: "I believe that wherever we were before this life is the same place we'll go after. So in other words, also a no. Do you wish you'd been born male?"

Me: "Usually. Guys have it way easier. We came full circle. Let's stop playing this."

"One more round," Lion pleads. "Let's do which and then we'll stop. I promise."

"Fine," I grumble. "You start."

Lion: "Tommy, which girl is hotter, Mya or Ella?"

"Fuck you Lion," I say.

Tommy: "Depends on the day." He stares at his feet. "Uh Mya, which color gummy bear is your favorite?"

Me: "The clear ones. I like transparency. Which fairy tale is your favorite?"

Ella: "Hmm...Snow White because the Prince is both Jesus and a necrophiliac. Which is your preferred way to die?"

Jed: "By my own hands."

"Yeah, but how?" she asks.

"I'd strangle myself."

"You can't strangle yourself, you'd lose consciousness before you could cut off the circulation to your brain," I respond.

"I want to be tar and feathered!" Lion exclaims.

Jed: "I could suffocate myself. Or I'd fall to my death. Zigzag like a dying bird. Lion, which super power would you choose?"

"X-ray vision," he says, pointing at my chest.

"Game over," I declare.

My body threatens to crumble like sand. The Dreamachine's blue light bulb, suspended inside a rotating cylinder on a turntable, shines through perfectly patterned holes. It beats like a heart between eight and thirteen pulses per second, depending whom you ask to count.

Jed and I built the thing from scratch, although he did most of the handiwork. We are the resident Aquarians: logically abstract, metaphysically methodical. We built it to alter our brain's quirky chemicals, to induce lucid euphoria, to merge consciousness, to let our inner Burroughs shine. See, we built the Dreamachine to sustain ourselves, to live inside the light.

"One more, one more."

"Dammit Lion, enough."

"Wait, this one's just for you, Mya." Lion does a drum roll in the air. "Are you a good witch or a bad witch?"

Oh, Lion. "I prefer to remain ambiguous."

Jed stands on one leg: "In each of us two natures are at war, the good and the evil. All our lives the fight goes on between them, and one of them must conquer. But in our own hands lies the power to choose: what we want most to be we are."

"What's that from?" asks Ella.

"*Jekyll and Hyde*, or at least from the restaurant's napkin."

"Duh," says Lion. And we all fall down.

A circle is sustainable only by the notion of infinity (right?). According to most scientists, everything is finite; if you could create an algorithm to calculate every on and off switch of every single life and death, from animal to animal and species to species, you'd discover the specific numbers. If you were small enough to count the leg of every insect or singular cell of thoughtless organisms, if you were big enough to accurately count the stars (or suns) and all their planets and rings and rocks and clouds and national anthems, you'd figure out the grand sum, at least for the millisecond.

But what if they kept going? Maybe the universe folds over itself like a Möbius strip, or a gigantic circle without a finishing line. What if space and time and matter navigate cyclically through a vast and endless plane? Perhaps the universe is self-reflexive, like an intelligent horror film...it refers back (and forth) indefinitely, the viewers left scratching their heads and pondering the director's intentions.

I'm in love with the notion of continuity. Every parking lot I've ever walked through: one and the same. Every brick, tag sale, telephone wire, traffic light, gas station, restroom stall, Church altar, Mac store, every Laundromat coin machine, plastic utensil, taxicab, sidewalk gum-stain and missing sock. The guardrail on the highway runs on and on and rarely takes a bathroom break. It stretches across the planet like a smile.

Our manic-depressive god glances over his shoulder and spots us in the corner: drowsy daydreamers, with shadowy shapes dancing at the backs of our eyes. We are melancholic alchemists, quote unquote lazy bums. We are smooth-talking psychonauts with commitments to nonconformity and a distaste for the constraints of our generation. We twist and shout and kiss and tell; we order Chinese and read the Beats and play drunken Scrabble until four a.m. We pollinate the house and feed the cabinet's live-in mice. Surely we must register low on god's fine-tuned radio or Richter scale. What are we doing? Ella brings home boys with asymmetric haircuts and obvious fetishes. Lion brews his mushroom tea or bakes pot cookies with icing faces. Tommy shuts himself away to read Beckett or *The Tempest* over and over hopped up on Ella's Adderall. Jed sets out on mini-adventures, hitchhiking across the state with zero cash; since arriving in New York he's trespassed into abandoned asylums, jailhouses, and cemeteries.

I've developed my own winter routine. I light a candle in the dark and smoke my nightly joint while sitting on the edge of the bathtub, feet in scalding hot water, leg warmers hugging my thighs. Last night, I could hear Tommy's acoustic from two doors down, and Lion and Jed engaged in a loud debate about whether or not randomness is at the root of any "formulaic masterpiece." I drew spirals in the water with my toes, telling myself that the universe runs on everlasting energy and will never dry out. If matter's neither created nor destroyed, then, in some form or another, we're here forever (right?). Our energy is trapped in the windowsills and the soles of our shoes in a pile by the door.

Listen closely: above the white noise of our communal dream, you can hear the internal tick tock that counts down the seconds. The incessant heartbeat, brainwave static, nervous impulses of interwoven lives. Our lines of vision waver like heat. We are Freudian field days, with tricks up moth-eaten sleeves. We are altogether altering the vantage point, relatively and without much to say. We're all just trying to hang onto our lighters.

What do I do (you ask), day in, day out? I am gathering anthropological data. I document these incidental muses making misconceptions seem inventive. The rest of the world fades like disappearing ink. Perhaps this is all I will ever be. Perhaps tonight's fleeting moment is all that ever was. Perhaps the Dreamachine won't elevate our consciousness or bring us any closer to discovering who we really are. Tommy looks tired and Jed rather stern, Ella looks restless and Lion's just bored. What I really want to ask, what I long to shout into the wavering air and downcast eyes is the same question I ask the bathtub every night: What are we doing? Why am I here? And then, what do I want?

Well, perhaps I will live under staircases, between couch cushions, within microwavable ecosystems, escaping every-so-often through hyperspacial tunnels! Well, I want a cat named Oz and a mouse named Oscar to keep me sane while I rewrite and revise my history, while I tinker with the laws of time. And yet, I don't want to be anywhere, know anyone, wear anything, don't want to speak at all. Sometimes I walk home with eyes closed, unafraid of the cold piercing my neck, listening only to my boots and my bones. There is nothing I want (to be) except sunlight.

We're growing old in this cold and spring's the only hope. Last week, Ella and I smoked my nightly joint in the bathtub together, wearing our bras. Clogged-up inhales and exhales synchronized like metronomes: yin and yang, cyclic fish, we were right and left brain forming one self. I am logic-minded, an observer of observers. She detects shapes and shadows, aural outlines, colors and clouds on smudgy countertops. She spins vinyl on her eyelids and offers the room a sultry gaze. *Ella, you are the moon's heartbeat. The accidental downpour. You know*...we're all trapped inside our geometric heads, our crooked backbone daydreams. Chalk marks on the ceiling and nicotine pulp between wood planks, duct-tape on the doorknobs, and hunger pangs stashed in the bathroom drawer. When in doubt, blame it on the weather (blame it on the traffic, blame it on genetics, blame it on your father).

We are living in a postmodern fairy tale. I want to distill this moment and construct a diorama of our shared existence, our present-tense time. I want to shout into the room, into outer space, into our collective unconscious...

"We should listen to ourselves more."

Who said that? Was it me?

"That wouldn't be a bad idea," Tommy says, seeming farther away.

Lion and Ella toss an imaginary ball back and forth. Jed stares into the empty fireplace, feeling the last of its warmth. "It's never too late to be a saint," he says.

Lion swallows the ball; his eyes as dark as night, he fades in and out of this pulsating light. We are all deities in our own right.

I realize now: I am only what they see. The light bounces off our molecular designs and through the retinas of their eyes. So, what does that make me?

Maybe I will say: The sun in this room is dying, and we'll need an umbrella to cover our bones. We're disappearing; I see our atoms scatter like the dust of human existence. But do the others yet know it? I wonder...*Hello?*

THE TEST

AS USUAL, HEATHER HADN'T SEEN IT COMING. Aaron's anger—or in this case, *hanger*—was a laser beam aimed at her heart. No one but her could discern the laser, and she doubted anyone else had ever been its intended target.

"I don't understand why you won't eat the vegetables," Aaron carried on as they walked. "Subways are the same all over the world. They don't wash the lettuce in the sink. The vegetables come pre-washed, like baby carrots at the supermarket."

Heather shivered. May meant November in the Southern Hemisphere and she hadn't been cold in months. A dreary afternoon drizzle was killing their plan of exploring the Royal Botanic Gardens. That and Aaron's laser.

"You've never worked at Subway, you don't know that for sure."

"It's a well-known fact. Look it up."

"We're still in a foreign country. You know exactly how I am about contamination and tap water. I want to be careful."

"We're in Australia!" He waved his hand around as if to say 'See, everything's in English, just like home.'

It was true that Sydney felt more familiar than all the other cities through which they'd traveled. A slew of business people, mostly Caucasian and much taller ("guess they have more room to grow here," Aaron had joked), hurried past. So many people with somewhere to be. Clop went their shoes. Swish went their slacks. The architecture—colonial and conventional, sleek and reserved—mirrored everyone's attire, aside from some alternative kids with gauged ears. Heather thought the city and its inhabitants would look more...different. She kept singing *I come from a land down under* to remind herself where she was. She had made it this far—the final frontier.

"Look," she said, turning toward Aaron, "my gastroenterologist said people get sick toward the end of their trip because they stop being cautious and get overly confident."

"You got sick in Bangkok and were *very* cautious."

"Just get your sandwich and I'll find something else. Why does this sort of thing always have to be a fight with you?"

"Because your irrational fears keep costing us money. And the worst part about it is you're doing it intentionally, fully aware of how selfish you're being."

Heather paused to grab a lamppost. She wished someone would intervene to confirm her suspicions about Subway using tap water and tap water generally being unsafe for travelers even in places where people spoke English. She could hardly understand what people were saying here anyway. *Can't you hear, can't you hear the thunder? You better run, you better take cover.*

"I'm trying to compromise with you," she told Aaron, gripping the post as if she might fall. "I said I would get Subway because you're starving and I settled on avocado because that's what I feel comfortable eating."

"Newsflash, Heather. You're not compromising by spending *our* money on a veggie sandwich when you're not going to eat *any* of the veggies and will *only* eat avocado, which costs extra!"

"A dollar extra. Which is less than a dollar in US fucking currency."

"That is not the fucking point."

Heather understood the point perfectly well. They were nearly out of money, and money had always been Aaron's greatest concern. Ironically, he'd quit his job as a vegan chef to embark on this belated quest to the other side of the world. He hadn't made a dime in the seven months they'd spent backpacking the Pacific Rim, and it was currently biting them both in the ass.

They'd done things on the cheap since day one—bargain-shopping, D.I.Y. adventuring, trading second-hand books, walking with their packs instead of taking cabs, washing their clothes in the sink, and "making" their own water by boiling then cooling it whenever their room came with the appropriate amenities—but spending funds on fun was becoming difficult to justify. How much fun was an adult allowed? Aaron was thirty-one, Heather twenty-eight. They'd been a couple for three and a half years. By societal standards, they should have been saving for a wedding, or a house, or a baby, or all those things in quick succession, yet they lived in a railroad apartment in Greenpoint with a diabetic tattoo artist, who had agreed to babysit their betta fish Bluey, and neither had ever owned property or ever seriously considered raising a child, much to their mothers' chagrin.

"What are we saving for, if not life experience?" had been Aaron's mantra when Heather, who'd rarely left the country, was still on the fence about spending eight months abroad. She'd weighed the pros and cons, took trusted friends for brunch, and then asked Aaron to meet her on the rooftop, where she'd propped a poster board that spelled the word "Yes!" Aaron had given her the longest, wettest kiss and Heather knew she had made the right choice.

Yet the more money they spent, the more things seemed to bother Aaron, inducing his laser beam rage. She could list these things off the top of her head: her exasperated sighs, utter inability to finish a cup of tea, haphazard method of packing her bag, and addiction to posting sub-par photos on Facebook when they were supposed to be cultivating a commendable travel blog they could pass off as "work." He hated the way Heather left most of the logistics to him while she took online quizzes or perused fashion sites, the way she walked too slow and talked too fast and failed to properly pronounce foreign words and sometimes became too assertive with strangers, and especially the way she outright refused to adhere to obvious social customs, like the time she wore a tank top at Angkor Wat ("It's a hundred degrees! And nobody cares!"). Then there was the fact that Aaron kept having to accommodate her needs, like not staying in dorms (she wouldn't be able to sleep) and taking more flights than bus rides (she sometimes got motion sick), and avoiding boats whenever possible (another irrational fear).

He'd said, "I would do this trip very differently if you weren't here."

She'd said, "Well maybe you should have done this alone."

He had acted offended, then dismayed, and finally leaned in close and said, "But I wouldn't be happy unless I was doing it with you."

The compromising went both ways, of course. Heather had subletted their room and put her job as a wardrobe stylist and window-dresser on hold. She'd abandoned the life she had built to travel to places where Aaron was literally the only person with whom she could hold a conversation. She hadn't even been interested in Asia, but Aaron had convinced her it was the best place for backpackers, humming with ancient history and postcard-worthy sights. And he'd been right! She had stood atop the Great Wall feeling gigantesque—the wall slithered across hilltops like a heavenly caterpillar and she'd waved to the sky even though she knew seeing the wall from space was only a myth.

What Aaron had failed to predict, however, was how isolated she'd feel as a vegan in the Philippines, or a black girl in China, or an interracial couple in Korea, or an American here in Australia, and how much she despised wearing the same clothes every week and using condoms that didn't feel right and trying to find lotion that wouldn't whiten her skin and walking two miles to eat a suitable meal when she was so famished she could shove a herd of cows in her face. Yes she was getting in shape and "toughening up" (which her father had assured), yes that "journey not the destination" adage was turning out to be pretty damn true, and yes she and Aaron were making lifelong memories and inside jokes, but she longed for a bath with Epsom salts and big bars of soap and a nothing-night of ordering scrambled tofu, watching *Family Feud,* and venting to friends who spoke the same language. Scratch that, ordering salad, with glistening hunks of iceberg lettuce. And an Arnold Palmer, ice cubes fat as ravioli.

She had to wonder, wasn't it enough that she'd been willing to come along for this ride? Hadn't she made the ultimate compromise by fulfilling Aaron's dream? She had tolerated cold showers, beds of stone, sleeper trains with screaming babies, squat toilets with no doors, and gut-churning scents of indefinable origin. She'd pushed bikes up dirt hills, paddled a sinking kayak, climbed three thousand steps up a steep mountainside, and squirmed through claustrophobic caves. She'd been bitten by hundreds of bloodthirsty mosquitoes, walked under sheets of monsoonal rain, sweated all night through intermittent blackouts, watched people spit and piss and fight and hogtie pigs, and had to pee so badly she thought she would suffer permanent damage. She'd played pitiful games of charades just to find the right bus, accidentally ate chunks of yak meat in bread, suffered the brutal poundings of a deaf and mute masseuse, came face-to-face with a wild horned bull, and had a hundred dollars stolen from her locked bag. Worst of all, she'd endured stares upon stares for hours on end—men gawked, children pointed, and women couldn't stop touching her hair. Everywhere she went, her mere existence incited awe and amusement. They even snapped photos, with and without her permission, as if she were some exotic bird they might never spot again.

So one might say Aaron owed her. Besides, she didn't pick a fight with *him* when he decided against using the hostel's kitchen because the European bros kept cooking bacon. He should have known how expensive Australia would be and how little they'd have left after all the countries on his list. Sure, his "if we don't visit now, when?" logic still applied, but bottles of water in Sydney cost three bucks and forget a proper lunch!

Heather sighed. Even though she knew Aaron hated it.

They ate their sandwiches in miasmic silence. The avocado by itself wasn't very good. At the adjacent table, a father gave his two-year-old a bottle of Sprite with a straw. The son slurped happily while Heather seethed. Couldn't he have given him orange juice or something? She wanted to point it out to Aaron, but imagined him saying, *Give the guy a break, that's just how they do things here* and making her feel shittier.

When they exited the food court, the sky was still gray: layers and layers of lanky clouds. Raindrops splattered the pavement sporadically, as if they couldn't decide whether or not to fall. Heather and Aaron walked through an outdoor mall without saying a word. An old man with a battered acoustic sang "La Bamba." Tourists danced and tossed him coins. Locals swigged coffee and swung shopping bags. Heather roved like a Mars robot. At the very least, nobody stared.

They began heading south toward the hostel. The day was a bust; there was no denying it. Earlier, they'd gone back to the Museum of Contemporary Art because Aaron had finally agreed to see the five-dollar light show. "You're going to regret it if you miss this!" the ticket girl had told them when they'd visited two days prior. But they hadn't accounted for a rainy Sunday—days of the week no longer meant a thing—and the museum was mobbed. The line for buying tickets had snaked out the door, and then Aaron felt faint and the Subway battle ensued. Now it was time to admit defeat, return to the room, take a nap, and attempt to start anew.

Heather walked ahead, her legs keeping pace with her swiftly beating heart. The word "selfish" kept appearing in her mind—it was one of Aaron's favorites, along with "lazy," "oblivious," and "stubborn." She hadn't felt this down on herself since she was in high school.

They rarely went a full day without some kind of squabble, which typically began when Heather said or did something Aaron disliked. One fight had erupted amid picturesque rice terraces. Another in the middle of a fishing village. Yet another in a crowded bus station, after which they sat apart for a full six hours. A few of these fights had become truly epic—tears shed and objects thrown. Twice Heather had looked up flights home, but they were so long and expensive they had made her cry more. She didn't want to phone home for funds and admit she was no longer having fun, so she was stuck with Aaron on this side of the globe, and she'd started to resent him for prioritizing what they saw and ate over how they treated one another. Day in, day out, she worried their relationship might never recover. Perhaps the whole trip had been a mistake.

Aaron's voice floated behind her. "Don't walk angry."

She moved faster to get away from him—and to atone for all those times she'd struggled to keep up while he barely glanced back—but then eventually slowed. Walking by his side, their silence was insufferable. She knew better than to expect an apology.

A sign appeared at the edge of the sidewalk: "Free Personality Test!" Out of the corner of her eye, Heather noticed the building behind it: Sydney's Church of Scientology. They walked a few more steps, then stopped dead in their tracks, facing one another.

"Did you see the sign back there?" Heather asked, breathless.

"Yup. Did you see the building?"

"Yup."

Momentarily forgetting her anger, Heather felt as though she were standing atop another Great Wall.

"Should we do it?"

"I don't know," he said, a mischievous glimmer in his eyes. "I mean, you saw the documentary. The spaceships dumping billions of bodies into volcanoes? And the thetans and crazy Tom Cruise and tax evasions and shit."

"Oh, I know," Heather said. "But that's why I want to do it. To see what it's really like inside. Plus, it's free! You love things that are free."

"I do." He played with the scraggly beard Heather detested. She'd accidentally thrown out his razor in Manila and he hadn't shaved since. "Can you go in there with a straight face, though? We shouldn't do this just to laugh at them."

"No of course not, we'll pretend we're genuinely interested. Like, super earnest. 'Hello, we saw your sign out front and we'd really like to learn more!' And we won't mention the thetans or Tom Cruise or anything."

The more Heather talked about it the more excited she felt. She was convinced that this ridiculous excursion could, ironically enough, get them back on solid ground. The silence between them had already thawed.

She continued to dangle the idea, like enticing a horse with a carrot. "Free entertainment in a pricy city…something to do on a crappy, rainy day…"

"Fine. But *don't* laugh."

"I won't, I swear. You can do the talking."

They turned around and approached the Church, which was just a modern building with horizontal windows. Heather had envisioned dungeons and chambers, but the presence of these windows didn't necessarily negate that possibility. She wondered if Aaron would save her, if need be.

They pushed open the glass doors and approached the Asian lady sitting behind a big white desk. Aaron flashed her a friendly smile.

"Hi there, we saw your sign out front and were wondering if we could take the personality test."

"That's great! Yes you can!" The lady rose up like an exclamation mark. "Are you familiar with Scientology?"

"Not really, ma'am," Aaron responded. "But we're open to learning more."

He was a natural! Heather beamed.

The lady wore a silver and black vest with a matching man's tie and collared shirt. Her nametag read Sue. On the wall behind her hung a dazzling cross with a four-point star and the Sydney Harbor Bridge arching in the background. Did Jesus or the crucifixion play a role in Scientology? If so, Heather felt less inclined to go through with this experiment. She'd been raised in a family with Deep South ties, a family that confessed their sins and believed in miracles. Her parents had never been dogmatic, but Heather still dodged anything remotely Christian. Aaron felt similarly about Judaism after growing up with Orthodox grandparents. They'd bonded over their religious detachment (along with a mutual love of smoothies and hatred of toe socks) on their first date, a discussion that went surprisingly well with ice-skating.

Sue ushered them into a spacious main room, which looked like a futuristic library, except this library's books were all by the same author: L. Ron Hubbard, the mad scientist, or mad science-fictionist, who'd brainwashed believers and fooled the IRS. The room was designed to resemble some high-end science fair, with curved partitions bearing flat-screen TVs demarcating the space into themed sections. Other vest-and-tie scientologists with nametags appeared out of nowhere, trotting over to greet them like waiters on a space station. Heather imagined trying to convince her clients that this was the hot new style to emulate. Vests and ties for all!

After a few hellos had been kicked around the room, they were seated at a small table with more pencils and erasers than two people could possibly need. A second lady, Lorna, came over with the tests. Her blond hair formed flawless ringlets that encircled her face like a hair-sprayed halo.

"As you answer these questions, try to be as honest as possible," Lorna said softly. "Don't sit too long with each question and don't go back to look over or change your answers. Just answer quickly and honestly, and please do not speak."

Lorna handed them paper booklets with 200-question Scantrons, which reminded Heather of high school exams. She shuddered. Were you supposed to study your personality first, cramming *you* into your head before putting pencil to paper? She'd imagined something less formal, more vocal, and certainly funnier. So far, this wasn't exactly funny.

She opened the booklet and got to work, pencil poised in mid-air so she wouldn't chew it. There were only three options for every question: *Yes*, *No*, or *Uncertain*. The test started innocently, asking about her ethics, emotions, relationships, productivity, and communication. It almost felt like a job interview. Double negatives and awkward phrasing kept tripping her up. And then things got weird.

Do you ever get disturbed by the noise of the wind or a "house settling down?"

Didn't everyone sometimes? But "sometimes" wasn't an option. *Uncertain.*

Do you bite your fingernails or chew the end of your pencil?

She looked at the pencil's tooth marks, which closely resembled the ones she had left on countless pencils throughout the years. *Yes.*

Do you get occasional twitches of your muscles, when there is no logical reason for it?

Heather snuck a glance at Aaron to see if he seemed equal parts puzzled and amused. His face looked as stoic as a monk locked in prayer. She returned to her test. *Uncertain.*

Is your life a constant struggle for survival?

She was starting to feel edgy. Was she allowed to explain her answer on a piece of loose-leaf? Was her definition of "survival" the same as theirs? Let's be honest…*No.*

Do others push you around?

Did "others" include the boy sitting serenely beside her? The boy who had just called her selfish? *Uncertain.*

Do you sometimes feel that your age is against you (too young or too old)?

Now this test was touching a nerve. She was older than most backpackers and up-and-coming stylists, but still too young to be taken seriously. *Yes.*

Does life seem rather vague and unreal to you?

She stifled a laugh. Here she was inside the Church of Scientology in the land down under! So… *Yes.*

Have you ever considered suicide?

She paused, pencil hovering above the sheet. *No.*

Wait, that was a lie. No, she wasn't the typical candidate for suicide because she'd never really go through it…but she'd certainly *considered* it. She knew what would happen if she answered truthfully, yet she grabbed an eraser. *Yes.*

The test continued. Questions about her past and future. Her habits and hobbies. Her self-esteem and tone of voice. Her sense of trust and grasp of logic. Whether or not she gossiped or loaned items or took risks or paid debts or felt like a failure or spoke up when she had an opinion. *Yes. No. Uncertain.* Had she passed, failed, or skated by?

By the time she finished her armpits were damp.

Aaron was still filling his Scantron circles when Lorna took Heather's test and led her to the flat-screen TV closest to the front desk. She instructed her to sit on a cushioned bench and watch a five-minute video about the reactive and analytical minds. The film was poorly acted (where was Tom Cruise when they needed him?) and overly dramatic, but otherwise well produced. One scene showed a boy getting food poisoning from deviled eggs; when the same boy, later in life, attended a jovial picnic and someone brought out deviled eggs, he felt sick and couldn't touch them. This was supposed to prove a point about how childhood trauma negatively affects the adult subconscious, but Heather knew she would have done the same thing.

Aaron finished his test and watched the same video while Heather browsed a timeline of L. Ron Hubbard's life. There he was at a typewriter, wearing a blazer. Then in a captain's hat, steering a ship. He'd certainly kept busy all those years, and probably indulged in a lot of sex. All those poor gullible women—women who'd worshipped Hubbard and followed him to the ends of the earth—and not a single one had made it to this wall. Was she doing the same thing on this journey with Aaron, sacrificing her own plans and savings to follow him around the globe?

Aaron joined her by the timeline; his eyes looked glassy, as if he were high.

"What'd you think of the test?" Heather whispered.

"Dude." Aaron ran his fingers through his beard again, giving it a tug. "The one about letting someone else fill in the last words of the crossword puzzle? Or killing an animal to put it out of its misery?"

"I know! What about the noises in the wind?"

"And being a slow eater."

"And the muscle twitches."

"Excuse me," a voice said, and Heather and Aaron darted apart as if they'd been caught smooching at a middle school dance. A short man named Wayne was waving a piece of paper like he'd just won an auction. "Heather, I have your results, would you please come with me for a private discussion?"

"What about Aaron?" She felt the sudden urge to cling to Aaron's pant leg and never let go.

"His answers are still being processed, but Bernard will grab him soon."

"Can't we just wait and talk over everything together?"

Wayne smiled and wagged a finger. "You need to have separate consultations to understand your results. That's how we do things here."

It was then Heather realized that her plan had backfired. Okay, they could still laugh about this later and continue to share thoughts and experiences, but she wanted to see Aaron's reactions in the moment and team up with him against these bozos. She wanted to fight *with* him, not against him.

Aaron waved goodbye as Heather followed Wayne to a small glass cubicle in the same large room. There was no door, but the glass was strangely soundproof, since she could no longer hear the videos playing for a handful of other guests.

Reluctantly, she sat catty-corner at Wayne's desk. His nose was bulbous, head balding, and complexion ruddy, as if he'd just run a few laps in the cold. He was stout like a hobbit, with a middle-aged-man gut she hoped Aaron would never acquire. She'd bet money that Wayne's feet were square and his back hairy.

"It's so nice to sit and talk with you today, Heather," he said in a cartoonish accent. "Where are you from again?"

"New York City," she said. Saying "New York" (never "America") was a point of pride, even though she'd lived in Virginia most of her life.

"Wow, big city," Wayne said, appropriately impressed. "I'm from Tasmania myself. Ever been out there?"

"No, but we're traveling there soon, and then on to New Zealand, and then home." *Home,* she thought, *finally.*

Wayne launched into a few tips about sights to see in Tasmania, which Heather mostly tuned out. Aaron would research that later.

"All right," Wayne said, "let's get down to business."

He presented the precious piece of paper, smoothing its edges. It revealed a large graph with numbers up the side, but unlike geometry or calculus, ten words—*Happy* vs. *Depressed, Composed* vs. *Nervous, Responsible (Causative)* vs. *Irresponsible*, and more—were horizontally opposed. The middle of the graph bore long swaths of gray with a thick line running through. All numbers above the line were positive and all numbers below it were negative.

"This is you," Wayne said, calling Heather's attention not to the graph itself, but to a thinner line that peaked and crashed across it. She assumed that the coordinates corresponded to her answers; he'd magically tallied all those *Yes, No*, and *Uncertains* to create this bizarre triangular mountain.

"What do you notice about this, Heather?" He folded his hands across his belly like an imitation Santa.

"Well, this line is all over the place...pretty high and pretty low."

"Exactly right, highs and lows." He nodded and extended his finger again. It might have been the ugliest finger Heather had ever seen. "With more lows than highs, you see?"

Heather trailed her own finger along the line, riding it like a roller coaster.

"This is the desirable zone," Wayne continued, aiming that appalling finger at the dense gray swaths, "but most of your points are out of range. I have to tell you, Heather, I think you can really benefit from the courses and lectures we offer here."

"Courses and lectures for what?" *For learning how to manipulate people?* she wanted to say.

"Let's discuss *you* more first." Wayne nudged his chair closer to the desk. "Your lowest score is this one, *Lack of Accord*. Now, this means that your personality can be very hard for others to deal with. You argue with people and instantly contradict them. If I say, 'The sky's blue,' you'll immediately tell me, 'No it's not!' without even looking up."

Heather bit her lip and scrunched up her face. "I don't do that."

"I think that you do."

"No, I really don't."

"Would you like to know how I *know* you do?"

"Because some algorithm spat out these coordinates saying I do?"

"No Heather, because you just contradicted me, less than a second after I'd finished speaking."

As if he'd just won a Supreme Court victory, Wayne leaned back in his chair and grinned. Heather tried to stay calm.

"Just because I disagree with you right now doesn't mean I disagree with everyone all the time," she said in her most rational tone.

"Do you and Aaron get into disagreements?" Wayne motioned to his left and Heather turned toward the next-door cubicle, where she found Aaron sitting across from a man she assumed to be Bernard—older, stooped, and hook-nosed, with a head of silver hair that perfectly matched his vest and tie. Bernard seemed to be doing all the talking while Aaron listened with hands in his lap.

"Sometimes we fight, sure," she said. "Doesn't every couple?"

"Tell me Heather, how did you meet Aaron?"

Heather loathed this question; her answer was so unoriginal, so millennial. A list of past lies flicked by in her head—she'd met Aaron at jury duty, in a stopped elevator, in the crossfire of a protest, at an animal shelter while trying to adopt the same blind kitten. But why lie to Wayne? If she had to suffer through this private psychotherapy session, she may as well try to gain something useful.

"OK Cupid," she mumbled.

"OK what?"

"It's a dating website, based on algorithms actually," she explained. "It matches you with someone based on how you fill out your profile. So we met that way and texted a bunch and then went ice-skating in Prospect Park."

"I see." He scratched the bald part of his head. "Do you trust Aaron, Heather?"

She was starting to hate how often he said her name. It reminded her of the high school guidance counselor who tried too hard to be everybody's friend.

"What do you mean?"

"I mean simply, do you trust him?"

"Yes?" she said, trying to ignore the seed of doubt in her voice.

Wayne folded his hands. He looked ready to deliver a deathly diagnosis.

"Deep down, you don't trust people. You lack the ability or desire to trust, which causes a lack of empathy for others." He took a deep breath. "This makes it hard to experience real love in your life, Heather."

"Trust and empathy are not related like that," she responded sternly, crossing her arms. "And I have plenty of real love in my life." But how could she be sure? Maybe the OK Cupid algorithm was as distorted as Wayne's graph. How did she know that Aaron really loved her?

It happened in her childhood home. They'd been dating for barely three months when Easter rolled around and she invited him to attend her family's annual celebration. As soon as Aaron agreed, she regretted the invitation.

The bus ride to Richmond took seven long hours and she gnawed gum nervously the entire way. Her cool veneer would dissipate the second Aaron stepped into her magenta-walled bedroom that still housed Beanie Babies, a million *Betty & Veronica* comics, and a framed Janet Jackson poster. And what about the image of Jesus blessing the kitchen, the photos of twelve-year-old Heather wearing a tattoo choker and platform sneakers, not to mention the quintessential prom picture where her date looked cross-eyed, and the fact that her family prayed before dinner and actually said "may I be excused?" like *The Cosby Show* meets *Leave It To Beaver*? Aaron's parents, on the other hand, had been divorced for fifteen years. His father was a documentary film producer and his mother a professor of women's studies, both Orthodox defectors who'd raised Aaron in Park Slope back when it was rough. As young as thirteen, Aaron had gotten into serious hijinks: tagging walls, running from cops, and playing drums in an anarchistic punk band. He had some street cred; Heather did not.

"It'll be fine!" he'd told her, but she held her breath all through the holiday. He was as much of a spectacle as the birth of Jesus Christ. Behold, an auburn-haired Jew! Behold, a Brooklyn accent! Behold, Heather's hipster boyfriend!

Her twin brothers, home from college, teased her every chance they got, and her teenage sister kept making kissy faces behind Aaron's back. Her father tried to perform the old-fashioned "you better be good to my daughter" routine, which Jamie parodied and Jordan filmed. Her nana told him about calling the fire department to get Heather down from her tree and her mother mentioned the hot dog eating contest that had made Heather puke and then Uncle Dennis said something vaguely offensive like "slavery was worse than the Holocaust."

By the time the two climbed into bed (the Beanie Babies shoved aside), Heather burst into tears.

"What's wrong?" Aaron asked, rubbing her back.

"I feel so embarrassed."

"Maybe you feel like I know the real you now. Or the old you."

"Maybe," she sniffled, "and I'm afraid you don't like her."

"I love her, in fact." He turned Heather to face him and looked deep into her eyes. "I love *you*."

It was the first time he'd said it, and she knew he had meant it with all of his heart.

Wayne clicked a ballpoint pen. Emphatically, he began adding marks to the graph while elaborating on Heather's deficiencies. Soon enough, the page was littered with arrows, question marks, and words like *confusion, Dianetics, attitude, betrayal (fear of), poor decisions*, and *TRUST* in barely legible handwriting. Heather could hardly make sense of what was happening. She'd entered this so-called Church to remedy a rotten day and now she was stranded with a trollish Tasmanian hell-bent on explaining everything that was wrong with her, as if she didn't already feel terrible enough! Still, she tried to listen to his statements (and pitches for fifty-five dollar courses), jumping in every so often to rightfully defend herself.

"You let things happen *around* you," Wayne stated, "because you don't feel safe making decisions for yourself."

"I let things happen because I'm a go-with-the-flow kind of person."

She felt like she was climbing Mt. Everest with no oxygen mask; the air kept getting thinner and thinner. Wayne, on the other hand, seemed to grow stronger with every breath.

"I don't think that's a bad thing," she continued, cracking her knuckles. "I mean, isn't it better than being a control freak?" She recalled the avocado debacle: who was the controlling one in *that* situation?

Wayne fanned his metaphorical feathers and puffed out his chest. "Not at all. 'Control freaks' *cause* things to happen in their lives, but you won't take on that responsibility. You convince yourself that whatever happens is fine by you, even if you don't like it."

Heather sighed. She thought of Aaron leading her up Chinese mountains, and how much she'd wanted to ask him *why?* What was the point of this uncomfortable journey, and of making her mother worry? What were they trying to prove and to whom?

She glanced to her left again. Through the soundproof glass, Aaron's mouth was now the one moving while Bernard nodded in rapt attention. He picked up a hardcover Dianetics book and quickly leafed through it as Aaron sat back with a satisfied smile. Was he stumping Bernard? She felt a little sorry for the guy; Aaron was *winning* at this, if such a thing were possible. Did Bernard even suspect this was supposed to be a joke?

Blood rushed to Heather's face. It wasn't fair. She wanted Bernard to rattle Aaron to his core, to tell him he was too anxious and cocky and critical. She wanted Aaron to see the error of his ways, to realize that he *needed* her, and that he couldn't have done this trip alone, even if she'd told him *No.*

No, I have my own life. No, I don't want to turn into Siamese twin travel buds who fight about vegetables. No, I don't want to spend my hard-earned cash on your hedonistic dreams.

But then again, *No, I don't want to sit side-by-side on separate laptops, an inevitable habit born of boredom and stable wifi. No, I don't want to be that woman in the nursing home who's never taken risks. No, I wouldn't want to miss this.*

Heather knew that most of Aaron's gripes were valid; she didn't wake up early and didn't help plan and let most of the stress fall onto his shoulders. She lost track of the number of times he'd said, "If only you'd focus less on our relationship and more on actually planning things with me!" She knew she didn't "respect his time," she knew she complained about trivial things—like missing her faux leather jacket and boots (which she couldn't justify lugging for eight months) while starving Cambodian children begged outside the Killing Fields—and she knew she'd been retreating into her own inner world. She knew, above all, she was holding him back.

Everyone expected her to grow and change—to become a better person, a brand new self—but she couldn't tell *what* she was learning or how she was changing. She was seeing new things at such a rapid rate that she'd stopped paying attention to make herself more comfortable in the absence of a comfort zone.

"What do you think is the root of your trouble with decisions,

Heather?" Wayne's dull brown eyes were burrowing through hers, trying to unearth pearls of trauma. What was her damage? Her *deviled egg?*

"I have no idea."

In her peripheral vision she watched Bernard leave his cubicle. He was speaking with another Scientologist, perhaps seeking her advice. Aaron looked at Heather and gave a subtle thumb's up. She forced herself to smile. If she let on that she wasn't having fun, he'd probably say, *But this whole thing was your idea!*

"Tell me about your parents," Wayne said eagerly. "Are they still together? Both alive?" He was grasping in the dark now, attempting to crawl into the corners of her mind.

"They're great," she said bluntly, "they're still together and still alive. I couldn't have asked for a better family."

"What about other aspects of your childhood? Your friends, say?"

"It was all pretty standard. Nothing dramatic."

"Tell me then," he persisted, "is there anything from your past you would change if you could?"

Heather longed for a pencil to bite. "No."

"How about something you wish would happen now? Something you've been dwelling on and don't want to admit."

She watched Bernard return to his cubicle with yet another hardcover book. No wait, *two* hardcover books! He'd clearly needed backup to compete with the likes of Aaron. You couldn't convince Aaron of anything he didn't already know to be true.

And then it hit her: she wished for *more* from this man she adored. Hers was a simple fantasy, though it had gathered details as each month passed, growing into an elaborate tale for which she'd secretly conducted a little research. The scene replayed in her head at night when she couldn't sleep, and she refused to let go of it, even now.

One morning in China, a voice appeared in his head—*do it now!* It was just like the Fugazi song he used to play while folding laundry, only louder, more persistent. It followed Aaron like a thick trail of smoke. Followed him across borders and bridges, inside trikes and tuk-tuks and jam-packed jeepneys. He started feeling helpless, restless, then resolute. There was no question really, nothing to figure out except how to go about it.

The first order of business was to buy a ring. Not just any ring, of course—for someone like Heather, it had to be special. A diamond was too conventional. He tried to remember her jewelry collection in Greenpoint; she preferred silver to gold and her birthstone was sapphire. She liked rings with some bulk, but also thinner bands with etchings. He made mental notes whenever they passed local markets, paying close attention when something caught Heather's eye.

"What do you think of this?" she said in Vientiane, holding a plain silver ring. "It was made from a US bomb dropped here in the '60s."

"Hmm," he responded, "how much do they want for it?"

"24,000 kip. How much is that?"

"Like three bucks. Too much."

"Can't you bargain it down for me?"

"No, let's go."

A ring from a bomb wouldn't do, and neither would Heather buying her own cheap jewelry. Still, the experience inspired him—she admired things imbued with history, and infused with meaning. He wanted to take what he'd learned and find a ring by himself. He wanted to impress her the way she'd impressed him all those hard months on the road.

One day in Hanoi, Heather awoke with awful cramps and wanted to stay in. It was humid and drizzling anyway, so Aaron offered to go out and grab breakfast.

"Let me get this straight," she said, raising an eyebrow, "you're actually going to *buy* me breakfast and not make me eat peanut butter and jelly?"

"That's right," he said, grinning.

No part of him wanted to purchase breakfast, but he knew he needed to keep up appearances. He quickly hopped on their rented motorbike (he'd tried to teach Heather to drive, but that didn't go well) and embarked on a whirlwind tour of Hanoi's Old Quarter. He was determined to use this opportunity to his advantage, and as luck would have it, he soon found what he'd been seeking.

A kind old lady in a conical hat explained the significance of one particularly gorgeous ring. Its deep pink gem was tourmaline, native to the Luc Yen region of northern Vietnam. It was smooth, round, and sparkling, encircled by tiny sculpted leaves and set in sterling silver. The old lady's husband, a hardworking miner, had discovered the stone while digging for rubies in the early '80s, and she'd crafted the ring soon after. It was the first elaborate ring she'd made and she had worn it for years until her knuckles swelled and she decided to sell it with the rest of her wares.

Her timeworn hands moved Aaron so deeply that he didn't even bargain. She pecked him on the cheek and protected the ring in a tiny cardboard box, which Aaron placed inside the travel wallet he wore beneath his shirt. During the ride back to the hostel—stopping for veggie dumplings on the way—he imagined this stunning pink stone (like the pink of Heather's childhood walls, the pink of her lips and the pink of her heart) bright as a star against a white gown.

Do you, Aaron Cole Levy, take this woman, Heather Autumn Clark, to be your lawfully wedded wife?

But he couldn't do it right away; he had to find the right time. He brought the ring everywhere, guarding it more fiercely than his passport. The dark pink stone pulsed against his stomach, beating in sync with his heart. He almost took it out in a rice field flecked with long-necked birds, on the decaying steps of a deserted villa, amid wavering sand dunes beneath a full moon's glow, and in the serenity of a temple where monks chanted low. He'd chickened out each time. The pink pulsed harder and the voice cried louder, *DO IT NOW!*

When they landed in Sydney, with only a month until their pre-booked flight home, he decided this was *it.* And when they finalized their Australia itinerary, The Great Ocean Road revealed itself as the perfect moment. They'd be renting a car for the first time; he would pull off the road on an empty scenic overlook, waves as tall as trees crashing down below. Perhaps a rainbow would arch overheard as he bent down on one knee. She would scream, "Yes!" like the poster board she'd propped on their rooftop, the one word that assured him he had made the right choice.

Heather shook her head. She damn well knew Aaron hadn't bought a ring, and hated herself for nurturing such clichés. But glancing again at Aaron—were there seriously *more* books stacked on Bernard's desk?—she couldn't help hoping that part of her fantasy was true. At the very least, she hoped she had impressed him. She wanted him to look past her flaws the same way she'd tried to look past his. She didn't think Aaron understood how hard this journey had been on her, or how much fear she'd battled along the way. Wayne hadn't delved much into fear—perhaps this was the deepest trauma he had yet to expose.

"You see this little flower shape here?" he said, switching topics. "This point is highly unstable. You bounce up and down like a yo-yo between happy and depressed, but with more depression than happiness."

"Okay."

She remembered Aaron telling her, "Chill the fuck out—you either love me or you hate me! Can't you find a middle ground?"

"It seems to me that someone keeps knocking you off balance," Wayne declared. "And when you're down, down, all the way down here," his disgusting finger was far too close, "well now that's a dangerous place to be. Tell me, honestly, have you thought about killing yourself?"

There it was—the question she knew would come back to haunt her. It was almost a relief. Here was something she could wrap her mind around. Wayne was getting warm.

"I wouldn't ever do it," she whispered in case Aaron could hear. "But doesn't everyone think about it sometimes?"

"No," Wayne said. "What makes you feel this way, Heather?"

"I don't know." She paused. "I just feel really hopeless sometimes, and I start to wonder why I'm here at all. Especially now, after seeing how so many people live in the world. Like, what's the point of all this? What do I have to offer anyone? The feeling comes out of the blue and sticks with me for a day or two, until it passes."

Wayne scratched his head. "You are in danger, Heather." He wrote *DANGER* on the page and underlined it twice. "Your head is above water, which is what everyone sees, but you're held down by chains under the sea." His voice rose like a preacher at the pulpit. "You're struggling and flailing but no one knows it! We can help you get through this, Heather. We can help you survive."

Survive. More than anything, she wanted her relationship to survive. She wanted that pink stone (or sapphire, or ruby, or even a predictable diamond, who cared?) and that white gown and that "I do" at the nondenominational altar.

Wayne kept on, his voice like a sledgehammer, "You are *not* your own best friend, Heather, but you need to be. This is very important. This is life or death."

Until death do us part. Death was the ultimate release. Freedom. And Heather realized that she'd finally learned what true freedom meant. As much as it scared her, it was liberating to exist in a land full of strangers you would never see again. It was liberating to have so few clothes and possessions, to go days without cell service or the comforts of home, and to share every waking moment with the person whose love you both feared and desired.

Suddenly she remembered curved trees reflecting in Aaron's helmet as they zipped through Bali like a bullet on motorbike, her arms wrapped around him tight. She remembered the crammed night sky in Kampot, constellations expanding like the freckles on Aaron's shoulder blades. She remembered fireworks exploding on a beach in Bohol, a manic swirl of sparks forming spider webs of smoke. She remembered spilling stories and secrets as they roamed around Cat Ba eating cassava and waving to workers. She remembered chasing sunsets on Koh Lanta as the Muslim call to prayer rolled across the sky. She remembered sailing seamlessly through pine trees on the Cangshan Mountain chairlift, and how she'd lifted her shirt with not a soul in sight. She remembered kingdoms of coral and forests of kelp as they swam amongst florescent fish in the Andaman Sea. She remembered midnight ping-pong in a Xi'an courtyard, where she beat Aaron three times yet he still smiled wide. If she closed her eyes now she could choose any moment from their trip, not only seeing it clearly but reliving the heat of the sun and the sting of the sand, smelling crops as they burned and herbs as they steeped. Time had slowed down as the world opened up.

There was a palpable sweetness to each place they discovered, like arriving in New York all wide-eyed and woozy. Like climbing trees as a kid and entering a bright green world that bore little relation to the one down below.

Maybe she *didn't* want this trip to end; maybe she wanted to stay in an alternate reality with the present moment at her fingertips. She needed to welcome the fear that clogged her veins because it meant everything was new again, like those first few weeks with Aaron when she treasured each kiss because she didn't know if another would come, if the two of them would last.

Here was a boy who held her hand when they crossed the street, who offered the window seat, who sang her to sleep, who mapped their routes, who calmed her down, who carried her bag, who saved the last bite, who was showing her the world and she was a better person for it.

Ultimately, though, it was all up to her: the power to stay or go, to fight or flee. The question wasn't, *Does Aaron want to marry me,* but, *Do I want to marry him*? But that wasn't the point, either. They had survived these seven months together: the two of them against the world.

"You look upset, Heather." Wayne's egg-shaped head came into focus. His concern was phony, this whole place a sham.

"I *am* upset, *Wayne*," she said, standing up, "but I don't give a shit."

"Excuse me?"

She picked up the graph and tore it in two, then four, then more: words, lines, and numbers falling like raindrops onto his desk.

"Thanks for the chat, but I know *I'm* not perfect and *we're* not perfect, and that's okay with me."

He sat there stunned and stuttering as Heather backed away. She barged into Bernard's cubicle and strode to his desk. He held up a hardcover book like a shield.

"What are you doing?" Aaron cried out as Heather snatched his graph and tore the thing in two. She didn't want to see what it said; she already knew.

"Come on, let's get out of here."

He recoiled for a moment—the horror of upsetting a stranger, of causing a scene, of taking *this* kind of risk—but then a devilish smile appeared. She took Aaron's hand and felt his fingers grip.

"I'm sorry," he said.

She didn't know if he meant it for Bernard, who hadn't the nerve to speak, or for Wayne fuming behind the glass, or for *her*, atoning for earlier that day or all the days prior. It no longer mattered.

Still holding hands, Heather led Aaron out of the Church and back onto the streets of Sydney, laughing as the rain fell. They ran away into the great unknown, the only freedom one can ever know.

BEAST OF BOREDOM

LOGAN IS ON TOP OF ME. Would it be cliché to say he feels miles away? Would it be blasphemous to admit that I'm trying to fantasize about someone else? Or would it be worse to confess that I fail even in doing that?

To my credit, Logan and I have been at it a long time. Long, anyway, for my thirty and his thirty-two years. We're bound not only by our bodies but also by god and the law and the one hundred people at our summer wedding. We've been at this eight years straight. Some women would envy such a thing. Some would keel over and die if I showed them the ring with which he proposed: a family heirloom as big as a mushroom.

His penis inside me hardly feels like anything, as if it were already there. As if it has always been there. His body parts and mine revisit the same terrain night after night, or more like once or twice a week.

A strand of his sandy blond hair falls into my eye. This is something different, slightly whimsical. Maybe that hair will scratch my corneas and I will go blind. I will learn to walk with a stick, get a seeing-eye dog, whom I will name Gus or Verne or Hamlet, and eventually read and write Braille. This might take months; I'm slow with new languages. While blind, I might find Logan all over again, using my nose, mouth, fingertips. I'll rediscover the scent of his hair, the calluses of his feet, and the sounds in his stomach, like tiny geysers.

He moves his head, and the hair moves too. So much for that.

I hear myself moan, but the moaning sounds distant, like a police siren way off in another part of town. What is this sound rising from my throat? How does it relate to the metronomic thrusts of Logan's hips as he digs deeper, deeper? We are at it again: clammy and naked, unconcerned with what the downstairs neighbors and their little kids might hear—the *creak creak* of the boxspring or the jangle of beads I've strung across the headboard. Logan licks my neck like a thirsty pup and holds himself above me with both hands pressed into the mattress. I feel my fingers clasp around his wrist, strong as a tree branch, as I consciously try to moan again. It comes out like a flickering streetlight. I do not look him in the eye.

My mind curls into itself and a litany of thoughts commands my attention...what I ate today and what I might eat later; how many papers I still need to grade; why I found one of my students crying in the bathroom; why most of my students can't resist checking their phones every five minutes; how bees have to deal with our wireless beams cutting across space; last night's dream about elephant-sized books that doubled as boats; the other night's dream about sleeping with the soccer coach while Logan shoveled bones; what I'm going to do this weekend, what I did last weekend, why I never invent anything exciting to do on the weekends and thus spend too much 'quality time' with Logan, which inevitably leads to an argument about whether the toilet paper should hang *under* or *over* the roll; what my students do on the weekends, like getting drunk or stoned or laid; why so many friends and acquaintances post pictures of their unborn babies, which all look like demons; how by this age my mother had birthed my brother, my sister, *and* me; how enough time has passed that the clothes I wore as a teen are back in style, only now the jeans are elastic and pre-torn; how my students think thirty is equivalent to fifty but how magazines say forty is the new twenty, which must make thirty the new ten?; how I pulled out three gray hairs today even though supposedly I'll grow back nine more; how I miss my old bicycle, the one with the banana seat; how my father promised to fix that bike and never did; how it was strapped to his car when he swerved off the road twelve years ago; how it's hard to muster emotion these days except when I have my period and cry at commercials for life insurance; how I used to go into churches, even though I'm Jewish, and pay a quarter to light a candle not only for my father, but also for myself, and how watching that flame sputter in its long red tube was like crying the most beautiful tear, a big sparkling one just like my big sparkling diamond that once belonged to a woman who died in her sleep; how, in a way, my father died in his sleep, too; how we are all sleeping, every 'waking' moment we think means life; how reality is subjective, time relative, past, present and future illusory and imperceptible; how Logan has gone limp. The deed is apparently done.

He rolls off and offers a hearty sigh to the room or the moon or to me. I open my eyes. I didn't even realize they were closed; that I *had* been blind in some small way.

I turn toward him and prop myself up on my elbow, giving a seductive little grin for his sake. A token of my gratitude for time well intentioned.

"Hey there," he says, leaning in for a kiss. His lips taste like Logan. Nothing more.

I heard somewhere that John Lennon used to scrawl "Johnandyoko" as his signature. The couple had become one entity, one word—not a contraction and no hyphens needed. He also said something like, "Just as I have my right hand, so I have Yoko." Have I ever felt that strongly, that surely, about anything? Logan's right hand performs its post-coital sweep of my torso. I think about friction, static electricity, excitable electrons. My sister, Becca, used to rub balloons on her head and stick them to our wall.

"Did you come?" Logan asks.

I suck in my smile. I have forgotten to fake it. I've been forgetting lately. I realize now that the awkward moans emerging from my throat were just short of palpable. I'm too caught up in an endless cycle of thoughts, all meaningless and badly timed.

"Well...no. But it felt good."

He frowns. "Do you want to wash up and I'll go down on you?"

"I'm fine."

"What's wrong?"

"Just have a lot on my mind."

"Like what?"

"I dunno...things." I search my thoughts, shimmy down my mental list, but all of it has been vacuumed by some other part of my brain.

"Is it school?"

"Oh! One of my students was crying today."

"Why?"

"I don't know."

"Who was it?"

"Ashley DiCarlo."

"Does she often?"

"Often what?"

"Cry."

"How should I know? I'm her history teacher, not her guidance counselor."

He falls silent. We've reached the natural end of *that* conservation. My mouth is dry.

We get up to pee and hop in the shower, fulfilling the duties of our daily routine. We are, after all, married adults. My parents were married for twenty-seven years, before, well, before my father left the house that day. It was raining, I remember.

I stare at Logan, all of Logan, as the water turns us red and splotchy. If we actually grow old together like we promised we would, if we survive long enough to acquire age-spots on our skin and seats in the shower, I hope I feel grateful for this moment right here. I hope I find the whole thing endlessly poetic.

He soaps his skin and it glistens like the tiles. Most girls would relish the man standing before me, who hardly looks different from when I first met him—a few more smile-lines and a tad less head hair, but he still wears it long. Otherwise he's got the right amount of hair in all the right places, high cheekbones, an angled chin, sharp brown eyes, muscular forearms and biceps from lifting actual people as opposed to weights, lean legs from running, and even decent-looking pinkie toes. And his penis, well there's enough of it to satisfy, when one feels one *can* be satisfied. We used to shave once a week, getting right up into our naughty bits and laying everything bare for ultimate pleasure. We haven't bothered with things like that in a couple of years...likely when I started faking.

"So," he says, looking down at me from a few inches above. Actually, he's looking at my tits, or perhaps the water flowing over my nipples. I can't help but feel ashamed of the way my prized D-cups have been drooping, inch by inch.

"So," I answer.

"How was your day, besides that girl crying?"

"It was okay. Nothing special."

"Are you counting the weeks yet?"

"Five left, not counting finals."

"Anyone destined to fail?"

"Some pass, some fail, just like every year."

He does his secure-the-shower-curtain thing to make sure we don't soak the floor and then goes back to staring at my tits, which I take as a blank kind of stare. Maybe he's in the midst of an optical trick where the longer you look at something, the more you realize how absurd it is. Surely I've done that with his penis.

I can't muster the energy to ask him a single question. My thoughts begin racing again as I picture Ashley in the bathroom. She hadn't reentered the classroom, not even after the bell. I picked up her bag and poked my head into the nearest bathroom, expecting to find her smoking, or texting, or talking, or changing, or not in there at all, but she was sitting on the radiator, crying with her head in her hands. Maybe she'd just finished cutting her arm or purging her lunch. The kids watch videos about these things in Health, and I always thought watching someone self-mutilate or succeed at bulimia could almost convince you to do the same. But maybe Ashley had just gotten her heart broken for the first time, or maybe she was the one who did the heart-breaking; she's pretty enough, with straightened hair and smoky eyes and glossy lips like most of the sixteen-year-old girls I teach.

When she glanced up, her face in a knot, the two of us locked gazes. I had no idea what to say. I haven't dealt with real emotion in god knows how long. I lecture about things that happened to people who died before any of us were born. I put strangers on pedestals and take off points if the kids misspell their names.

All I could utter was, "Do you need a minute?" What I *could* have said, I realize now, was "Oh honey, what's wrong?" or "Would you like me to write you a pass?" or "Please see me later if you need to talk," but I simply left her bag on the floor and dashed to the faculty room for my hundredth cup of coffee, all while feeling jealous that Ashley had something worth crying over. Like all the high school kids who gossip in the cafeteria, smoke cigarettes in the parking lot, and give each other piggyback rides up and down the stairs, she's in the thick of it. Every minor issue is a major crisis, every moment some glorious or traumatic "first" worthy of a longwinded "Dear Diary." There's simply no recreating the drama of teenage existence. The gory spectacle of youth.

I suppose I could tell Logan this whole story, and even elaborate on my recent feelings about the aging process: how childhood is elusive and teenage years are spotty—as if I'd only been conscious every third day—and how college years define you until you realize you're more than that, or at least should be, and how adulthood is one long stretch of days—endless, relentless, utterly futile—like a winter that never wakes up, a volcano that never erupts, and how old age looms in the graying distance but we never think, not for a moment's breadth, that *that* will be *us*. Or I could tell him it's my turn for the soap that smells like sea vegetables. I don't.

I glance at the faint scar on his wrist, which his silver watch would otherwise cover. I gave him that scar eight years ago when all we wanted to do was fuck each other's everything and had no idea it would lead to holy matrimony. In my bed, in his bed, before we had the same bed; on my couch, on his couch, before we had the same couch; in my shower, in his shower, in this shower?; on the floor, against walls; blinds shut, blinds open; in a skirt, in a dress; in heels, in boots; to music, to silence; on my knees, on top, on bottom, side by side; quick, slow, loud, quiet; hands held, hands cuffed, hands tied; tongues out, heads down, legs up; late night, early morning, mid-day; red-lit, blue-lit, pitch-black, stark-bright; his back, my nails, his bones, my mouth.

Those were the days.

For the past year or more, all the fantasizing I aim for when he's on top of me, always on top for some reason, is about boys I fucked before him, as if every Logan-related flashback, no matter how titillating, can't even do the trick. Flesh-and-bones Logan gives way to memory-induced Logan, the version of him stored in my cells, but neither Logan takes me from here to, well, *there*.

"I'm gonna hop out," he says, jarring me.

He hands over the vegetable soap and pets my wet hair. I squeeze my fingers around the soap the way I squeezed them around his wrist. That's how I gave him that scar—my nails digging in like claws.

He turns from me, steps out, and wraps his favorite towel around his waist. I hear him open and close the medicine cabinet. "We need more toothpaste." Logan always brushes his teeth after a shower, regardless of the time of day. Come to think of it, he used to brush his teeth *in* the shower, when we first started dating.

"I know," I respond. "There should be a little left in the tube, so use that. I can Listerine." I'd love for him to leave so I can ruminate freely, without the guilt of having nothing to say.

He turns the faucet on, then off. "I'll just run to the store. Be back before you're out." Sometimes I hate how efficient he can be.

Water travels the length of my spine as I stand in silence. I twist the H knob to get my blood pumping and heart pounding, to make me feel alive. "Be right back!" I hear. The front door slams. The water burns. A sigh escapes my throat. Unlike the ones that emerged during sex, this one is meaty. Rooted deep.

Before I became Rachel Merrick; before I gave Becca the dog I had rescued (Logan was allergic); before I set foot in Delaware; before I gained a few pounds 'round the hips; before I thought I'd lost Logan's family heirloom at a coworker's party, when I'd casually slipped it into my purse so I could flirt with a musician I might have actually kissed if drunken panic hadn't set in; before the routine of planning, grading, lecturing, and presenting Powerpoint slides in rainbow colors, I was a girl who *indulged* in this thing called life. I ate up life like chocolate ice cream.

From the age of my students until the day I met Logan, I created a pattern of spontaneous choices, if they could even be called choices. Once, I picked up a gutter-punk in Pioneer Square (spikes, scars, scrappy dog, the works), brought him to my dorm at Reed, smoked him up, unbuttoned his pants, and fucked him 'til we couldn't move. I don't remember all of it, but those are the basics. Maybe I was still mourning my father, maybe I started to find street-kids more alluring than my privileged peers, maybe I didn't take sex all that seriously, maybe I liked making bold anti-decisions, or maybe I wanted to take some self-indulgent risks before society deemed it unacceptable to do so. At twenty years old, I was reluctant to consider the future-Rachel I'd become.

Zoning out, I stare at the multicolor world map on our shower curtain, which always seems to taunt me. I studied history because I wanted to explore and discover this blocky puzzle—a world in which I never felt at home.

It all comes rushing back: how badly I wanted to defy expectations, to live a fascinating existence, to become a travel writer, or cultural anthropologist, or one of those experts who gets long voice-overs on documentaries about the Dark Ages, Stonehenge, Atlantis, the Silk Road, Babylon, Zionism, Zoroaster, the Zulu, the tombs of Lycia, the celestial science of Egypt, or

Ayurvedic medicine in ancient India. But after a plethora of thesis papers and focusing my mental energy on people, places, and ideas that had nothing to do with modern-day life, I had to admit that most of what I'd studied had one purpose and one purpose only: to teach it to *other* people in a classroom setting. My future depended on blank faces staring at a map behind my head.

I wish someone had told me that history doesn't extend into the dreaded "real world." I wish a professor had admitted that I was destined to end where I'd begun: coming full circle to teach what I'd learned so that another student could teach it to someone else. The chain must remain unbroken: someone must preserve the past as time charges forward, as continents and galaxies move further apart, as species die and people kill each other. I didn't want to live out my days in the stuffy libraries of academia; I wanted to set foot on every continent, and maybe I could have done it too, but somehow I let Logan carry me from Portland, Oregon to Newark, Delaware, where he wanted to start "a life." A life, that is, with me. He convinced me to obtain that oh-so-sensible Masters in Education. With his help, I kicked Rachel Solomon to the curb…and all the gusto that came with her.

But really, it wasn't that simple; nothing ever is. And I wasn't that passive; people usually aren't. I made choices too, and I panicked late at night about what I was going to do. I chose the safest route, stayed with the safest guy. A man who was obviously too good for me.

I trail my finger across the planet in plastic, stopping at the places I've visited: Jamaica, Mexico, Costa Rica, Japan, Iceland, Greece, Spain, Italy, and Israel—my fingernail scratches the purple surface of that volatile country. My birthright. Though my feet met these landscapes, it never felt like I was there. I was merely walking inside this synthetic shower curtain, taking generic pictures for a future self to sift through. Even the sea felt artificial.

I'm never really anywhere, am I? My mind is too distracted with itself.

By the time I'm done washing, I feel like I'm about to faint. I ring out my hair and dry off my limbs. Steam fogs the mirror. It's best I don't face my face right now, with all these thoughts I've been thinking.

In the bedroom, I search for my terrycloth bathrobe, which

Logan's mother bought me along with a heated back massager for the big 3-0. Cheers to aging, here's something to make your tired bones all better! Tonight feels like the right night to wear it.

On one of the shelves in the closet I come across our "bag of sex." Inside I find one fuzzy handcuff, a silver vibrator, sexy dice from my bachelorette party, half a bottle of massage oil, chocolate flavored lube, marmalade flavored lube, an empty birth control pack, and a misplaced lipstick. I can't remember the last time we used anything from this bag.

I lie down on my side of the mattress. Our spacious duplex is quiet; the little kids downstairs must be fast asleep, and lord knows their parents don't create any sex sounds. I feel vaguely in the mood now that I'm all by myself, or maybe now that I've looked into the bag, which represents an entirely different Rachel-and-Logan, as if the two of us, once unstable atoms, have together formed a balanced compound. We have, in essence, plateaued. This, I realize, is not a new discovery. Not in the least.

Just as I'm slipping into a reverie about another boy from the pre-Logan years—a Reed boy named Brandon or Brendan who stopped by my dorm one night with a plate of macrobiotic food he had made just for me; a boy I stripped as swiftly as the squatter, but with Brandon/Brendan I remember doing it on the kitchen table while my roommates were out; a boy who used to stare at me across the round table in our ethnomusicology class and who actually wanted to be my boyfriend, though I decided he'd work better as a habitual fuck until he replaced me with a girl who swooned over those rice-heavy dinners, made with love—in comes Logan with the toothpaste. He flips it in the air like a snack for a dolphin and then jumps down onto his side of the bed. It's as if he simply materialized there, filling his rightful place. I rarely get more than an hour alone at home and this was more like twenty minutes.

"Hey cutie." He holds up the toothpaste and gives me a little wink with his little eye.

"Hey you."

"You look spiffy in that thing."

"Thanks."

Staring at him, I can almost see the boy I met eight years ago. I've replayed our "first day" in my mind so many times it feels like fiction.

That afternoon, I was visiting my buddy Blake at the Portland Rehabilitation Center, where he spent a few weeks after a vicious car accident fucked up his legs and back. He was in a wheelchair, but he'd walk again, which was a relief to us recent Reed grads. For the past four years, my circle of friends had never considered *real* tragedy in any real way. Of course I knew differently, and Blake's accident peeled the scab my father's death had caused. I felt raw and riotous. Blake had taken uppers and then gone out for a joy ride, so his accident served as a much-needed reality check for us subcultural kids who equated self-destructive tendencies with real-world experience.

Blake and I had screwed around a bit, but were never remotely in love; it was just one of those male-female friendships I formed in college. The two of us swallowed E and made out all night; free-based THC oil and took a bath; ate shrooms and frolicked naked in the woods...that sort of thing. So I visited him with a stack of comics I'd found on the street and a pot brownie or two. I arrived at the hospital in a D.A.R.E. t-shirt and a very short skirt; not quite the right attire for the place or occasion, but what did I know? My friend Olivia was in tow; she too had fooled around with Blake, and she too worked a non-resume-building job while searching aimlessly for something that required her degree (for Olivia, that was Classics and Philosophy, even more impractical than History).

When we entered the room, there was Logan helping Blake into a wheelchair for the visit. I didn't want to cry over my dad, who had not been so lucky, stare awkwardly at Blake, or acknowledge that he needed a wheelchair like an old man, so I ended up scrutinizing Logan instead. His hair was in a tiny bun and he wore wire rim glasses. I had been expecting some kind of doctor get-up, like a long white lab coat, but he was wearing a crewneck sweater, hemp necklace, khakis, sneakers, and a nametag...pretty dorky, but something about him struck me. Maybe it was because a young attractive guy was literally carrying another young attractive guy and that automatically made him a better person than most. Or maybe it was one of those unexpected moments when you catch a glimpse of your future unrolling before you like a red carpet.

When Logan was done, he wiped a morsel of sweat from his hairline, then stared at me and smiled. Our lines of sight met in the middle. Ten minutes later, while Olivia steered Blake through the landscaped courtyard, I took a little stroll with Logan and admitted that I'd just snuck in a pot brownie. I was testing him to see how innocent or goody-goody he was. Logan laughed softly and winked his little wink from behind that dorky lens, promising he wouldn't tell a soul what I'd done. We traded numbers and met up for coffee. After a prolonged conversation during which we analyzed the pros and cons of waiting to have sex versus getting it out of the way early on, we had really hot sex at his place. I was, I think, in love.

It dawns on me, as if for the first time: I miss that combat-boot girl, that idealistic, masochistic mess who did things her own way and made no apologies. Yes, I miss the me before Logan, before Delaware, before grad school, before the sixteen-year-old students I envy, and before this marriage. Nostalgia must be the theme of the day. Or maybe angst.

"Whatcha thinking?" Logan asks. He reaches over and taps my nose like I'm his little kid.

"I don't know…nothing."

"Oh come on. You babe, you're always thinking something. Tell me."

I want to say, *Well Logan, I miss those days of chaos and misdirection. You see, I feel stagnant, distant, unfazed. Our love is sameness nowadays. My passion has been replaced by a steady paycheck and a robe from your mom.*

He smiles a dopey grin and keeps at it. "Come on, what's twirling around in that magnificent brain of yours? You've been quiet lately."

My dearest, I continue internally, *I regret to inform you that, really and truly, I have nothing of value to say. I am merely hectic thoughts replayed in fast forward. I am capable of only the most basic responses to your most basic questions.*

I sigh and groan. "Nothing, really really nothing."

We leave it at that.

He caresses my bottom lip. His fingertips stick a bit. Then they scurry to my collarbone and slowly trace its shape.

A wave of warmth enters my bloodstream. I want him to whisper, "Hey baby, fuck me," so I can do it right this time. I want to be fucked out of my thoughts, beyond my body, straight up to heaven. I want it to be like some random guy at a party who's been eyeing me for hours, feeding me compliments and booze, trapping me in a doorway while he snakes his arm around my hip and leads me into a bathroom, or closet, or laundry room, or backyard...but then I remember that Logan and I already fucked tonight. For all intents and purposes, I should be satisfied.

Logan leans in for the whisper. I lean in to receive it. His breath excites me.

"Guess what?"

"What?"

"I bought Extra Whitening this time."

I cross my arms over my terrycloth chest. "Great job."

"What's the matter?"

"Nothing." I want to fight. I want to fight so bad and so hard that we end up bloody and bruised and then have the best fucking make-up sex two people can have. But what are we fighting about? Toothpaste? My *attitude*?

"I have another question," he says.

"What?" *Ask me something deep, something real, make me tell you a secret, or make me explain myself all over again, the way I tried to eight years ago.*

"Did you clean your hair out of the drain because I'm always the one who has to snake it out, you know?"

Did he really just ask that? "No, but I will later."

"Thanks babe, you're the best."

He plants a kiss on my forehead like my fairy godmother. And maybe he is. Maybe, despite my tangled thoughts tonight, his kiss is the one thing I've needed all along. But then again, history is destined to repeat itself, and nothing ever changes for long.

"No problem," I say. No problem at all.

BUZZ

A HELICOPTER CIRCLED. Perhaps because it was New Years, perhaps because it was New York. Nina wanted to mention it to Anthony, but walking at this pace pulled the voice from her throat.

She took three gulps of air and asked, "Are you mad at me about Ruby?"

"No." He looked ahead.

The sound of the helicopter oscillated. Nina sang to herself and buttoned her coat. The tips of her fingers stuck out from her gloves and she resisted the urge to gnaw them.

Music, drugs, and alcohol—a customary combination—had fueled the party they'd just left. At midnight, when thirty-some-odd guests stood around a blaring TV and balloons drifted from makeshift ceiling rigs, Nina and Anthony had found one another. No one had noticed their tiny kiss (it was over before it began). None would have guessed he'd been crashing at her pad all week, the floor littered with hastily torn condom wrappers neither of them picked up.

As usual, a drunken Ruby had shown up fashionably late, well after the midnight balloons and awkward kisses. Nina had seen Ruby swing-dance with Trevor and sneak into the bathroom to do blow with Mitch, after which Ruby straddled her on the window seat. She had tried to pry Ruby from her lap when she caught Anthony watching from the kitchen-turned-dance floor, but suddenly Ruby's mouth was on hers, lipstick smearing, before she could hold her down on a chair. By then Anthony had found his way to the tequila, perhaps to occupy his tongue.

It was a new January, a new year, but just as bitter as December. As they walked east, Anthony didn't seem to notice the brash

Brooklyn wind or the scavenging helicopter. He stared straight ahead and said nothing until they reached 181, several blocks from the party. He buzzed, peered through the door's dirty window, and gave Nina that look—one of many. This particular look meant he was drunk, looking to get drunker, and didn't want to answer questions or be held accountable for her fluctuating emotions. At other times, when they sat side-by-side yet didn't speak, he gave her a look that meant *I'm sorry, but this is the way it's got to be.* The only look Nina liked was the one Anthony snuck her secretly among friends, the one that meant *I want you.*

Mitch answered the door wearing his thrift store blazer, white dress shoes, and oversized grin. "I thought you were going to bring over more girls."

Anthony shrugged. "More might come later?"

Mitch shook his head and threw up his hands, one of which landed on Nina's shoulder. He drew her close and she detected a heavy dose of cigarettes and whiskey. "The girls always go where the drugs are," he said, dragging them inside and locking the door.

He led them through a disorganized room, with '60s and '70s album covers tacked to the walls, into a long, dimly lit space. Nina noticed an aluminum ladder lying on its side, as if fallen-down-drunk. They approached an enclave of weathered couches over which Christmas lights cast clashing colors. An archway opened into the recording studio and engineering room. Mitch brought them into the studio.

The room was larger than Nina had expected. Oddly shaped slates of wood, like giant artist palettes, hung from the ceiling. Power cords snaked beneath the Oriental rugs like the floor's risen veins. Amplifiers lounged on these overlapping rugs and a drum kit stood amid freestanding microphones. An upright piano and organ sat across from one another, each pressed against soundproofing foam, while a keyboard stood near a row of guitars. There were crates of percussive instruments, a few tables full of half-spent candles, and one glass wall revealing the soundboards and electronic console in the engineering room.

"Who else is here?" Anthony asked as he walked to the piano and struck a minor chord.

"The owner Hank Loom, Owen and Tate, the band minus Trevor, and that girl Maddie. Where's Ruby Tuesday?"

"Don't ask," Nina muttered. Anthony ignored the question and plopped down on the piano bench.

"Hey hey, play some Cal stuff," Mitch declared, handing Nina a tambourine and moving toward his guitar. The surface of his blue acoustic bore numerous scratch marks, dents, and initials. Remnants of duct tape clung to the body, demarcating the spot where he'd proudly displayed photographs of girlfriends, one after the next. Mitch always liked to think of the girls adrift in the audience, beaming when they saw their face plastered on his guitar.

Mitch pulled the strap over his shoulder and started strumming. He bounced around, a shoelace dangling from the guitar neck, nylon strings jutting from the tuning keys, his eyes half-open and vocal chords about to gush as he let loose on the first verse of "New Matter." When Cal had written these lyrics, the boys in his band, Fissure, hadn't known anyone else in their Midwestern town. The song had been written over a year ago, just after Cal drove across the country with Fissure, which Mitch would later attempt to seize and christen Moonshine. Mitch only managed to pluck Trevor from Fissure's ashes because Anthony and the drummer wanted nothing to do with his reincarnation.

Fissure had hoped to sequester for a year, if not longer, which they thought all serious bands should do. Nina had argued with Cal about the decision to move from the tri-state area to the middle of nowhere. "Do you know how many bands come from the middle of nowhere to try to make it in New York, and you guys are already here!" Of course Cal hadn't listened, failing to grasp that deep down she simply wanted him to stay. To Nina, the Midwest felt like Mars.

That summer—holed up in their ramshackle house near a lake in Wisconsin, smoking hash and drinking beer—the band churned out dizzying commotions of distortion. Layer upon layer, the sounds swirled and amassed, brimming with tension. Soaring melodies would escalate to maddening heights, pressing against the ceiling and swimming along the walls until the cacophonies infiltrated the slumbering neighborhood.

But when alone, Cal wrote the prettiest, simplest songs—tiny windows into his otherwise impenetrable soul. If the boys set down guitar picks and drum sticks at three a.m., Cal would slink to the humid basement and sit at his electric typewriter for another two hours. He would garner lyrics from his dreams, finger-pick his

Washburn acoustic or A-style mandolin, and record on a four-track. These songs made their way onto several conceptual demos packaged with homemade cover art. Pen-and-ink monsters acted as distorted self-portraits; each bore Cal's bright blue eyes.

Nobody in the group, not the members of Fissure or Nina, who didn't make it to Wisconsin in time, witnessed Cal's creative process. Like much of his life, it was confined to basements or attics: any musty place he could occupy alone.

Nina gripped the tambourine and glared at Mitch, who was botching words as he attempted to emulate Cal. He let out a yelp between verses, Cal-style.

Cal was in a different kind of middle of nowhere now, but Nina wondered if he was glancing through the pitch-black skylight, as high as the helicopter, or sitting next to Anthony at the piano. Anthony, who had taken over Cal's bedroom for six months before the boys parted ways and Fissure broke up. Anthony, who didn't have the heart to take Cal's drawings off the wall. Anthony, who never seemed to realize what it meant to Nina, when she finally arrived.

As Mitch carried on, Anthony's fingers danced across the keys. His dark hair had grown long and chaotic, hanging in a clump over his eyes. His outstretched hands flew as his foot pumped the sustaining pedal, occasionally drifting to the una corda to soften the fury. Nina watched him, hoping Cal could find his way into her peripheral vision.

Mitch shouted from the center of the room, "Nina, play that thing already!"

She threw down her bag and beat the tambourine in her hands, dancing around him on the rug. It was a rare chance to chime in with the boys, to feel as young and alive as she thought she ought to feel. A chance to play music in a room drenched in history—a room none of them had truly earned.

"I'm Nico!" she shouted, keeping perfect time. Her long hair swung and the scenery blurred. Mitch nodded and raised his gaze to the ceiling, as he often did in the midst of performing. Knees bent, he threw his wrist into motion, tearing at the steel strings with calloused fingertips. Nina thought she could hear Cal's voice curl around Mitch's like a snake.

Three minutes later, when they reached the final note, Mitch crumpled theatrically to the floor. He played dead for two seconds, then bolted upright and dashed off.

Nina stood idle, lowering her instrument. There was no reverberation, no remainder of their rendition; she was Nico no longer, and Cal was still gone.

Anthony shifted key and began playing some classical adaptation. She wanted to take that empty place by his side, to press her fingertips to the black and white keys; it was safe now, since they were the only ones in the room. More than that, she wanted to climb backward through time into his Fissure-house bedroom, dawn bursting through the blinds, summer sunlight in her eyes, she and Anthony sweat-stained and humming Cal's songs, mourning him together. She wanted the two of them, one inside the other, to be inside of her again. Under the sheets, under the painted ceiling, under the sloping rooftop and the moonless blue hour of new-day, under the searchlights of any helicopters that had been persistently hunting the night. Instead, she left Anthony at the piano, alone. All the boys Nina loved came with big broken hearts.

A Sonic Youth record spun—Nina couldn't tell which—in the engineering room, where Hank Loom sat with feet propped on his console. His gray ponytail hung down the back of the chair as he blew into a silver harmonica. Nearby, a wall of stereo equipment and shelves were at full capacity, while two computer screens, bookending the mixing board, emitted royal blue light.

Everyone sat around a coffee table strewn with naked discs. Two empty CD cases, marred by razors, were covered with fine powder. Owen and Tate were huddled at one end of a sinking sofa; Tate had short, bleached hair that resembled a wig and Owen had a boyish face that almost looked innocent. Maddie, the token groupie Nina hoped she'd never become, and Gabe, Moonshine's bassist, were draped arms over knees on the other end of the couch. And then there was Flip, Moonshine's drummer, balancing his body on an exercise ball; his bandmates often called him the Scottish Bob Dylan thanks to his untamed poof of orange-red hair. Mitch was crouching on the shabby carpet, shaking dust from a vial.

Nina moved an empty flask and sat down on an unoccupied folding chair. No one said hello. Hank's harmonica served as irritating background noise, Mitch was busy cutting lines, and Owen and Tate seemed lost in some other world. As usual, a heated debate was well underway between Gabe and Flip. Maddie, in a skirt even shorter than Nina's, smiled plenty, but didn't say a word.

"Okay," Flip said, rocking back and forth on the oversized ball, "Ray Manzarek versus Brian Jones, go."

"Jones, no question," Gabe answered.

"Jones? Are you high?"

Everyone laughed, except for Nina, who wasn't high and who was waiting for her turn to answer.

"Come on," Flip said, "if it wasn't for Manzarek, The Doors would be nothing, nowhere, nonexistent."

"Yeah, yeah, yeah."

"How 'bout Bowie versus Bolan?" Flip continued, fiddling with his lip ring.

"Bolan came first."

"That doesn't make him better."

"There's no question." Gabe pushed up his vintage horn-rimmed glasses. "If it weren't for Marc Bolan and T. Rex, there wouldn't have been Bowie. End of story, Bolan wins by default. Can we speed this up to date?"

"You're way off, but okay. Thom Yorke versus Thurston Moore."

"Yorke, for sure."

"You are so fucked up!" Flip rolled his head in his hands.

"Radiohead is the modern generation's Pink Floyd," Nina said, then immediately felt foolish. She wasn't a real musician, and she knew they didn't consider her qualified to offer such opinions. She wanted to explain that music was her one true love, yet she'd spent her whole life in a dark audience watching men perform. She pulled lint off her purple stockings as Mitch handed Owen a jewel case bearing six skinny lines.

Owen placed the case on the table, re-rolled a dollar bill, and lowered his head. His nostril gobbled the powder in one fell sniff. He rubbed his finger in the residue, careful not to disrupt the other lines, and smeared it across his gums. He motioned to Tate, who took the bill, pushed her bobbed, bleached hair behind her ears, and hunched over. She lingered above the white line, inhaling in little spurts: pinching her nose, tossing her head, sniffling, running her fingertip through the ghost of the drug, and wiping it against her teeth.

"Yo Hank, put some Pixies on," Flip said, slapping his thighs like a snare drum. He sang, "I got a broken face, uh huh uh huh ooh!" while Gabe and Maddie took their turns with the dust.

Owen's eyes met Nina's—his were bloodshot and shimmering. He offered the slightest sliver of a smile, muscles bulging at the edges of his face. They barely knew each other, had never really spoken; he was Hank's apprentice and had helped record Moonshine's EP. He hadn't been at the party down the street.

It was like seeing Cal for the first time. Owen was thinner, haggard, strung out on cocaine rather than hash, but still she found the same wild eyes, the same secret smile tossed across the room. She could never identify the meaning, the longing, the exigency, the innermost echo of words half-uttered and hardly remembered. Only in poetry could she spit out and promptly stash away the moments she didn't dare speak of.

One September night three years ago, she had followed Cal along sidewalks and back roads, all the way up a stairwell to a rooftop, trespassing to the one place he would go to be alone. This was back before the move, before the Fissure house, before his cells devoured him, before the city consumed almost everyone else. His eyes had said *I want you* and he'd carried a condom in his pocket. The rooftop was damp, seeping into her pores. She had tried to stop him, if only for a minute. He stuck his tongue down her throat and told her not to worry, not to think so much. So she caved, and they fucked in front of the moon. But the aftermath wasn't pretty. His girlfriend never found out, but Nina often woke in the middle of the night with her fingernails digging deep into her flesh. Thick red lines ran the length of an arm, from collarbone to collarbone, and from hairline to spine.

They'd kept on with it: rooftops and basements, dirty hair, cold walks home, four a.m. showers (so the girl wouldn't detect Nina's scent), and once, in his bedroom, she had fished bracelets from the space between mattress and wall, double-checking her ears for missing rings. Their mutual friends never told, never let on that they knew. But they did.

Anthony rested on A flat. He needed a cigarette. Shaking his hair from his face, he lit one and kept playing. Chord after chord, sound waves spiraled out.

Like always, his thoughts wandered to Ruby. He thought of her at the party, in ripped kaleidoscopic leggings and a furry vest. Ruby, a black pearl pinned to her cartilage. Ruby, a twin, Aries, former dancer, wannabe artist. Ruby, an F minor seventh. He saw Ruby parading around in his clothes. Ruby eating a snow cone, charting his horoscope, collecting soda tabs and bottle caps, rubbing his feet with homeopathic oil. Ruby with a xylophone in her eyes and castanets for teeth. Ruby underneath him, above him, before the move, before the next several rooms he would occupy alone. Ruby with a perfect spine and splotchy birthmark on her right inner thigh. Ruby who spoke to him now only when he spoke first.

F minor seventh, sustained.

Anthony lifted his foot from the pedal, rose from the bench, and let the sound die. He walked into the engineering room. Nina was sitting with her back to him, but she quickly turned her head and looked him in the eye—a look that meant, *Are you okay?* He tried to ignore her. Hank waved him over.

"We should record you sometime," Hank said, cleaning the spit from his harmonica and chewing the lone filter of a cigarette. "Just you, doing your thing on the piano."

"That would be cool," Anthony said. Cal would have liked Hank, he thought, even if he'd despise Moonshine.

"I mean it, man. You're really something."

"Thanks."

"Next time you're in New York, have the guys let me know."

Flip walked over and stood between them, balancing the scratched CD case on his upturned palms. In an exaggerated version of his slight Kentucky drawl, he said, "I believe this is for you, colonel."

"Wait, isn't Hank our chaperone for tonight?" Gabe shouted from the couch.

"Only by default," Hank said, laughing. He grabbed the dollar bill from behind Flip's ear, took the case, and snorted a line. "I have to head out so you guys will be on your own. Try not to wreck the place."

"Hank, if you didn't have a wife and kids I'd tell one of these fine ladies to service you first," Mitch said, gesturing toward Nina, Tate, and Maddie. Nina rolled her eyes. "This great man right here," he said a notch louder, "this is the man behind the green curtain, the great and powerful wizard responsible for Moonshine's success!"

"Here, here!" Flip said, raising his beer and making trumpet sounds. As everyone lifted their bottles to toast, Flip attempted to stand on the exercise ball. He crashed to the floor.

"Don't cheer to me, let's cheer to Moonshine," Hank said while lending Flip a hand.

"To Moonshine," Mitch announced, louder than before. "Better than any of these fucking hipster bands, better than ninety percent of music today, better than Fissure!"

Anthony groaned under his breath. Nina glared at Mitch for belittling Fissure and indirectly Cal. Mitch blew her a kiss.

Hank sniffed one last line and reminded Owen to turn off the equipment and lock the door before they left. Flip commandeered Hank's rolling chair and spun himself in circles. Anthony coldly asked Mitch for more coke and Mitch handed him the half-empty vial. Anthony took two key bumps and returned the vial to Mitch, always the supplier.

Nina might have tried it, if anyone had offered. Perhaps she could transform into somebody new, the way she did in poems. The way she looked at things symbolically, detecting patterns across the landscape of her life. The way she floated above the rooms, omniscient and observing. But none of them offered. They all knew Nina didn't do drugs. So she sat there like a patient ghost, wondering when one of them might need her. If she kissed Anthony for real tonight, her lips would buzz.

Mitch scrolled through contacts on his phone to convince people from the party to come to the studio. "Ruby, Ruby, Ruby, Ruby!" he sang into her voicemail. He tried Trevor next. "I bet they're passed out," he lamented.

Anthony recalled Ruby dancing with Trevor in the kitchen at the party. The group's sexual politics were agonizingly liberal, though he'd made the first move toward "open season on friends" by sleeping with Nina in that doomed house, in Cal's old bed. Ruby was free to do whatever she pleased, with Trevor or with anyone. He had done this to himself. Leaning back, he waited to taste the nasty drip.

Maddie whispered into Gabe's ear and the two stood up, holding hands. They moseyed out the door as if no one else existed. Anthony grabbed a beer and stole their empty seat on the couch. Flip skimmed through vinyl. Mitch tried several more contacts until contending to retrieve his blue acoustic from the studio. He returned with a pick between his teeth and plopped down on the exercise ball. Owen asked for the vial and helped himself to another bump. He rolled off a list of potential record choices to Flip, who presented album after album like Vanna White. Tate broke her silence and asked Anthony for a smoke; a tiny flame came alive and just as suddenly died. Owen jumped up to wrestle Foreigner from Flip. Nina watched all of them, chewing her lip.

Tate always caught people in the act of it—Anthony was staring. Tate's hands were warped and pinkish, and the skin looked smeared. He was probably wondering if the scarring spread elsewhere.

"I know it's bad," she said in a gravelly voice. "I suppose you want to know the story."

"No, you don't have to tell me," Anthony said, embarrassed that she'd caught him staring. "You hardly know me."

The two had met briefly at a bar three days earlier, the place where everyone had landed for the night. Tate knew Anthony was visiting from some other city, and she preferred talking to people she wouldn't have to see again. She also preferred talking when she was high, and only to one person at a time.

"That's why I can tell you," she said, then took a drag of her cigarette. With her left hand, she held her roaming jaw in place.

From the other side of the coffee table, Nina watched the girl's lower jaw shift sideways, top and bottom teeth scraping. Tate had an ancient face: long straight nose, close-set eyes, high cheekbones. She could have been from any generation, any era of time, any European civilization, except of course for the bleached hair and plastic jewelry. She could have been born a thousand times.

"It was over a year ago," Tate whispered, leaning in close, her dilated pupils like two black lakes. "I was stupid, I'd lit a candle or two. I liked to, you know, unwind at the end of the day. I'd been drinking, I guess I was pretty drunk, and then I passed out. This was back when I was living alone in Chicago. I worked for this asshole photographer I was dating...fucking, to be exact."

Anthony tried to swallow the unsavory taste in his mouth. Owen and Flip continued to quarrel over records. Mitch strummed one of his songs and faced Nina, who couldn't quite hear Tate over his voice.

"I woke up in the hospital the next day and realized I'd been in a coma. Smoke inhalation, you know. It was a three-family house, and the whole thing went up in flames. Everyone got out except me. During the coma I kept drifting up to the surface, hearing faint voices and making shapes in my mind from those sounds, but then the current would pull me back down to the ocean floor. When I was fully conscious, I saw my mom sitting in a chair beside my bed. It took me awhile to understand what had happened. Really, I had no idea, no memory of anything leading up to the fire. I must have been at that guy's studio all day, and I think we had a fight or something. We must have, we always fought, it kind of got us going. Anyway, he never visited me in the hospital."

Anthony hated the idea that someone you loved, someone like Ruby, could abandon you like that. But then again, Tate hadn't said the word love.

"Maybe he thought it was his fault and felt guilty," he offered.

"No, he just didn't care. I didn't show up for work the next day and he probably assumed I'd had enough of him and skipped town. He was fifteen years older than me and seeing another woman."

"I see," Anthony said, trying not to judge her. "What did you do after you realized what had happened?"

"Oh god, I was terrified. I mean, fast forward through time and space and I'm in a hospital with third-degree burns on forty percent of my body? I started screaming when I saw all the bandages. I was a monster."

She paused and blew smoke in deformed circles. "And then I heard my voice, you know, my speaking voice. I didn't used to sound like this...something rattling around in my throat, like an aluminum can. The doctors said it was temporary damage to the vocal chords. I guess not so temporary. When I calmed down, my mother said, 'At least it didn't get your face.' As if it had been some kind of disease, some *thing* unto itself, like an animal...at least it didn't bite me there!" She let out a terse laugh, coughed and said,

"At least I can pass for normal, that's what she meant."

"But you're not," Anthony said. "I don't mean you're...you look fine. It's just that you've been through all of this. You're forever changed. You're not the same person at all."

"Oh, I know. I woke up in a different body and a different reality. Like a parallel fucking universe." Tate inched closer to Anthony and lowered her voice, as Mitch shouted at Flip to shut off the music so he could hear himself play. "I moved from the ICU to the Burn Unit for a few weeks. When I left, I had to go to physical therapy for my arms and hands. I couldn't work, I couldn't do photography, and I didn't want to either. Two months ago, I moved in with Owen. I lived in Brooklyn before Chicago, but it's different now. I mean, I used to go out, pick up guys or whatever, and now I'm afraid of them seeing my body and feeling the scars. It's torturous, trying to gauge how they'll react."

"But you said you're with Owen."

"Oh yeah, we're friends. Only friends. Besides, he's too young for me."

Tate looked at Nina across the table. Their eyes met before Nina lowered hers and began picking her cuticles. When Nina looked up again, she shifted her gaze sideways to Mitch, who clearly wanted her attention. He swayed on the exercise ball, singing directly at her, while Owen and Flip loitered by the mixing board passionately discussing the evolution of math rock.

"Are you with that chick?" Tate whispered to Anthony. She scratched her mop of hair, motioning with her head to avoid being obvious. "She's been kind of...staring."

Anthony looked at Nina: purple legs tightly crossed, fingertips in the midst of being ravaged, full bottom lip in its typical pout. He thought of Nina's mattress on the floor. The way she wanted the wall side. The way she would crawl over him to use the bathroom. The way her hipbones fit inside his. The way she would trace the tattoo on his chest. The way she licked his ear when he fucked her. The way she left marks on his neck, even when he asked her not to.

"No...well...no, I'm not. She does that. Staring, I mean." He cleared his throat and abruptly changed the subject. "Do you want to hear my story? The similarities might shock you."

"Sure."

Anthony took a deep breath, which hurt somewhere deep in his chest. "I was seven, I lived way upstate and spent a lot of time outside in the summer. I was playing with friends in this huge lot where they were building a school. The construction must have been on hold because nobody was working there, and we were running around, climbing on top of things and jumping off, like you do when you're seven. I don't remember that day...I remember other days when the three of us did this sort of thing, but I don't remember the day it happened. I fell off one of the high platforms, flat to the dirt. That put me in a coma for a couple days."

"Oh my god," Tate said, gripping her jaw. Nina's eyes shot in their direction. "You were lucky."

"I know."

"What was it like when you woke up?"

"Well, I remember my mom and older sister on the bed. There was a tube in my throat. It felt so weird; I wanted to swallow, but couldn't. They pulled it out and a horrible chill ran through my whole body. My throat was scratched up for days."

"How bad were you hurt?"

"My right leg was broken in half, there were steel pins holding the bones together. Other than that, it was all bruises and scrapes, plus a serious concussion. I was in the hospital for almost three months. I had to relearn to walk, broken leg and all."

"Jesus Christ, that's awful. And you were so young. You remember all of that?"

"Not all of it. But I remember things like...you know those tile games where you have to slide the square pieces to make a picture? My sister gave me one of those when I woke up. She was waiting there to give it to me. The tiles formed the face of a tiger. I liked tigers, I remember that."

They looked down at the carpet, at the couch's crisscross stitching, at Tate's wounded hand lying flat on her jeans. They listened to Mitch's song and caught bits of Owen and Flip's conversation. No one could hear the helicopter, still rattling the sky.

"It's the dying and coming back," Tate said after a few minutes, when the words took shape in her head. "Or, the *practically* dying, the almost dying, the near-death lingering, and the coming back in a state very different than before."

"Yes," Anthony said, "and no matter what changed inside you, there's never enough evidence to show it."

"Most people, they die and then they're dead. There's no coming back."

"Most people."

They fell silent, as ghosts loomed above.

Anthony wanted to ask Tate if Cal had been some sort of sacrifice—statistically, one of them had to die first. Perhaps Cal had raised his hand, held his breath, and taken the plunge to save everyone else. Perhaps he and Nina and Ruby and Trevor and even Tate were only alive right now because Cal was gone.

Anthony had always admired Cal: a crooner and a charmer wise beyond his years. He'd preached experience over education and actually lived it, working manual labor jobs while the rest of them studied to fulfill their parents' dreams (or so they had thought). But now he would never write more songs or tell more stories or bask in the heat of stage lights and applause. Anthony admired him for the way he'd lived his whirlwind life, but also for succumbing to death, for burning out rather than fading away. Anthony had tried on death as a child, but Cal had gone all the way. Though it hadn't been his choice, Anthony knew Cal would have wanted to go first.

He tried to shake the morbid notion from his head—he always thought of Cal more in the company of their shared friends—and grabbed another beer.

Tate asked Mitch for more blow. Flip spun in the chair. Mitch lowered his guitar and fished the vial from his blazer. Flip placed the needle on a Patti Smith record, asking, "Wasn't *Horses* recorded here?" Mitch let Owen divvy up the lines, declaring, "That's one hell of a rail!"

Nina watched them crave their collective buzz: those miniscule vibrations like swarming bees sending every atom into a tizzy. The bees could fly up their noses and down their throats—high-pitched purrs inside their heads. She couldn't stand to watch them anymore, so she left to find a bathroom.

When Nina opened the door, she caught Maddie straddling Gabe on the lid of the toilet. Gabe still wore all his clothes, glasses on his head, while Maddie was down to a lacy black bra that matched her skirt and thigh-highs. Gabe was clutching a large chunk of her hair.

"Shit, I'm sorry," Nina stammered, cheeks flushed. Couldn't they have locked the fucking door? She glanced at the sink, expecting a used or yet-to-be-used condom. Maddie turned her head and grinned.

Jealousy twisted like a knife in Nina's gut. She wanted to scream.

It could have been her and Anthony in there; he could have said *I want you*, could have led her by the hand, could have ripped off her shirt and left the door unlocked in the heat of the moment. They'd fucked just yesterday and the day before that, her hands against the wall and his hair in her eyes. In a breathy whisper he'd said, "You're so hot." Not beautiful, not special, not incredible. Not loved.

They had been friends for five years, and she'd often been the third wheel on his and Ruby's dates. Back then, she had loved their love. To her, sex was sacred act—two separate beings could create one self, however impermanent. But then she'd gone up to that rooftop with Cal. Then she'd left his room at three a.m. with arms crossed and head bowed. Then she'd fucked him at a party much like this, their friends left wondering, *where's Nina, where's Cal?* And then she'd found herself entangled with Anthony in Wisconsin, chasing a memory of shame and loss. Their intimacy surprised her—she hadn't known Anthony could *move* like that—but the more they touched the fewer words they said aloud.

Now she understood the truth: sex was anything but sacred. Somehow that didn't seem to bother Gabe, Maddie, or anyone else in their group of friends. The others were thriving in debauchery, free-falling into temptation, allowing their hearts to wither and decay as if they'd never intended to use them at all.

"Hey Nina, are you gonna leave anytime soon?" Gabe asked matter-of-factly, still clutching Maddie's hair.

"Unless you want to join us," Maddie joked.

Nina slammed the door. Alone, she sank to the concrete floor. The cold stabbed her knees.

Anthony stalked the mixing board, pacing like a caged animal.

Owen and Tate slouched over the table, lapping up powder. Flip stood on the folding chair, emphatically telling a tale about feral children. Mitch stared at nothing, fingers scooting up his guitar's wooden neck. Nina was nowhere to be found.

Gabe and Maddie sauntered into the engineering room holding

clammy hands. Mitch snapped back to life and immediately gave Gabe an overenthusiastic thumbs-up, his face breaking into a clownish smile.

"Way to go, buddy," he said to Gabe, "she's my favorite too."

Blood rushed to Gabe's face. He lunged at Mitch, grabbed his thumb, and bent it back with force. It looked like he wanted to break it off.

"Fuck you, stop!" Mitch cried as his guitar hit the floor.

But Gabe didn't stop. Mitch yelped like a dog.

Flip stood stock-still, his orange hair on end. From the corner of the room, Anthony watched with a smirk. Cal would have gotten a kick out of this. He would have cheered Gabe on.

"Fucking stop!" Mitch shouted.

Gabe released his grip as Mitch tumbled backwards off the ball and landed on his head. Owen and Tate, freshly tweaked, couldn't stop laughing. Tate smashed one discolored hand against her gums to stifle the sound. Anthony looked on in awe, wondering if Gabe would bash Mitch's head into the floor. He started to feel a little bad for Mitch—he was obviously down for the count, and humiliated at that.

But a second later Mitch picked himself up, regained his balance, and charged at Gabe. Taller and stronger, Gabe raised his elbow like a shield and easily blocked Mitch's half-formed fists.

"What's your problem?" Mitch huffed. He resorted to tugging his blazer and smoothing his hair.

"You're a disrespectful, narcissistic fuck, that's my problem. And quit being a pussy, I didn't even hurt you."

"Unlike replaceable bassists, *these* fingers are actually worth something in this world." Mitch spit on the floor, lifted his guitar, and swung it over his shoulder as he stormed out of the room.

In the studio, Nina atop of a table between a browning cactus and a Virgin Mary candle. She had closed the door behind her, and though she could see everyone through the glass wall and sense some commotion in the engineering room, she couldn't hear Mitch's shouts or Owen's laughter. There was only a low drone, slow hum, which sat on the air like syrup. Perhaps it was the amplifiers' buzz. Perhaps the sound of silence. Perhaps the room remembered everything it heard.

She watched Anthony pace like a fish swimming complacent laps, misremembering himself and his globular little world with every lap. Was he thinking of her? she wondered. Or was he thinking of Ruby again? Was he wondering if Ruby and Trevor had tasted one another in the bathroom at the party? Did his wondering mirror her own, and, if so, could he feel her there wondering, watching his sharp turns and quick steps? Or perhaps he was also remembering Cal, whose death had brought them together and then pried them apart.

Now that she was alone, she had time and space to ask herself *why*...why did she care so much? Why did she keep going back to the same painful moments and the same hurtful people? The same songs and stories, shows and parties?

They'd shared jokes and hopes, ash and smoke, beds and couches, confessions and secrets, early morning rituals and late nights of mischief, and then they shared one tragic death. They all shared *him*. But why had she fallen into some lopsided version of love—that masochistic emotion—with Cal and then with Anthony?

She didn't have to rack her mind too hard for an answer. She was in love with Cal's art, with the way his art defined him, or at least rendered him more sensitive than he'd ever let on. She loved the way his fingers moved along the strings, the way his drawings took shape on the page, the way his voice spilled out so free. She was in love with him for what she wanted to be. Cal could express himself without fear, and she needed his voice to make sense of her own. She wanted to sing loud and clear into the blackest night, so loud that the whole world would shake and then wake to her melody. But Nina couldn't sing...and for the two years she'd loved Cal, she'd been the moon to his sun, the darkness to his light, the open ears to his every song. She hadn't known how to say no to him, even when it might have saved her, and when Cal's hands and voice disappeared off the earth, like many musicians they'd admired, she was left in the wake of wanting so much more.

Nina hopped off the table and marched resolutely to the piano. At first she tapped the keys, lowering each with delicate precision. Then she pressed one key at a time, causing single notes to float like tendrils of smoke.

Her hands guided her as if a ghost had been waiting for his song to be released. She wanted music to fly from her body the way it did from Mitch's, Anthony's, Cal's. Cal didn't even have a body anymore; the moments between remembering and forgetting him, between realizing his mortality and inventing his presence, were disquieting still. One night, early in their friendship, she, Ruby, and Anthony had slept on Cal's mattress while he worked some shitty job. When he entered the dim room at dawn and found them lying there together, lullabies escaped his throat like fireflies lighting the dusky sky.

On a tattered couch in the long entryway, Mitch held his guitar. He couldn't quite bring himself to play it. He listened to the sounds in the engineering room: a Black Sabbath record, which Owen probably chose, grating coughs that could only be Tate's, Flip's ongoing story and the word "glockenspiel" over and over. Occasionally, he heard an upsurge of laughter. He imagined them laughing at his childish departure, but attributed such paranoia only to the drugs. He fingered his pocket for the vial, then realized he'd left it for them to devour. He groaned, crossed his arms on the upright edge of his guitar, and lowered his head.

"You okay?"

He perked up as the girl walked in. He couldn't quite see her face; one light bulb hung at the other end of the room and the flickering Christmas lights distorted all perceptions.

"Nina?" he called out, as if she were farther away. "Is that you? Come here."

Nina sighed and sat down. She leaned back against the prickly couch and counted the blinks of the tiny twinkling lights.

Winter seeped through the walls. She wrapped her arms around her chest and double-crossed her legs, patches of dirt on purple knees. Part of her wished she had never followed Anthony to this studio, but there was no going back to the beginning of the night, just like there was no going back to the rooftop's watchful moon, or the abandoned bedroom's lambent sun. Anthony could never become Cal—only symbolically, in poetry. He could spit Cal's ghost to the ceiling, or enter her body as if playing Cal's role, but his body was his body, and no one else's. Nina thought she must be the only one who wouldn't accept fate, who would never reduce Cal to an echo.

"What are you thinking?" Mitch asked. His sudden interest took her by surprise.

"Do you really want to know?"

"I wouldn't have asked if I didn't."

"I was thinking about Cal," she said bluntly, feeling relieved to speak honestly. "I was wondering why no one really talks about him anymore. He's supposed to be here with us; it's only been a year since he died. No one thinks about him in moments like this...not as much as I do."

"Ah," he said, nodding. "Why do you think that is?"

"Because what we had, or *didn't* have...there's no way to define it. I held our story inside of me. It was supposed to be a secret, but everybody knew."

"I didn't know."

"You weren't there."

Mitch and most of Moonshine were newer friends, and she liked the idea of him not knowing. She thought of Cal's cells, how the cancer lay hidden for months, or possibly even years, as Cal played cat and mouse with life.

"It's funny, I was thinking of Julia before," Mitch said, sucking air through his irritated nostrils.

"Who's Julia?"

"My dead ex-girlfriend decaying in a box."

"That's not funny."

"But she is. She'll be nothing but bones soon enough. She died in October. The maggots must be stuffed by now. Fatso maggots."

"Shut up, that's disgusting."

"That's the only way I can talk about it, Nina." Mitch's voice changed pitch. No longer forced and abrasive, his tone softened like snow. "She was my first love. I can't believe she's dead."

Nina sighed again. "It's like there's this little hole inside of you, sucking up all the memories, every real moment you can remember having shared, and ones you didn't but wish you had, or ones you did but wish you hadn't...all the bullshit, and the final moments you can only imagine...the person exists inside of that hole, and nowhere else."

She thought of Cal as he lay suffering many miles from her touch. His girlfriend had been there, though by then she wasn't his girlfriend anymore. Anthony and Trevor had been there too, keeping watch in that Wisconsin hospital. Anthony had been the one to call Nina and tell her, "He's dying." Cal, filled with morphine, had said, "I don't understand it"—his final four words. His family and friends had coaxed him into slumber, weaned him into death, helping him let go of life. That winter, the year died with him. Their secret did too. He was twenty-two, and would be forever. He didn't exist in this brand new year.

"I had her initials tattooed on my arm," Mitch said, avoiding Nina's eyes. "That was well before she died. I have other initials, you've seen 'em. I guess it's something about absorbing someone's energy, someone you admire...it's like owning them, or proving you know them. Proving they know *you.* But it doesn't work. Nothing is permanent, not even a tattoo."

Nina thought of Cal's unfinished songs, and the ones he would never have the chance to write. Their friendship, or love, or whatever that *was*, had been left unfinished too. She glanced at the guitar resting atop Mitch's knees, eyeing its carved letters and duct tape residue.

"Did you have her picture there?" she asked, pointing to the prized spot.

Mitch touched the sticky shape. "Yeah, long after we broke up. My next girlfriend tore it off and ripped it to shreds."

"How did she—"

"Aneurysm. One day she just collapsed. A swollen blood vessel. Popped, like a balloon." He made a smacking noise with his lips.

"I thought it was because of the drugs," he continued. "She had a heroin problem years ago, when we were together. This other jackass had gotten her hooked on the stuff. At first I used to do it with her, but I had control over it and she didn't, so I stopped. I knew she needed to stop too so I locked her in her room for a week. This was in her parents' house...they'd gone to Europe and left her there alone, so I stayed with her the whole time, cutting school and everything."

"And she went through withdrawal? Cold turkey?"

"Yup. I had to carry her back and forth to the bathroom because she couldn't make it by herself. I had to wash the sheets and the carpet, rinse off her sweat. By the end of the week, though, she was okay."

"And she stayed clean?"

"She did while we were together. I broke up with her when I moved to London for six months...okay, I didn't so much break up with her as take off without explanation. Either way, we didn't talk much after that, so I don't know if she dipped back into it or not."

Nina suddenly remembered Cal's typewriter, and how it was almost hers. He had offered to sell it to her just before the grand odyssey that ended in tragedy, but then he'd recognized its value and taken back the offer. It ended up in the basement of the Fissure house and was still sitting on the table when she visited the following summer. One morning, while Anthony slept, she had typed a paperless letter to Cal, pressing his leftover fingerprints.

"You're a pretty good guy when you're not acting like a jerk," Nina said, with more confidence.

"I am a good guy, deep down. I can't even look at you right now, I'm being so honest."

Mitch thought of the way Anthony looked at Nina—his eyes always rested on her face, but his mouth never said much when people were around.

"Can I ask you a question?" Mitch asked.

"Okay."

"What do you want?"

She couldn't believe someone had asked.

She wanted the aching to pass and the ghosts to materialize so she didn't have to remember so much. She wanted music at every moment of every day, and a song written just for her. She wanted Anthony to admit that all of this—their moments in Cal's room and in her bedroom this week—had amounted to something sacred. Or, at the very least, she wanted him to admit that he'd been curious to feel what Cal had felt. That together, the two of them could recreate Cal. That all might be resurrected.

"Chamomile tea," she told Mitch. "What do *you* want?"

"For this godforsaken night to be over." He smiled for her sake, like he did for Julia in that locked room.

"It must be near dawn by now," she said.

"Yeah, but does it matter?"

They looked at one another. They both knew that in this windowless cave in Bushwick, with infinite sounds, streams of smoke, amphetamine laughter, and the ghosts of dead idols watching from the walls, time ceased to mean anything to anyone, least of all the living.

"Happy New Year, Nina."

"Happy New Year." They could have leaned in to kiss, but didn't.

Nina considered waiting for Anthony like she'd done at parties and bars and Moonshine shows for the past few nights. But wasn't she sick of waiting for boys like him? Yes, Nina thought: she was sick of watching them play, sick of hearing them talk, sick of kissing their mouths, sick of praising their art, sick of stroking their egos and mothering their wounds. She was sick of secrets and drugs and loss and love, sick of wondering when they might understand who she was.

As Mitch plucked his strings with newfound strength, Nina left the couch and waltzed past the open door of the engineering room. She picked up her jacket and bag in full view of Anthony, then turned on her heel and walked out.

Nina took one last glance into the studio. Through the skylight came a gentle blue; she'd been right about the dawn. She expected to endure a chilly walk to the L and then a ride on the train where she'd stick out as one of those girls who hadn't yet slept, who was going home alone. Tonight, or rather this morning, Nina didn't mind. She didn't look back, and she didn't say goodbye.

ACKNOWLEDGMENTS

First and foremost, I must thank Amanda Miller for her friendship, guidance, suggestions, massages, and writing dates. Along with Amanda, I must thank the other wonderful Ponies in our writing group, Scott Hess and Britt Canty, as well as Ponies of the past—Thea Cook, Nicole DeWalt, and Naomi Kriss—for the invaluable editorial feedback and unconditional support over the past several years. My writing would not be the same without you, Ponies! Also, thanks to Lorin Taylor, Emese Tot, and Tyler Nesler for your creative contributions to this project.

I am grateful to my former professors Darryl Pinckney, Dale Peck, and Mary LaChapelle for your thoughts on a few of these stories, and I'm equally grateful to professors who taught me a great deal about fiction—Kathleen Hill, Shelley Jackson, Nelly Reifler, and Helen Schulman—as well as the teachers and mentors who not only instilled a lifelong love of language but encouraged me as an aspiring writer: Ellen O'Connell, Pamela Matott, Marion O'Connor, Mary Therese Goldman, Eileen Curran, and Jackie Morelli. The New York City Writopia Lab community has also been vital for the past four years, and I must thank Rebecca Wallace-Segall for allowing me to work with creative young writers whom I find endlessly uplifting and inspiring.

I am indebted to friends who acted as muses (whether or not they knew it), including Bob 'Shaggy' Crawford, Joel Remland, Ariana Brooks-James, Rachel Druker, the Kim's Video crew, my extended Fleetwood family, The Stevedores, and the incomparable Spencer Bell.

Lastly, I am eternally thankful for the support of my mother Angela, sister Laura, stepfather Skip, father Danny, partner Joel, and the rest of my family.

CREDITS

"The Garden" was previously published in *Runaway Parade* Issue 28: Abyss.

"Ten Days" was published in *Hypertext Magazine.*

Song lyrics that appear in *Dust* were written by the Beatles, Nirvana, Bruce Springsteen, Virgin Prunes, Smashing Pumpkins, Men At Work, Fugazi, and the Pixies.

43157785R00125

Made in the USA
San Bernardino, CA
15 December 2016